DECEPTION

Also by Alex Connor

The Caravaggio Conspiracy
Isle of the Dead
Memory of Bones
Legacy of Blood
The Rembrandt Secret

THE BOSCH DECEPTION

ALEX CONNOR

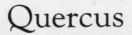

First published in Great Britain in 2014 by

Quercus Editions Ltd
55 Baker Street
7th Floor, South Block
London W1U 8EW

A CIP catalogue record for this book is available
from the British Library.

PB ISBN 978 1 78206 507 4
EBOOK ISBN 978 1 78206 508 1

Printed and bound in Great Britain by Clays Ltd, St Ives plc.

Typeset by Elliptis Digital Limited, Glasgow

'The Garden of Earthly Delights' [detail]

After Hieronymus Bosch

'The like of which was never seen before
Or thought of by any other man.'

Albrecht Dürer, 1471–1528

*'Who will be able to tell of all the weird and strange
ideas which were in the mind of Jeronimus Bos, and his
expressions of them by his brush? He painted gruesome
pictures.'*

Karel van Mander, 1548–1606

London

The pain of the hammer blow cut through his sleep and he slumped back against the door of St Stephen's church. Alarmed, he struggled to open his eyes, smelt burning, then jerked his legs up. His trousers were on fire. Someone had poured petrol on him; he could see the man standing over him with a can, emptying the last drops on to his body. Terrified, the victim screamed, writhing in pain, the flames soaring up his legs and into his groin.

Stumbling to his feet, he was suddenly engulfed, the fire eating into his chest and face. He could feel his skin melting, slipping off his bones, his eyes boiling in his skull. Hysterical, desperate, he screamed again, the flames licking around and inside his mouth as he staggered down to the gravel path. But he was going nowhere in the darkness as he shrieked and spun like a firework and the smell of burnt flesh filled the air, smoke rising from the blackening shape. He was still screaming as his attacker watched him fall forward on to the path, flames flickering over the dying, stinking body. Finally the screaming stopped. His flesh crackled and the flames died down, the smoke thick and cloying.

Moving over to his victim, the attacker kicked at the body. It didn't move. Then, dropping the petrol can beside the corpse, he calmly walked away.

Book One

Prologue

's-Hertogenbosch, Brabant, 1460

It is a fallacy that killing a bird brings ill luck. For the members of the Swan Brethren, it was a form of tribute. On an early evening, barely into a bitter November, two men carried in the swan on an ornate silver plate. Its feathers were clotted with blood from the arrow point, its head lying listless, its throat ice-white, long, fragile, leading to the open ebony eyes. Its closed beak, redly defiant, seemed like a full stop.

Ten years old, he watched his father, Antonius van Aken, receive the offering. He was wearing the insigniu of the order, his position as artistic advisor to the Brotherhood of Our Lady marking him out from his peers. The order had been established in the religious Netherlands to venerate the mother of Christ, but Hieronymus knew of the politics involved. Even a religious sect had a pecking order. There were the ordinary members of the Brotherhood and the sworn members – the glorious 'Swan Brethren' who donated a swan for the yearly banquet.

3

Glossy-faced and perspiring, Antonius studied the swan and nodded approval. Applause broke out among the assembled company, clerics, nobility and magistrates clapping the tips of their elegant fingers in muted appreciation.

Hieronymus gazed at the dead bird. He thought it was a little like him, overwhelmed by circumstances just as he was overwhelmed by family. His father, two grandfathers and five brothers were all painters, all gifted men, healthy and dismissive of a sickly runt of a child. Suddenly he saw the bird move and he blinked, leaning over the banisters and staring down into the hall beneath. Without warning the swan rose up, webbed feet stamping on the silver tray, threatening to topple off as the men beneath panicked and struggled to hold on to their charge.

Hieronymus could see his father's eyes widen in terror as the bird opened its bloody wings and turned towards him. Its tremendous span seemed for a moment to envelop the entire Brotherhood in shadow, the men cowering beneath. And then the swan's beak – that molten arrow – jabbed into Antonius's skull. The bone cracked and Antonius van Aken was thrown upwards, landing bloodied and mangled on the silver platter where the bird had previously lain.

For the second time that night, Hieronymus woke up screaming.

One

Church of St Stephen, Fulham, London, the present day

'Father?'

The priest turned, staring at a face he didn't recognise. At first. *'Nicholas?'*

He nodded, moving towards the older man. Nicholas Laverne, forty-one years old, a man who had left London ten years earlier and had – to all intents and purposes – disappeared. Nicholas Laverne, the ex-priest who had railed publicly against the Catholic Church and been excommunicated for his pains. The same Nicholas Laverne whose very name was inflammatory.

'Is it really you, Nicholas?'

He nodded in reply.

Hurriedly the old priest looked around, but there was no one on the street and, without thinking, he beckoned for Nicholas to follow him into the church. They entered by the back door, skirting the anteroom where the priests prepared for Mass, and moved into a gloomy kitchen. Turning on the light and pulling down the blind at the window, Father Michael gestured for Nicholas to sit down.

He hesitated, then took a seat. 'I'm sorry I came here. I hope no one saw me—'

'It's a church. Sanctuary for everyone.'

'Which is why you took me round the back,' Nicholas replied bitterly.

'You don't change.'

He knew he should have been ashamed of the remark, but Nicholas was unrepentant. He stood over six feet tall, his hair black and dusty looking and his eyes blue. Well-fed and well-dressed, he could have been handsome. As it was, he had the appearance of someone recovering from a long illness.

'Where have you been?' Father Michael asked, making a drink for both of them and passing Nicholas of cup of tea. 'D'you want something to eat?'

'Why?'

Father Michael paused. '*Why what?*'

'Why did you do it?'

The older priest shrugged. 'What did I do?'

'Nothing changes, does it?' Nicholas replied. 'Denial all the way.'

'I don't know what you want me to confess.'

Nicholas stared at the ageing priest, taking in the foxing of grey hair, the narrow face, the pale, appealing eyes. Perfect for confession, forgiveness oozing from every compassionate pore.

'You turned on me.'

The priest shook his head. 'You turned on yourself. And on the Church.' He leaned towards Nicholas. 'You acted like a madman. What did you expect? For the Church to sanction what you said? You had no proof—'

'*I had proof!*'

'Which wasn't reliable. Or so you said,' Father Michael replied, eyes hostile now. 'What d'you want? No one's seen you for years – why come back now?'

'I need to talk to you. It's important. I wouldn't have come back to London otherwise.'

'Where were you?'

'France.'

'Doing what?'

'Why d'you care?' Nicholas countered.

'You don't look well.'

'But I'm better now. Much better.' He glanced at his watch. 'I won't stay for long – don't worry. But I need some help before I go. And before you refuse, remember you owe me—'

'*Nothing.*'

'Think back, Father. Examine your conscience,' Nicholas replied, pulling a cloth bag from the inside pocket of his coat. Silently he shook out the contents, a heavy gold chain falling on to the bleached wood of the kitchen table. With his forefinger he straightened it out, the gold weighty, its value obvious.

The priest put on his glasses and stared at the chain. 'It looks old.'

'It is old. Centuries old,' Nicholas replied, 'and it's worth a fortune. The gold itself could fetch thousands, its provenance millions. But the real value lies in what the chain *held*.'

'What are you talking about?'

'The past. You're a historian, Father – you know all about the religious organisations of the old Catholic Church,' Nicholas replied, weighing the chain in his hands. 'What d'you know about the Brotherhood of Mary?'

'Brotherhood of Mary . . . let me think for a minute.' The priest gathered his thoughts. '. . . It was also known as the Brotherhood of Our Lady. It was one of many groups which worshipped the Virgin in the late Middle Ages.'

'In Brabant?'

'All around Europe, especially in the Netherlands. There was a Brotherhood of Our Lady in 's-Hertogenbosch.' The priest was unable to resist the temptation to flaunt his knowledge. 'Devotion centred on the famous miracle-working image of the Virgin, the *Zoete Lieve Vrouw*, in the church of Saint John, where the Brotherhood had a chapel.'

Nicholas was listening intently. 'What else?'

'The congregation consisted of members from Northern Netherlands and Westphalia. It supported the religious and cultural life of 's-Hertogenbosch.' Father Michael leaned back in his chair, suddenly suspicious. 'Where did this chain come from?'

''s-Hertogenbosch. The same city Hieronymus Bosch came from. Apparently he was commissioned to create

8

paintings for the Chapel of Our Lady there.' Nicholas continued, 'Bosch's father managed to get most of his family employed by the Brotherhood. Hieronymus was the most talented, the most famous of all of them, but his grandfather, father and brothers were painters too. They must have been quite a force to reckon with. You knew that Bosch's father, Antonius van Aken, was artistic advisor to the Brotherhood?'

'You've obviously read up on it, so why are you asking me for information?'

'You're the expert; I'm just learning as I go along.'

Abruptly, Father Michael rose to his feet. 'I don't want trouble!'

'I'm asking about a religious organisation and a painter. What trouble could come from that?' Nicholas asked. 'I've found out some facts, but you know a lot about Hieronymus Bosch, the artist. You've always been interested in him. So tell me what you know.'

The priest hesitated, then sat down again.

'Bosch lived and died in his hometown. There's no documentary evidence that he ever left the place where he was born. But then again, there are very few details about his life. Sometime between 1479 and 1481, he married Aleyt Goyaerts van den Meerveen. She was older than him, a wealthy woman in her own right. After they married, the couple moved to the nearby town of Oirschot because she'd inherited a house and land from her family.'

'Did they have children?'

'Apparently not.'

The elderly priest was regarding his visitor with caution. Perhaps if he gave Nicholas Laverne the information he wanted, he would leave – and stay away. He brought with him too many memories, too many reminders of scandal. Once he had been a friend, a colleague, but that was a long time ago.

'The final entry in the accounts of the Brotherhood of Our Lady notes that Bosch died in 1516.'

'Are his paintings valuable?'

The old priest nodded. 'Of course! And rare. He's highly collectable. Sought after by connoisseurs and galleries everywhere.'

'So the art world would be interested in anything to do with Hieronymus Bosch?'

'Naturally. Who wouldn't be?'

Nicholas stared at the old man. 'You were always a fan of his.'

'I studied History of Art before I entered the Church. You know that, and that's why you're picking my brains now. Hieronymus Bosch has always fascinated me. He was a great religious painter.'

'You preached his vision of Hell often enough—'

'It was important in the Middle Ages for people to be scared away from sin,' the priest retorted. 'Bosch served a purpose. He warned the congregation of what would happen if they turned from God. He painted images that everyone could understand. He was a visionary.'

Nicholas toyed with the heavy chain in his hands, as the priest watched him.

'I shouldn't have let you in,' Father Michael said at last. 'You never brought anything but trouble. We were glad to be rid of you. Things have been quiet for the last ten years. Until . . .' He paused and Nicholas picked up on his hesitation.

'Until what?'

The priest thought of the homeless man who had been burned alive outside the church only days before.

'Nothing of any interest to you. There was an incident, that's all.'

The priest was unsettled, suspicious. Was the re-emergence of Nicholas Laverne connected with the murder? Was the man sitting across the kitchen table, only feet away from him, somehow involved in the death of the homeless man? The victim no one could place. The man without identification, or history. Burned to death in the porch of the church. His church. The church where Nicholas Laverne had once listened to confession and given absolution of sins. From where the Church had exiled him as a traitor, a liar, the Devil's recruit. Excommunicated because of his exposing of a scandal, his complete rejection of the Christian faith and, worse, his abuse of the Host at Mass . . .

Father Michael remembered it as though he were watching it take place before his eyes. Nicholas had been hounded for going to the press, but although barred from the Church, he had entered their neighbour church, St Barnabas's, one

11

day and made his way to the altar rail. Father Luke had been giving Mass and had looked at Nicholas in horrified disbelief as he knocked the wine and wafers out of his hands, the red wine spotting his white and gold vestments as the congregants fled to the back of the church.

It had been an unholy sin.

The old priest closed his eyes against the image. Nicholas had then left, shouting at the top of his lungs, white-skinned with fury. A madman. No, not a madman . . . But now he was back, a decade later, and what had he become in the meantime? the priest thought uneasily. A murderer?

'What is it?'

His mouth dried as Nicholas stared at him, unblinking. 'What are you afraid of?'

'You, Nicholas,' the old priest replied. 'I'm afraid of you.'

Two

Paris, France

Sabine Monette glanced at the phone once more, her hand hovering over it. Should she ring him? Should she? Why not? But then again, why risk it? She pulled on her coat and walked out into the street, skirting a motorbike propped up against the kerb.

For a woman in her late sixties, Sabine moved quickly, her posture erect. Widowhood suited her, the death of Monsieur Monette providing her with money *without* benefits. How sad, her friends told her, to be alone. Without a man, in a cold bed. Sabine put on a show of sorrow to please them, but relished her release from wifely tedium. Monsieur Monette had been irksome in the main and to live alone was a glorious indulgence. There were no irritating reminders of male vanity, aftershave unsuitable on sagging skin. No haemorrhoid cream in the bathroom. No newspapers thick with finance and thin on gossip. No tiresome denials of affairs. No wheezing, dry coughing in the moments before sleep.

13

Monette had had few good points, but dying was his masterstroke.

His demise had left Sabine free to pursue her obsession with the arts. With enough money to invest in Dutch painting, she had amassed a limited, but prestigious collection of Bruegel and Bosch, fighting off dealers and established collectors. In her secluded château outside Paris, she hung her trophies, ensuring their safety by the addition of alarms, intruder lights and dogs. In this cosy little blister of plenty, Sabine could have lived out her days in peace. But then something happened that changed everything.

Madame Monette became a thief.

Three

London

Working late at the office, Honor rubbed her temples to keep herself awake then turned back to the file she had been reading. It was a dry case about fraud, a subject she loathed but one which would ensure the long overdue promotion she had been promised. If she won this case, she would become a partner at the law firm. After eleven years. After harassment, bigotry and prejudice. After long days and longer nights in the office she had come to know better than her flat. But it would be worth it to get her name on the bloody door. Yes, it would all turn out to be worth it.

Or then again, maybe it wouldn't.

Standing up and looking out on to the street below, she checked her watch and frowned. Ten thirty at night – no wonder she wasn't in a relationship. What man would put up with hours like this? Her husband certainly hadn't. Perched on the edge of her desk, Honor turned a framed photograph around to face her. She should put it away. After all, who had a photograph of their brother on their desk? But then again, her brother was all she had.

And she didn't even have him now. Not unless he re-appeared. He was troubled, abusive, uncontrollable. Made himself into a nuisance. Yes, Honor thought, you certainly did that. Made yourself into a bloody nuisance asking all those questions. And getting no answers for your trouble . . .

Her mind went back to their childhood. After the car accident that killed their parents, the three of them – her and her two brothers, Nicholas and Henry – had been taken in by their unmarried uncle. David Laverne was a man who had made a fortune in plastics and retired to the countryside with a selection of old 78 records which he played at full volume. It hadn't mattered when he was alone, but when three children arrived unexpectedly, David found his self-imposed – if noisy – seclusion breached. Henry, aged sixteen, was not too much of a shock for him; he was responsible and old for his years, even professing an interest in the vintage 78s and the overgrown vegetable garden. But Nicholas, at fourteen, was a loose cannon.

It was down to Honor to become her brother's willing apologist, because Henry seldom took Nicholas's side. Short-sighted without the glasses he avoided wearing, Henry soon assumed a paternal role over his younger siblings. Clever and talented, charming by instinct but mean when ignored, Henry made Nicholas appear even more of an outsider and as the years passed Henry grew to despise his younger brother's recklessness and teenage lasciviousness. Everyone knew Henry was earmarked for success, Nicholas's dark nature and appearance the flip side to his classy charm.

Honor had loved both of them, but Nicholas she found fascinating. So she had covered up for his misdeeds, lied for him, made excuses for him, soothed their exasperated uncle when he came close to having Nicholas put into care. All through their growing up Honor had been a constant: an admirer of Henry and a protector for Nicholas. But I wasn't really the nice kid everyone believed I was, Honor thought. Fraud, she mused, glancing back at the file on her desk. We're all frauds really. All pretending we're something we're not.

'You *are* here.'

She looked over at the door, where a man stood watching her: Mark Spencer, slightly senior to her, wanting to get personal. And failing. 'Like to go for a drink?'

'Can't. I've got to finish this.'

'But I've just heard something gross, and I have to share it with someone,' Mark went on, moving his stocky little body further into her office. 'Some down-and-out's been burned alive. Only a couple of streets from here. Outside a church.'

'Jesus. Who was it?'

'No one knows, but the security guy told me he'd been hanging around for the last few weeks. On his uppers, sleeping rough apparently.'

He slid further into Honor's office, facing her full on so that she wouldn't notice his bald spot. Thirty-five, due to be a slaphead at forty. Using fibre powder to colour in his scalp. No one told him it left residue on the back of his collar when he sweated.

'How old was he?'

Mark shrugged. 'Not old, not young. Who knows? They look older when they've been sleeping rough. He just dossed down in the church porch and someone made a firework out of the poor bastard. Christian charity, hey?'Mark paused, ready to try his luck again. 'Sure about that drink?'

She ignored him.

'But the police will have to find out who the man was. I mean, it's murder. He can't have just turned up out of the blue. He had to belong to someone. There must be someone looking for him.'

Her voice dropped, an unwelcome thought coming into her mind. *Surely it couldn't be her brother?* After so long, it *was* possible that Nicholas had come back to London to look for her. And finding his sister doing well, would he have hung back, too ashamed to contact her? It would have been like him to watch, wait for the right time to approach. Maybe one evening when she left the office late. Or mid-morning when she sneaked out for a coffee at the Costa on the corner.

The last time Honor had seen her brother he had been belligerent, rejecting help, even pushing her away. No, he didn't want any of her fucking money, he had said. But she had slid it into his pocket anyway when he wasn't looking. And despite his temper she had gone to the station with him and waited until past midnight for the last train up to Liverpool. He had got on board without looking back, but as

18

the train pulled away he had leaned out of the window and called her name.

Was it him? God Almighty, Honor thought, was it him? She tried to be logical. After all, why should it be her brother? But the thought stuck, gnawed at her. Had Nicholas finally come back only to be murdered streets away from her?

'Where did they take the body?'

'How the hell would I know?' Mark replied curtly. 'He was a down-and-out. Who cares?'

Four

Startled by a sound outside, Father Michael got to his feet, lifted the blind, and peered out of the kitchen window. He could see nothing. Nicholas Laverne was still sitting at the kitchen table behind him.

'You're jumpy.'

'I want you to leave,' the priest said flatly. He could catch the noise of a car horn sounding in the next street and knew that the church was empty and locked up for the night. His housekeeper had gone home and no one would be calling now. Not so late. Or maybe someone *would* come to see the priest and find him talking to a stranger. Or maybe find him alone. Dead.

His gaze moved to the chain in Nicholas's hands. 'What did you mean about the chain *holding* something?'

'See these?' Nicholas asked, pointing out the engraved gold connectors between the links. 'They're hollow. And when I looked closely, I could see that one of them had a

20

crack in it. Inside someone had hidden a tiny piece of paper. It was the same with all of them—'

Father Michael shook his head. 'I don't want to know.'

'You don't know what I'm going to say.'

'I know it's going to bring trouble.'

'You used to be brave.'

'I used to be young.'

Nicholas nodded, continuing anyway. 'Inside every connector was a tiny scrap of rolled-up paper. Very small, twenty-eight of them in total. And on each there were a few words. I found the first note by accident, then I found the others and pieced them together.'

'How did you get the chain?'

'I was given it for safe keeping.'

'You? Safe keeping?' The old priest snorted. 'You couldn't keep anything safe. Who would entrust you with anything valuable?'

Nicholas was stung by the remark. 'You think I stole it? Is that what you think of me now? That I've become a thief?'

'I don't know what to think. And I don't want to hear any more. Go now, while you can. I don't care what you've done or what you're going to do – just get out.' The priest moved to the door and opened it. Outside the night was misty, slow with rain.

Nicholas didn't move. 'Shut the door and sit down. I'm not going, not yet. Sit down!'

The priest reluctantly closed the door and took his seat at the table again. 'I remember how you used to be. You were special, Nicholas. One of the best priests I've ever known—'

'I don't want to talk about the past. All that matters is what's going to happen *now*. Listen to me, Father.' He shook the object in his hands. 'This chain holds a secret. The words on each little piece of paper, when put together, spell out a truth that has been hidden for centuries. A truth kept secret for the good of – and in the protection of – the Catholic Church.'

'God forgive you.' The old priest sighed. 'What is it this time? Another conspiracy? You ruined your life once before, Nicholas, and for what? You were thrown out of the Church, your name destroyed. No one believed you then, and now you come back with another conspiracy. Only this time you're not a young charismatic priest, you're little more than a fugitive.'

'This chain carries a secret—'

The old priest snatched at the piece but Nicholas held on to it and used it to pull Father Michael towards him. 'You think I'd be so stupid as to bring this chain *with* the notes? You think I'd trust you, priest?' He let go suddenly, smiling. 'The evidence is safe. Only I know where it is. Or what it is.'

'And what is it?'

'Proof of a con so clever it's fooled people for generations. Proof of a lie perpetuated by the Catholic Church.' Nicholas took in a long breath. 'There was once a man called Hieronymus Bosch. He painted visions of Hell – a master of the damned, of monsters and chimeras, of all manner of grotesques. He was revered in his lifetime, famous, fêted, and he made vast amounts of money. Because – you know this already, Father, so forgive me for stating the obvious – no one could paint like Hieronymus Bosch. No one had his imagination. He was sought after. A celebrity of his day. A genius. A one-off. Now what if I were to tell you that—'

Nicholas stopped talking. A loud noise startled them both – the heavy clunk of the church door being pushed open and thrown back against the other side of the wall where they were sitting. Someone had entered the church of St Stephen. Someone was only yards away from them. They could hear footsteps close by, fading away as the stranger moved towards the altar.

Unnerved, Father Michael began to tremble and Nicholas glanced up at him. 'What is it?'

'I . . . I . . . Why are you here? What d'you want from me?'

'I just want your help. Your knowledge,' Nicholas replied, then turned in the direction of the sounds. 'Who is it?'

'Don't you know?'

'No. I came alone.'

The old priest was shaking uncontrollably, 'I locked the church door. I locked it and now someone's in there.'

'Maybe you forgot—'

'I locked it! And I have the only key,' the old priest blustered. 'But someone's in the church. Someone's in there now. And you're *back*.' He rose to his feet. 'A man was murdered here only a few days ago. He was burned alive. I came home and found him on the path . . .' His fingers fastened

23

around his rosary. 'For years this church has been a safe place, but now a man's been murdered here and someone's broken into a church that I secured, to which I have the only key . . .'

The priest paused, listening. The footsteps had ceased. There was the slow creak of the door swinging closed as the intruder left, and the church was silent again.

'Well, whoever it was, they've gone now,' Nicholas said calmly.

'And yet someone was here. And a man is still dead. And you're still in my kitchen. For ten years there's been no trouble. And now . . .' Shaken, the priest stood his ground. 'What did you bring with you, Nicholas Laverne? What in God's name did you bring to my door?'

Five

Carel Honthorst ordered a coffee as he watched Madame Monette take a seat outside. He sat down, facing in the opposite direction but able to see the Frenchwoman's reflection in the cafe window. She lit a cigarette and began talking rapidly on her mobile, then finished the call and threw it into her bag irritably. Honthorst was impressed. Sixty-seven years old and she hardly looked a day over fifty, he thought, taking in the slim legs and firm jawline. Still sexually attractive . . . Uncomfortable, he shifted his thoughts. What did she weigh? A hundred and twenty, tops. Height? Five foot six, possibly seven. His gaze moved to her neck. Fine, almost unlined, and long. Delicate. Easy to break.

Honthorst sipped his coffee and put his fingertips to his face, checking that the concealer he was using had not run. He had been assured that it would cover his bad skin and stay in place until he washed it off. Waterproof, the woman had assured him, trying not to smirk. A man

25

using concealer! her expression said. Ponce, obviously . . . Honthorst could read her mind – women always found it amusing. It wasn't their fault; he could put himself in their place and see what they saw. A hulking man, broad-shouldered and barrel-chested, with skin like orange peel. Cratered, burnt or acne-scarred. Not pretty, not pretty at all.

Which was where the concealer came in. Back in Holland he had a chemist make it up for him, so he could avoid the embarrassment of shopping around. But on this trip Honthorst had lost his potion and had had to endure the barely disguised contempt from the shop assistant. Trying not to laugh, she had tried out various shades on the back of his burly hand, matching the concealer closest to his complexion, and once he had made his choice she had said: 'Do you want me to wrap it, sir? Or will you be putting it on now?'

Honthorst flinched at the memory of the words, continuing to watch Madame Monette's reflection in the window. He knew that the shop girl would have laughed at him after he had left, shared the story with her colleagues, even – perhaps – her boyfriend. Who would have clear skin, naturally. But Honthorst took some pleasure in the fact that after the amusement of the day the shop girl would spend that night crying over the death of her dog.

Which he had run over outside her flat.

Finishing his coffee, Honthorst walked into the cafe, pausing beside Madame Monette's table. She was reading the newspaper and took a moment to look up, surprised.

'Yes?'

'I have a message for you.'

Her expression was curious, nothing more. 'Really? From whom?'

Without being invited, Honthorst slid into the seat opposite her. 'You were very wrong to do what you did, Madame.'

Even though his French was good, she placed the underlying accent immediately. Dutch. Leaning back in her seat, Sabine Monette said simply, 'Please leave my table or I'll have you removed.'

'You stole the chain which once belonged to Hieronymus Bosch.' He pronounced the name perfectly. 'I have been charged with its return.'

'Don't be ridiculous!' Sabine said imperiously. 'What *are* you talking about?'

'You bought a small Bosch painting from Gerrit der Keyser. It was hung with a chain—'

'Who are you?' she asked coldly. 'I don't know you.'

'I work for Mr der Keyser.'

'In the gallery?'

'As a consultant.'

She eyed him sniffily. 'Consultant of what?'

He ignored the question. 'The painting you bought was hung with a chain—'

'Which I purchased together with the painting.'

Honthorst moved his position slightly to avoid the sunlight. 'I'm not referring to the gold chain *you* put on the picture. I'm referring to the one which was on there originally.' When she didn't reply, he continued. 'It was a clever trick, Madame, but the chain wasn't part of the deal.'

She folded her arms defiantly. 'Are you accusing me of theft?'

'Not if you return the original chain. Mr der Keyser is more than willing to forget this little incident. Especially as you've been a valued client of his for some while – and an old friend.'

'*This is ridiculous!*' Sabine snorted. 'If the chain was so valuable, why leave it on the painting? Why wasn't it removed earlier?'

'My employer did not realise what the chain was.'

'And now he does? That's convenient. How?'

'We have proof from the original owner. He also didn't realise its value until he found the papers with which the painting had been originally stored. His solicitor had kept them for safe-keeping. When he read them, he contacted us and we checked the chain on the picture.'

'How could you?' Sabine said triumphantly. 'The Bosch is in my house.'

He was unperturbed. 'Photographs were taken before it left the gallery, Madame. Photographs of the picture, the frame *and* its backing. Which included the chain. It's done for every item sold, for the gallery's records.' Honthorst paused. 'So we compared our photographs of the Bosch when it arrived and when it left the gallery. The chains were different.'

28

Needled, Sabine stood her ground. 'So you say.'

'I can show you the photographs if you wish.'

'Which could have been digitally altered,' she retorted, unnerved but damned if she was going to show it. 'I think you're bluffing—'

'We have you on tape.'

'*What?*'

'We have you on tape, Madame. On video tape. And we can show that to the police.' Honthorst replied. 'We can *prove* that you removed one chain and replaced it with another. Your own.'

'Which is probably worth hundreds more than that filthy chain I took,' Sabine retorted loftily, knowing she had been caught out.

Irritated, she pushed her coffee aside. If she had left it on the painting and waited until the Bosch had been delivered she would have been home free. Yes, Gerrit der Keyser would have been told about the evidence from the previous owner, but by then the painting *and* the chain would have been in her possession legally. But instead she had given in to a moment of greed.

Keeping her hands steady, Sabine Monette sipped her coffee. She had spotted the chain at once, almost in the instant she had first viewed the painting. Gerrit der Keyser had been ill recently, was not on top form and was eager to make a sale. Unusually careless, he hadn't noticed the chain by which the small painting had been hung, and had left Madame Monette for a few minutes to study the picture alone. While he was gone, she had examined the chain and rubbed a little of the dirt off the middle link, finding the faint initial H, and a possible B.

Her heart rate had accelerated, but Sabine Monette had regained her composure quickly. Years of being cosseted had not made her soft. Her early life had been traumatic and her natural guile came back fourfold. Unfastening the chain from the back of the painting and slipping it into her pocket, she replaced it with the long antique gold chain necklace around her neck and called for Gerrit der Keyser.

And it was all on tape.

'Even at your age, the police don't look kindly on theft.'

Sabine's eyes narrowed as she faced at the Dutchman. 'I don't have it any longer.'

'What?'

'The chain. C-H-A-I-N.' She spelt it out for him. 'It's not in my possession any longer.'

And he shook his head.

'Oh dear, Madame,' Honthorst said quietly. 'You shouldn't have told me that.'

Six

Morgue, Hospital of St Francis, London

Illness terrified her, and the thought of death had worked on her senses ever since she was a child. The horrific death of her parents had affected the young Honor deeply, but the early demise of her brother Henry – in a fire – had shattered her. It had made the presence of death a real thing, not something she could ignore. Not for her the luxury of ignorance. She had seen the coffins and buried the ones she loved. Her family had been depleted ruthlessly and the brother she had loved most was estranged from her.

To others her actions would have seemed irrational, but Honor believed there was a distinct possibility that the man murdered outside the church might be Nicholas. And she had to know. Had to prepare herself for burying another member of the ill-fated Laverne family.

Walking up the hospital corridor, Honor caught sight of the pathologist in his white scrubs and green apron, his surgical mask pushed up on to his forehead. He nodded to her as she approached.

'You came to identify the body?'

Honor nodded. 'I spoke to the police—'

He grunted. 'Right, yes. Right. I got a call. They said you thought it might be your missing brother . . . You sure you want to view it?'

'I don't want to. I just have to . . . see if it's him . . .' She was unusually nervous.

'Have you ever identified a body before?'

'God, no!' Honor replied, then dropped her voice. 'It's probably not him. My brother, I mean.' Pushing her hands into her pockets she fought to keep herself calm. 'I'm not sure. I just want to know . . .'

'The body's badly burnt,' the pathologist went on, scratching the side of his nose with a biro. 'Not easy to identify.'

'His face . . . ?'

The pathologist shook his head. 'Not much left there, I'm afraid.' He glanced at the file in his hand. 'Did your brother have any identifying marks?'

'No . . . no, nothing.' She swallowed.

'There was no jewellery found on the body.'

'He didn't wear jewellery.' She looked at the pathologist. 'What about his teeth? You can identify people from dental records, can't you?'

'The victim doesn't have any teeth.'

There was a moment of shock, followed by relief.

'Then it can't be my brother! He had great teeth. People always noticed them.' Her hopes rose, the unease lifting. 'It can't be him. My brother had all his teeth.'

'So did the victim,' the pathologist continued, 'until someone knocked them out and set fire to him.'

Seven

Old Bond Street, London

Hiram Kaminski was setting his watch. Of course if he had any sense he would have bought a new timepiece, something expensive which was stylish and accurate, but he knew he could never part with the watch he had. It was the only thing he had left of his late father. Whom he had hated. Just as he hated the watch.

All through Hiram's childhood the watch had made its ghastly appearance. If he were late home, his father would tap the glass face to indicate his displeasure. If asked the time, his father would look hard at the watch and then make his son guess. Once in a while Hiram would be allowed the privilege of winding the watch, until one day he over-wound it and his father, furious, had to pay to have it repaired. It came back a few days later, its white face peaky, its thin black hands moving a little stiffly, like someone recuperating from two broken arms.

Hiram's father said that it never kept good time after his

son had over-wound it. It was, he said, 'just another example of how clumsy the boy is.'

So when his father died, Hiram was surprised to find the watch willed to him. For a while he had held it reverently in his hands, and then he had thrown it through the window of their first-floor apartment in Warsaw. The caretaker had found it and returned it to Hiram later, saying that it just went to prove 'how expensive things were made to last.'

Thirty years on and the bloody watch was still going.

Walking to the door of his office, Hiram glanced out into the gallery beyond. Only two places on earth looked good with flock wallpaper – Indian restaurants and West End art galleries. He let his glance travel along the walls and then settle on a small picture of a peasant, created by *A Follower of Bruegel*. A follower! Hiram thought. The art world had more followers than Scientology. What he needed was an original Bruegel, or a Bosch. He smiled to himself as a stout woman came down the stairs from the offices above.

'Hiram, a word,' she said, following him back into his office and taking a seat. Her legs were too plump to cross, her feet swollen in patent pumps, and her hands gripped a ledger. His wife, Judith. Still going after thirty years. Just like the bloody watch.

'We have a problem, my dear.' After a decade in London, she hadn't lost her accent. Their daughter spoke like a Sloane, but Judith's accent was Yiddish. 'Takings are down. We need a big sale, my love – an influx of money.'

'There's a recession on,' Hiram said, pecking his wife on the cheek. Maybe she wasn't so slim any more, but she was still clever with money. No one could touch her. 'People aren't buying the same at the moment.'

'People aren't buying from us, my dear.' She managed to make 'my dear' sound like a criticism. 'We need something splashy. Something BIG.' Her plump hands made a circle in the air.

'You want me to buy a round picture?'

She sighed. 'I want you to buy something people can't resist. There must be something out there—'

'There's a lot out there, but it's too expensive.'

Judith dismissed the remark. 'You have to speculate to accumulate. One fine painting is worth six mediocre ones.' She nodded her head vigorously. 'I heard something the other day. In the hairdresser's. I was sitting next to Miriam der Keyser and she was telling me about Gerrit being so ill, and—'

'And?'

'She told me about something I think her husband might have preferred her to keep to herself.' Judith looked round as though expecting Gerrit der Keyser to come in at any moment. 'He's had a heart attack, as you know. And I think it made her worry – and when Miriam worries she has a little drink at lunchtime, and then maybe another.'

Hiram tried to keep the impatience out of his voice. 'What did she tell you that she shouldn't have?'

'Miriam said one of their clients had stolen something from the gallery.'

'*Really?* Who?'

'How should I know! She shouldn't have told me so much, but she was upset, letting down her guard – you know what happens at the hairdresser's.'

He didn't, but let it go. 'So what was stolen?'

Judith leaned forward in her seat, her jacket buttons gaping at the front. 'Something about Hieronymus Bosch.'

'*A painting?*'

'Did I say a painting?' Judith asked, shrugging her shoulders. 'Did I mention a painting? This is the trouble with you men – you exaggerate. It wasn't a painting, it was something else.'

Silence fell and Hiram was the first to speak. 'Is it a secret?'

Judith gave her husband a long, slow look. 'All I know is that one of the customers stole something valuable to do with Hieronymus Bosch. Miriam didn't say "painting", so I thought maybe some personal artefact that once belonged to the painter . . .' She let the intimation work on her husband before continuing. 'Something worth a lot of money.'

'Anything that could be proved to have belonged to Hieronymus Bosch would be worth a fortune,' Hiram mused. 'So little's known about the man, there'd be a scramble to get hold of anything of his. I know three collectors who'd pay big money, including Conrad Voygel.' He thought for a moment, agitation rising. '*I'm* the specialist in painting from the late Middle Ages. I should have heard about this. How did it end up in the der Keyser gallery? Gerrit's more interested in the sixteenth century—'

'Gerrit's interested in making money. However it comes.' Judith tapped the account ledger. 'We need to get hold of this mystery object.'

'But we don't know what it is.'

'It's something connected to Bosch,' she said crisply. 'What else matters?'

'But you said it was stolen—'

Judith pulled a face. 'Maybe, maybe not. You know how this business works, Hiram. People put out rumours all the time to drum up interest. Maybe Gerrit's heart attack got him thinking. Maybe he's working up to a killing so he can retire and he wants to get everyone curious. This story about a theft could be a lie – maybe this phantom object's still hidden away in the der Keyer gallery. Or maybe he wants us to think it's valuable enough to steal.'

He glanced at his wife. 'Have the police been brought in?'

'No,' she said emphatically. 'From what I could gather it was all hush-hush.'

'Maybe there's no mystery object.'

'Oh, there's something,' Judith said emphatically. 'The way Miriam was talking she was nervy, like it was something big. Even bigger than a painting by Bosch. She knew at once that she shouldn't have said anything and changed the subject.'

'Then what?'

'She had her highlights done.'

Hiram stared at his wife, taking in a breath. 'I mean what else did Miriam say?'

'Nothing!' Judith replied. 'That's the point. She shut up like a clam. Which made me think that you should have a chat with Gerrit de Keyser.'

'I don't like him, the foul-mouthed barrow boy.'

'Foul-mouthed or not, talk to him. You've known each other for years. Take him out for lunch, suss him out.'

'Gerrit won't confide in me. You'd be better off taking Miriam out for lunch.'

'I won't get anything else out of Miriam der Keyser. No one will,' Judith said firmly. 'She looked like someone who'd just won the lottery – but forgotten where she put the ticket.'

Eight

Paris France

Unnerved, Sabine found herself studying every item of furniture in the room, each familiar piece collected during her marriage and afterwards, in her cosy widowhood. Cosy to outsiders, almost bland, but that wasn't the whole truth. Sabine let her hand rest on the lid of the grand piano. No one played it, no one ever had – it simply sat like a washed-up French-polished crab on the sand of the Aubusson carpet.

Impatient, Sabine turned away. She wasn't soothed by the sight of her belongings, rather she found them confrontational, mute rebukes to a life half lived. But that wasn't true. She had done more than any of her jaded neighbours. She had secrets; secrets that were long kept, treasured, but were now surfacing, called up unexpectedly from the wreck of history.

And all because of a thug of a man with bad skin . . . Sabine felt her age for the first time in her life. This was serious, something Decleor couldn't massage away. Something no plastic surgeon could eradicate or reverse. She was in trouble.

Her courage faltered, then her genes kicked in. Those genes from her earlier, tougher life. She was ready to fight, but just she had to write a testament in case the fight turned out to be a dead end, the demise of Sabine Monette. She glanced at the escritoire; she would write down everything that had happened. Not about the Bosch chain, but about her life and her own – most personal – secret. Something no one knew about. Not even Nicholas Laverne.

She had come close to telling him once, all those years before when she had called in at St Stephen's church. Instead she had confessed to a crisis of faith, and as their friendship developed there was never the right time to tell Nicholas the truth. But she would now . . . Because the Dutchman had frightened her and her future seemed suddenly bleak.

Putting in a call, Sabine was relieved when the phone was picked up. 'Nicholas, where are you?'

'London. I told you I was coming here.'

'Someone threatened me today—'

'*What?*'

'Some big Dutch bastard, who looked like he was wearing make-up, unless I'm losing my mind,' she snapped, sliding the lock on the door of her city centre apartment and then drawing the curtains. 'He didn't tell me his name—'

'What did he want?'

'The chain. He'd been hired by Gerrit der Keyser, the little runt. They knew I'd taken the chain off the Bosch when I

41

was in the gallery. *They have me on tape.*' She smiled suddenly, bleakly amused. 'Glad I was dressed up.'

On the other end of the line, Nicholas listened. Her bravado impressed him, but he was worried. He had been fond of Sabine Monette for years, his attentions filling the void left by her husband's death. Yet their meeting had been a chance one. Sabine had been seeing friends in London and had visited St Stephen's to make her confession. And it had been Nicholas Laverne, aka Father Daniel, to whom she had confessed.

Sabine had been a devout Catholic, but also a confused one. Ever since childhood she her put her desires into prayers, convinced of the presence of God by the continual granting of her supplications: deliverance from poverty, a wealthy husband, fine homes. Yet in her later years she had hit a crisis of faith. She turned from God not because He had been indulgent with her, but because He had been too lenient. The money had bought her what she wanted, but after that, what good was it? The wealthy husband had screwed other women, and then died. The fine homes required constant attention and staff, a never-ending bouncing from Paris to Lyon and back again.

The advantages for which the young and desperate Sabine had ached had turned out to be an anticlimax in her later years. To her surprise she realised that her faith was wavering and that she had nothing left to say to God. In fact, it was her lapse of faith that had propelled her to the church of St Stephen late one evening in winter, eleven years earlier.

Unlike the opulent, incense-bound atmosphere of Notre Dame in Paris, Sabine walked into a silent, narrow chapel, where the only lights had been dimmed, burning over the altar and beside the confessional booth. Her footsteps had announced her arrival, Nicholas hearing her entrance and moving into the church from the vestry beyond.

They never spoke of what Sabine had confessed that night or what Nicholas had heard. It had been a confession, after all, and his silence had been guaranteed. But from then on they became allies. In the week that followed, Nicholas had heard Sabine's confession several more times, until she stopped confessing. But she didn't stop visiting St Stephen's on her return trips to London and she didn't stop talking to Nicholas or listening to him express his own growing discontent with the Church.

His confusion ran parallel to her own and compounded her uncertainty. But she liked the priest's intelligence and wondered about his upbringing – a past he would avoid assiduously. Then one day his smoulder of discontent went up like a keg of gunpowder. Father Daniel was no more and Nicholas Laverne took his place.

'Gerrit der Keyser's got me on tape!' she repeated.

'Maybe he was bluffing—'

'I don't think so. He described exactly what I did.' She stared at the phone in her hand. 'You don't think this is being taped, do you?'

'Why would they tape your phone?'

'Because his *assistant* seemed very angry when I told him I didn't have the chain.' She paused, adding, 'I didn't tell him you had it, but when I said it wasn't in my possession any longer, he said, "You shouldn't have told me that." He was scary, I can tell you.' Her voice wavered for an instant. 'You *do* still have the chain, don't you?'

'Yes, and I've spoken to someone who knows about Hieronymus Bosch. He's an expert on Catholicism in the Middle Ages and art history. He was my mentor once – Father Michael at St Stephen's.' Nicholas paused, thinking back to the previous night. 'I didn't expect him to be glad to see me, but I certainly didn't think he'd be afraid of me.'

'Afraid of you – or what you told him?'

'That's just the point,' Nicholas replied. 'I was about to tell him the whole story and he didn't want to know. I tried to fill him in, but then something happened and I missed my chance. To be honest, he threw me out.'

She didn't know whether to be relieved or disappointed. 'So he doesn't know the chain's secret?'

'No. Only you and I know that.'

'And Gerrit der Keyser and the Dutch moose.'

'But *do* they?' he challenged her. 'They know you stole a chain off a painting which was connected to Hieronymus Bosch, but they don't know what was *inside* it . . . Maybe only we know that.'

'This isn't good,' Sabine said, shivering. 'If they're angry about losing the chain, what would they do if they knew about the rest?'

Nine

Sabine's words echoed in Nicholas's head. '*What would they do if they knew about the rest?*'

His mind slid back to the previous week, when she had returned to the hotel in London, brandishing the small Bosch painting. At once it had struck him that her actions were unusual: Sabine relied on other people and usually anything she bought would have been delivered. What he also hadn't been prepared for was her then ignoring the painting and taking something out of her handbag.

'There,' she had said, placing the chain on a side table. 'What d'you make of that?' She had beckoned for him to approach. 'I stole it. I can't believe it – I've never taken anything in my life before. I just saw and took it. I couldn't help myself . . .' She had watched as Nicholas stared at the object. 'Don't worry, no one will ever know. They were using it to hang the painting, can you believe it? If der Keyser had been his usual self, he would never have missed something like this.' Her voice had been almost childlike. It had been a prank. A moment's silliness. 'I saw some initials on it too.

An H and a B. I think it belonged to the artist . . . Well, don't just stare at me! Didn't I do well?'

'Are you still there?'

Nicholas's attention turned back to Sabine. Her voice was intense over the phone line, his own pretending a calmness he didn't feel. 'Are you on your own in the apartment?' he said.

'Yes.'

'Go to a hotel.'

'What!'

'Register at the George the Fifth. They know you there. You have to be somewhere safe.'

She was spooked, and could hear the anxiety in his voice. 'Why?'

'You just answered your own question, Sabine. "If they're angry about losing the chain, what would they do if they knew about the rest?" Gerrit der Keyser sent someone to talk to you, to scare you. He probably thought you'd give the chain back. That's why he was thrown when you said you didn't have it.'

She faltered, her legs trembling as she leaned against the sofa. 'The writings . . . Where are they?'

'Safe.' Nicholas assured her. 'But I'm not telling you where. I need to get them authenticated—'

'Without anyone hearing about it?' Sabine asked. 'You must be joking! The art world runs on gossip – you can't keep something like that quiet. And I've always been wary of Gerrit der Keyser; he's charming to his customers but a peasant underneath.' Her voice wavered. 'He hired a thug to threaten me—'

'Because he wants the chain. And he won't be the only one.'

'But I don't *have* the chain. You do.'

'Yes, I do,' Nicholas agreed, 'but not for long.'

Nicholas stands looking at the church. Dating back to the twelfth century, blackened with the passing of traffic and a build-up of petrol fumes, its outside walls are ebonised, its ancient window glass thickened and cream as sea ivory. Rain has nuzzled the corner-stones and weathered the overmantel of the door, the spire a weakling iron trying to head-butt Heaven.

I am back, he is thinking, pushing open the door and walking towards the nave. He can hear the rain outside and see the sloping red tiles before the altar, his gaze moving upwards towards the towering crucified Christ. Devotion has come back like warmth to frozen limbs and his knees bend in a welcome genuflection. Only the echo of a dripping outside tap disturbs the silence. A tap beside the outhouse where the garden tools are kept. An outhouse large enough to store old furniture and mowers, a cupboard at the far end secured with a padlock.

No, thinks Nicholas, I am not back. This is over . . . But he rises from his genuflection like a dancer and leaves the church. The yew trees plot his course towards the outhouse, three on his right, three on his left. He knows – he has counted them many times. At Christmas, lights are hung on them for the congregation's children, a wooden Nativity scene played out beneath a squatting oak nearby.

He is walking, then begins – as always – to run towards the outhouse. Inside it is silent, but under the silence is a sound – something barely human. A drowning noise of the lungs. In the virtual darkness he grapples his way between the gloomy ranks of discarded kitchen cupboards and garden mowers, making for the source of the noise. Then he stops at the locked cupboard door.

The breath leaves his lungs.

He calls out, as always.

Then inhales, waiting.

He doesn't wait long. Instead, hammering frantically on the wood, he tugs at the padlock. And from inside comes the sound he will never remember and never forget – the sound of someone dying.

I am back, he is thinking. I can change it this time . . . But the padlock stays shut and his hands can't break it, and the sound of the boy's voice – the voice that says nothing and everything – echoes to the scrabbling of his fingernails on the door. Nicholas kicks against the wood, because it is wrong. Something is very wrong here and he knows it. He kicks and kicks again, and suddenly the wood splinters and the door falls open in front of him.

The boy is dead. Nicholas can't have heard a voice or sounds of scrabbling – he is dead and has been for some while. The body is suspended by the rope, the arms limp, palms lying against his sides, the skin split like ripe figs; his head hanging backwards.

Nicholas moves towards him, lifts him – as he always does in the dream – then feels the hot rush of maggots fall out of the boy's open mouth.

Ten

Chelsea, London

Philip Preston was attempting to fix the cord on the sash window of his office. He had tried to jiggle the frame loose, but it was stuck at an angle. He hit it twice with his right fist and jumped back as it crashed downwards. Relieved that it wasn't broken, he locked it and returned to his desk. There he stared at the entry in his diary and sighed. He was hopelessly bored.

He knew he shouldn't be. With a mistress and a wife he should be knackered, not bored. And yet he was. His gaze moved towards the sign hanging outside the window. PHILIP PRESTON – AUCTIONEER. Before the malaise of his middle years he had taken pride in that sign, that emblem of his achievement. And it was not an undistinguished one. Despite being an enthusiastic womaniser Philip was a fine art historian and auctioneer; his auction house impressed with the quality of its sales. He understood art and pricing; he was adept at judging silver and a known authority on antique gold jewellery.

He was also ambitious. Greedy, if truth be told. His greed amused rather than shamed him. He had been an avaricious child, unwilling to share toys, demanding of his mother's attention. And she, divorced and devoted, lavished affection on her only child. As a boy Philip was taught that women existed for his benefit. To amuse, to cajole, to comfort. His mother denied him nothing, thereby setting in motion his pattern for life. To Philip Preston, women were a consolation and a beloved hobby.

The only female who escaped this judgement was his wife, Gayle. Driven to marry her because of attraction and her beauty – a beauty other men wanted to corral for themselves – Philip discovered that her face was merely an exotic doorway to an unstable mind. Her rages were amusing because afterwards they made love, but as she turned forty Gayle's emotional health, and her looks, began to falter. She had miscarried several times, Philip consoling and yet distant. Gayle's desire for a child seemed excessive to him, and her libido faltered as her neurosis grew. At the suggestion of seeing a specialist she had been enthusiastic, until she realised that her husband meant a psychiatrist.

Believing that Philip thought she was unbalanced, Gayle retaliated. She was not insane, she told him, merely emotional. But later she confessed to the psychiatrist that she had had a nervous breakdown in the past. A complete shattering of her system due to a broken romance and an overdependence on cannabis.

'I was ill,' she had told him, hands slapping together as though she were applauding her own diagnosis. 'But I'm not ill now. And I'm getting stronger by the day.'

But she gave up driving and a couple of times had lost confidence when she was out at lunch with friends, making excuses to leave early and going home. Because it was quiet there and she could go upstairs and lie on the bed, hearing nothing and not having to say anything – just stop. Gradually the periods of immobility increased, and at times the once stunning Gayle would 'stop' for days.

'Mr Preston?'

Philip looked up, startled out of his thoughts, at his secretary standing in the doorway of his office. She was wearing a tight skirt revealing the shape of her thighs.

'What is it?'

'You have a visitor, Nicholas Laverne.'

Surprised, he got to his feet and nodded, then remained standing. With a practised smile on his face he watched Nicholas enter. Nicholas Laverne, whose brother, Henry, had once been Gayle's lover, a fact that always surprised him. After all, Nicholas had been the lusty sibling, Henry less successful with women.

Philip snapped back into the present.

'Nicholas!' he said, shaking his visitor's hand and leading him to a seat. 'How good to see you after so long.' He was careful with his wording. How did you greet a man who had been excommunicated from the Catholic Church? His smile widened like a gate opening. 'How are you?'

'Thriving,' Nicholas replied dryly.

But he didn't return the smile, because he didn't like Philip Preston. Never had. The auctioneer had aged, but he still had an impressive head of thick hair – once sandy, now white – and a pair of pale eyes which twinkled like tea lights. Very inviting. Very false.

'It's been . . .' Philip paused, 'how long?'

'A decade.'

Philip nodded. '*A decade.*' He repeated the words as though it was the most amazing statement he had ever heard. 'How time passes. You look well – you've lost weight. I heard you were working for Sabine Monette.'

'True.'

'She's one of my customers,' he said, pleasant from practice, even though he found Nicholas Laverne an unsettling presence. 'I was thinking of your brother the other day,' he added. 'Poor Henry.'

They fell silent, Nicholas thrown by the mention of his sibling, the talented elder brother who had gone to Italy as a vaunted architect, squeezing his way in among the columns and the classical façades. Henry, too vain to wear his glasses. Henry, visiting spas to keep his health intact. Henry, sporty, talented and opportunistic.

The *late* Henry Laverne.

'Sorry, I didn't mean to hit a nerve,' Philip went on. 'How's your uncle? I haven't heard from him in a while.'

'So David hasn't been buying lately?' Nicholas replied, his tone crisp. 'You'll be pleased to hear he's still alive.'

Bastard, thought Philip, smiling at his visitor. Nicholas Laverne had always been blunt, outspoken to the point of rudeness. Philip imagined that he had prided himself on his truthfulness. But where had it got him? Looking like a deadbeat in second-hand clothes.

'And how's your sister, Honor? Such an attractive girl—'

Nicholas cut him off. 'I need help . . .'

Philip groaned inwardly. How he hated conversations that began '*I need help*'.

'. . . and I have something I think might interest you.' Nicholas reached into his pocket and brought out a thick envelope. 'But first I need to know that we're speaking in complete confidence—'

'Of course, of course—'

'No, Philip, not "of course",' Nicholas countered. 'This is important. You have to keep *everything* I say private, between us. Otherwise we can't do business.'

Philip was catching a whiff of money, inviting as frying bacon on a Sunday morning.

'You have my promise. Whatever you tell me won't leave this room.' He laid his manicured hands flat on the desk. 'What can I do for you?'

'I have this to sell,' Nicholas replied, shaking the chain from the envelope. 'It's from the late Middle Ages.'

Scooping it up in his hand, Philip studied the chain with an eyeglass, noticing the initials H and possibly a B.

He could tell at once that the piece was old and valuable, but when he glanced up at Nicholas he paused. Philip Preston had dealt with the art world for many years and had a heightened intuition when it came to his clients. He could sense greed because he recognised it. He could sense desperation. He could also sense trouble.

And he was holding it.

'Where did you get this?'

'That doesn't matter.'

'Actually it does,' Philip replied, weighing the chain in his hands. Loving it. 'Why me?'

'We've known each other for a long time. Your father used to do business with my late parents and my uncle,' Nicholas replied. 'When you took over we carried on working with you. Henry put a lot of business your way.'

'You, however, did not. Not when you were a priest anyway. You have to take vows of chastity and poverty, don't you? Wouldn't do for me.' He grimaced. 'But then again, now you've . . . changed direction . . . perhaps your fortunes have improved?'

Excommunication described as a change of direction. Nicholas almost laughed. 'There's more.'

'Not another chain?'

'Something the chain held.'

Nicholas leaned back in his seat, staring at the auctioneer. It was true, they had known each other for many years, but that wasn't the real reason he had come to Philip Preston. Of all the dealers, collectors and auctioneers in

London, Preston was the most slippery. Henry had taught his brother that, telling Nicholas stories of goods shipped out from London illegally, or imported under false names and papers. Of auction lots which had wildly exceeded their estimates because members of Philip Preston's staff had upped the phone bidding. He had heard about a Gainsborough which had not reached its target and had been burned – which meant, in art world parlance, set aside for a number of years until it could re-emerge on the market as a new lot. No auction house could afford to have a major artist fail to reach an estimate.

And that wasn't all; Philip Preston had perfected the art of the sleeper. Works supposedly by a master that came into his sales as *In the Manner of* Hogarth, or Turner or Bruegel. It meant that the work wasn't definitely by the master, but in his style. Then Philip went into overdrive. Deftly planting the rancid little seed, rumours would start circling that perhaps the painting was genuine after all. Then gossip would follow. If Philip had judged it correctly, greedy, stupid or novice dealers would want the painting, hoping to pull a fast one on their competitors. And if a few dealers could be enticed into action, a bidding war would start.

The rumour of the sleeper would incite that most creative of illnesses, auction blindness. The sketchy provenance was uncharacteristically dismissed as the duped blundered towards their acquisition of the sleeper. Philip Preston had made a lot of money that way, and the fact that the art world relied on risk ensured further profit. It wasn't illegal. It wasn't fair. But it was bloody good business.

Which was how Nicholas knew that Philip Preston wouldn't be unwilling to break the rules.

'Inside the connectors between the links in the chain were tiny pieces of paper,' Nicholas began. 'When the pieces were put together they told a story which was incredible and damning.'

Philip's merry eyes became stony. 'Go on.'

'The chain belonged to Hieronymus Bosch. There are papers proving this—'

'Is this a joke?'

'No,' Nicholas said calmly. 'The chain was used to hang the painting. That's why no one spotted it for so long. People were interested in the picture, not the means by which it was hung.'

Philip was trying to keep the excitement out of his voice. 'This writing. You've seen it?'

'I found it.'

'What did it say?'

'It told the truth about Hieronymus Bosch.'

'His work?'

'His life,' Nicholas replied, irritated as the door opened and someone walked in unannounced.

Immediately Philip waved the man away, but not before Nicholas noticed how tall he was. How heavily built, with skin so smooth it looked as though he were wearing make-up.

'*s-Hertogenbosch, Brabant 1468*

His father was waiting for Hieronymus at the bottom of the carved staircase, with its gargoyle heads and polished ebonised rail. He stood in his long tunic, stout in green hose, his face broad and square as a playing card. Antonius van Aken, artistic advisor to the Brotherhood of Mary, standing with his other sons behind him and the wheezing hook of his own father sitting watching them all.

Antonius looked up at his youngest son and said: 'We've waited for you all day.'

But as he went to take the first step, Hieronymus tensed. At eighteen years of age, he was already known as the most talented in the family. Thin, hardly more than five foot six tall, paint-spattered. Threatened on a staircase with gargoyles and chimera heads. His hand reached for the rail, feeling the slick smoothness under his fingers.

'I was working, Father.'

'Working,' Antonius repeated, managing a sneer and a raising of brows as he looked back at his family in mock astonishment. 'Our youngest teaches us to be diligent. What an example he sets – look at him and admire his devotion.'

Antonius moved past his youngest son, the others following. All but the old man, the grandfather, who sat evilly mute on the hall bench. Running after them, Hieronymus saw his father throw open the studio door, his movements heavy as he blundered towards the upright easel on which stood a scene of family life, sketched out, the finished details only in the portrait heads.

'So what I was told was right,' Antonius said, to the baying sniggering of his sons behind. 'This is not what the Brotherhood wants.' His arm went back and he knocked the wooden panel on to the floor. At once Hieronymus bent down to retrieve his work. But before he could, Antonius's foot came down hard on his hand, splaying out his fingers as he applied pressure.

'This is not religious!' he brayed, 'The Brotherhood paid for religious work. For the veneration of the Virgin. Not for pictures of peasants.' He increased the pressure on his son's hand. 'You owe your life to me. Your birth killed your mother, but I raised you anyway. I accepted God's will that He should take my wife and leave me a sickly boy, but in return you obey me, Hieronymus. You understand?'

'I understand, Father.'

Slowly Antonius raised his foot, then smiled, gesturing to his other sons. 'He has the Devil in him,' he explained, brushing imaginary fluff off his clothes, 'and the Devil must be subdued. Is that not right . . . ?'

They nodded, glad that it was – as always – Hieronymus who suffered. Only one son, Goossen, felt shame and pity for his brother. Not that he dared show it.

'. . . We worship and venerate Our Lady, the mother of Our Lord. That is our moral duty. We are employed to scare the wicked away from Hell and towards salvation.' He turned back to Hieronymus. 'I have arranged for you to undertake a commission.' It irked him that he couldn't give the work to his brothers or his other sons, but the Brotherhood had chosen Hieronymus. 'You are to paint an altarpiece for the church of Saint John. This is a great honour and you must make the family proud of your achievement. This means status and money for all of us.'

Antonius stared at his youngest son, irritated beyond measure. A sickly, whey-faced youth with miraculous hands. A boy with a marvellous, precocious talent and nothing to say for himself. Antonius wondered why God had chosen Hieronymus to bless, why He had ignored the rest of the family and forced them to play second fiddle to an awkward runt.

Uneasy under his father's critical gaze, Hieronymus coughed, doubling over for several seconds, bringing up phlegm. Disgusted, Antonius turned away, his gaze falling on a painting on the far wall. Hieronymus watched nervously as his father moved towards it, his revulsion obvious as he poked a plump finger at the panel.

'Why do you paint this depravity? Why paint ugliness and monsters? Why not paint God?'

'I have not seen God,' Hieronymus replied, timid but holding his ground, 'but I have seen, and known, many monsters.'

Unable to respond, Antonius left the studio, pausing outside to turn the lock on the door.

60

Eleven

Remembering what Sabine had said earlier, Nicholas watched the Dutchman as he backed out of Philip Preston's office, closing the door softly behind him.

'Who's that?'

'Him?' Philip pulled a face. 'God knows. But he's a pushy sod. He wants to talk to me apparently – sneaked past my secretary earlier. I told him to go away.'

'Why?'

'Because I don't have time for unscheduled appointments,' Philip continued, smiling. 'Unless, of course, I know the visitor.' His curiosity was like a lump in his throat. 'You were telling me about the Bosch chain. What it held.'

But Nicholas was spooked. 'Are you sure you don't know him?'

'I've never seen him in my life before.'

'Did he give a name?'

'Why d'you want to know?' Philip asked, then, exasperated, called his secretary on the extension. 'Did that man leave a name?' Nicholas watched as Philip listened to the reply and put down the phone. 'Carel Honthorst.'

'Dutch.'

'Sounds like it,' Philip replied. 'You were saying—'

'Has he been here before?'

'Christ!' the auctioneer snapped. 'No, I've never seen him before today. Why is it important?'

'Because he knows about the chain.' Nicholas replied, watching for any reaction in Philip's face. But there was none. 'He's been hired by Gerrit der Keyser to retrieve it. Which makes me wonder why he came here. Unless you know him. Or you already knew about the chain.' Nicholas leaned forward in his seat. 'Has the gossip begun? Has der Keyser already talked to you?'

'No, he hasn't! All this is new to me.' Philip crossed his legs, feigning nonchalance. 'When did *you* get hold of the chain?'

'Four days ago,' Nicholas replied. 'And four days in the art world is like a month in real life. A rumour could have gone round twice already.'

'Not one I've heard,' Philip replied coolly. 'Of course there is another explanation – that you were followed here.'

A moment nosedived between them and Nicholas fell silent. Had he been followed? They knew Sabine Monette had taken the chain, and they would have known Nicholas was close to her. Had they watched him with her? And watched him visit the old priest at St Stephen's church?

Spooked, he rose to his feet. 'I have to go—'

'We were talking!' Philip said incredulously, watching as Nicholas grabbed the chain and stuffed it into his pocket. 'What the hell is going on?'

'I'll come back. But in the meantime, keep your wits about you,' Nicholas said firmly. 'And don't talk to the Dutchman. Don't tell him anything.'

Twelve

Honor was sitting by the window of her office with a file on her lap. When anyone passed in the corridor outside she glanced down, as though absorbed with her client's case. But as soon as she heard the footsteps retreat she stared out of the window again. It *wasn't* her brother, she told herself. It wasn't Nicholas. The DNA test had finally confirmed it: the murder victim was not related to her. Related to someone, but not her.

Which meant that Nicholas was still alive, out there somewhere, and it meant that she was still waiting for contact from him. Suddenly the waiting seemed unbearable. Their uncle was old, irritable, slinking back into his Derbyshire home like a tortoise drawing in its head for winter. He had enjoyed his previous secluded lifestyle and was not prepared to let it be disturbed again. Even at Christmas.

So Honor had stopped visiting David Laverne, because she realised that he didn't want to see her. Phone calls were fine – remote affection but nothing more. Once handsome, David Laverne had shrunk into a grisly recluse, never revealing any hints about his past although Honor had once found photographs of him with a stunning woman. He had been holding her the way only lovers do, his face pressed against hers as though their skins were melting into each other. She recalled some vague memory of his being engaged – or was it married? – but nothing concrete. And she certainly didn't ask him.

No one asked David Laverne anything, because he wouldn't answer. Or he would tell them what he wanted them to know and nothing more. Irritation with the family that had been dumped on him led to David's withdrawal. When Nicholas ran off to London in his teens, it was Honor who rang the police and Henry who talked to them. David Laverne was listening to music somewhere in the house and wasn't to be disturbed. When the police demanded to talk to the children's ward he emerged reluctantly and stood, truculent in a patched cardigan, answering sullenly.

'No, I don't know where my nephew is. No, I don't know why he ran off. Nicholas is a very irritating boy—'

Honor had stepped in. 'He said he wanted to visit friends.'

The police and David Laverne had looked at her. Petite, black haired, intelligent. A good liar.

'You know who his friends are?' one of the policemen had asked her.

She had shrugged. 'No, but he's OK. Honestly. Nicholas will be back. He can take care of himself.'

And he did come back, several times. In and out of their lives like a visitor. Never one of the awkward, ill-matched family. Not really . . .

Finally making up her mind, Honor reached for her mobile and clicked down the stored numbers. She paused at the name Claude Devereux – a man she had spoken to many times, always about Nicholas. A man who had once worked with her other brother, Henry. She flinched at the thought of her dead sibling. Who would have thought Henry would die young? Henry, with his architectural practice in Paris, encouraged by Claude's father, Raoul Devereux.

Honor glanced back at the mobile and Claude Devereux's name. It had been nearly a year since they had last talked, when Claude had told her Nicholas was working for a wealthy widow, Sabine Monette.

'He seems happy there. She has an estate outside Paris, and an apartment on the Champs Elysées. Nicholas looks after her, does odd jobs.'

'*Odd jobs?*' Honor had queried. Her brother, doing odd jobs. 'He won't take my calls any more. I keep trying, but he won't talk to me. He was always difficult, but now he doesn't want anything to do with me. I didn't turn against him. Everyone else did, but not me. And yet he cut me out of his life.' Her tone had been injured, old wounds picked raw.

'Nicholas can't get over what happened to him.'

'It was years ago—'

'He was excommunicated from the Catholic Church.

For a priest, a believer, there's nothing's worse than being deprived of God.' Claude had hesitated. 'It shook him when he exposed the corruption and was punished for it.'

'He was naïve.'

'He was Nicholas.'

For a time Honor had suspected that Claude and Nicholas were lovers, but when Claude became engaged to Eloise she realised that the Frenchman was just – *just* – her brother's friend. And in running away from his disgrace in London, Nicholas had chosen France as his adopted home. An ex-priest, repelled by the Catholic faith, barred from Mass and destined for a heretic's burial.

Nicholas's religious fervour had been unexpected. A capricious mind, a restless character, he had teetered on the edge of criminality and promiscuity for years. As he entered his late teens he had bummed his way around London and the capitals of Europe, taken menial jobs, and then returned home only to be off again weeks later. Hardly the kind of person to choose a religious life . . . Honor thought for a moment. Perhaps the Church had offered him security. Nicholas had experienced a lot of danger, sex and excitement – perhaps he was tired. But why Catholicism? their beleaguered uncle had asked. You were raised as Church of England – why change? Honor had never understood that argument. In truth, the Laverne siblings hadn't been raised in any religion. They had been English, middle class, well-schooled and intelligent. Religious devotion had been nothing but an unwelcome moral cuckoo.

For another few moments she stared at the phone number and then dialled, waiting for Claude to answer. But it wasn't his voice that came down the line, it was his wife's, Eloise unusually flustered.

'Hello?'

'Eloise, how are you?' Honor began. 'We haven't spoken in a while and we should catch up. I was wondering if Claude was there. I'd like to speak to him if I may.'

Honor paused, waiting for the reply. It didn't come for several seconds.

'No,' Eloise said finally, 'you can't talk to him. Claude is dead.'

Thirteen

Church of St Stephen, Fulham, London

A wind was blowing, shifting the November trees and moving the dust around the basement yards. The street lamps were on, one flickering, the bulb about to fail, but the others blazing in a triumphant row. An ash tree, bark peeling as though sunburnt, shuddered in its yard of earth, while green wheelie bins stood like bouncers outside the row of doors.

Behind the houses, St Stephen's church drove its inky spire into the scatter of clouds. The church was locked up in darkness apart from a light burning in the rectory window. And behind the light, Father Michael sat thinking about Nicholas Laverne. Had it really been ten years? he thought. Ten years . . . Slowly he rose to his feet, unlocked the vestry door and moved into the church beyond. A single lamp burned over the altar, the gold crucifix throwing a gloomy shadow on the stone wall behind.

Genuflecting, Father Michael knelt down. His hands clasped in front of him, he tried to pray, but although the words came easily their meaning did not. After a while he sat back in the pew and stared at the stained-glass window. But there was nothing visible of the familiar pictures, because there was only darkness behind them. The figures had disappeared, their inspiring message blacked out. And outside the wind kept blowing.

He had prayed for the man who had been murdered only yards from where he sat. Had sent up supplications for the unknown victim who had been torched, burned alive. Sent into the next world screaming, clawing at the gravel as he died. And as he prayed, Father Michael had felt guilt because he had done nothing. Not on the night the man died, nor the week before when a stranger had come to the church and sought him out, asking to stay.

'No one can sleep in the church,' Father Michael had told him. 'It's against the rules. But you could go to the YMCA. Catch a number thirty-four bus at the corner and get off at Cromwell Street. They'll put you up for the night.'

'I want to stay here,' the man had persisted, talking with his back to the street lamp, his face half hidden under a hoodie. It had been raining that night, cold too. 'Please,' he had begged. 'Just let me stay. Who would know? I'll do odd jobs for you, anything you like—'

'I can't allow it,' Father Michael had insisted, touching the stranger's shoulder. 'I can offer you a drink and a sandwich, but not a place to sleep.'

There had been no further argument and no acceptance of the offer of food. Instead the man had walked off, turning at the corner, perhaps to catch the number 34 bus. But Father Michael knew he wouldn't, and three days later he hadn't been surprised to find the man sheltering in the church porch. It was after eleven at night, drunks calling out to each other from across the street, a police siren sounding in the distance, and the stranger waiting.

'What d'you want here?'

'I know this place,' he had replied. 'I lived round here once.' His voice had been cultured, his age around fifty. 'Won't you let me in? Just for one night, Father. Please, just for one night.'

I should have let him in, Father Michael thought, wracked with remorse. Sweet Jesus, why didn't I let him in? His gaze moved back to the blanked-out window, seeking comfort, trying to make out the familiar Biblical characters painted on the glass. In days his life had shifted from stability to a terrible unease. He could sense something dark coming for him, but he didn't know what.

The church which had comforted him for decades held only terror now. The shadows were dense, the cold forbidding, and the crucifix on the altar seemed more of a threat than a consolation. Was it just coincidence that Nicholas Laverne had come to see him only days after the stranger's murder? Laverne, the man of whom he had been so fond and was now so afraid. Laverne, exposing corruption in the Church and then forced out, disgraced and angry.

'God help me,' Father Michael prayed. 'God help us all . . .'

After his excommunication, Nicholas had raged in his letters. Had cursed God, cursed everything he had loved with a ferocity that was terrifying. After a while, the old priest had stopped opening the letters from Italy. But they kept coming, now postmarked Belgium. Later, France. He seemed to settle there, or so the letters indicated. But what Nicholas was doing, how he lived, what he did for work, the old priest never knew. When the stack of letters filled a drawer in the vestry, Father Michael took them out one night and burnt them in a brazier.

The paper took a while to catch, as though the Devil himself were blowing out the flames, but finally the fire took hold. In seconds every word, every thought that Nicholas Laverne had confided to his mentor, was gone.

Father Michael forgot Nicholas. The letters stopped. Nicholas seemed to be finally laid to rest. But something, *someone* else, came in his stead. A man looking for sanctuary in St Stephen's church. A man in a hoodie, sheltering from the rain. A man the priest had turned away, just as he had once turned away Nicholas Laverne.

Chilled, Father Michael closed his eyes, scratching around for a prayer. 'Bless me, Father, for I have sinned . . .' He clung to his rosary, the beads worn smooth. 'Bless me, Father, for I have sinned . . .'

And as the old priest sat, distressed and afraid, someone opened the vestry door and began, slowly and silently, to make their way towards him.

Book Two

Fourteen

Gerrit der Keyser's gallery, Chelsea, London

As comfortable as an onion in its skin, Philip Preston strode into the gallery, smiling flirtatiously at the receptionist. She smiled back, recognising him and wondering if he would invite her out again. After all, it was common knowledge that his wife was unstable – surely a man had a right to enjoy himself? Philip Preston might not be young, but he was successful and rich.

'How's your boss today?' he asked, leaning on her desk.

'Busy.'

'Too busy for me?' Philip lifted her chin with his left hand. 'You *are* a pretty girl. Now, run along and tell him I need five – no, make it fifteen – minutes with the old man.'

Gerrit der Keyser was spraying water on to a fern as Philip entered, his doleful expression winching itself up into a fleeting, and unconvincing, smile. His recent heart attack had forced him to lose weight and now his jowls sagged, the bags under his eyes pronounced even behind the bifocals.

'Philip,' Gerrit said by way of greeting. 'How are you?'

'Good,' he replied, sliding into a brocade sofa under a painting of Brouwer's *Peasants in a Tavern*. 'I was just passing and thought I'd pop in . . .'

Gerrit kept spraying the plant.

'. . . I heard something interesting about a Bosch painting, or rather the chain which held it up.' He could see Gerrit pause, his finger immobile on the water spray. 'Mean anything to you? I also had a visit from some man of yours. Honthorst, I think his name was.'

'I have so many fucking tablets to take,' Gerrit said, putting down the spray and moving to his desk. Once there, he opened the middle drawer and pulled out four bottles. 'Fucking tablets for this, tablets for that. To stop me getting breathless. To stop my heart racing like a BMW in a Brixton car chase. To stop my ankles swelling like some fat tart's.' He stared at the fourth bottle. 'I don't know what these are for. Probably to stop my bleeding arse dropping off.' He swept the bottles back into the drawer and slammed it shut. 'What d'you want, you smug fucker?'

'You always saved your charm for the customers.'

'Why waste an advantage?' Gerrit replied. 'What d'you want?'

'Do you employ a man called Carel Honthorst?'

'Yes. He helps me out, talks to people sometimes.'

'A heavy?'

Gerrit shrugged. 'A consultant.'

'You sold a Bosch painting with a chain attached—'

'I sold a painting with an old bag's necklace attached,' Gerrit said sourly.

He was weighing up how much to tell Philip Preston and how much to withhold. Obviously the auctioneer had heard the rumour and it would be pointless to deny it. Besides, Preston might be useful. He certainly had been in the past.

'Her own necklace?'

'She swapped them,' Gerrit snapped. 'Took off the original chain and put her own on. I'd never have missed it before I was ill. But I did, and I only found out when the previous owner told me about it. By then I'd sold it.'

'To whom?'

'"To whom?" You pompous git,' Gerrit mocked him. 'Is that how you get into so many tarts' knickers?'

Philip let the question pass. 'Who was the client?'

'You know her,' Gerrit said, putting his head on one side. 'But although she's still a looker, she's a bit long in the tooth, even for you.'

'Sabine Monette,' Philip guessed, remembering his infrequent customer. Then he frowned. 'She's loaded. Why would she steal a chain off the back of a painting she was buying?'

'Couldn't wait for it to be delivered. Probably thought that if she left it here I might suss it out.' The dealer waggled his wrist and his watch flopped around. 'See this – weight loss. More like fucking brain loss. I'm starving and that makes me slow. No dealer can afford to be slow – that's the way you make mistakes. Slip up, miss things.'

Philip steered the conversation back. Gerrit der Keyser was an East End trader made good. He had married into money, bought some sharp clothes, and hired the best spotters to trawl the world for paintings. And it was an open secret that sometimes his methods could be dubious.

'So you put the Dutchman on to Sabine Monette?' Philip asked. 'That was a bit heavy, wasn't it?'

'He didn't water-board her, he just asked for the chain back.'

The same chain that Philip had seen the previous day. The chain that had shimmered so fetchingly on his desk. He knew it was valuable – that much was obvious to anyone – but he wondered if Gerrit der Keyser knew that there was more to it? Nicholas's reticence had infuriated Philip and for the remainder of the previous day he had waited for his return – and for the full story. But Nicholas Laverne hadn't come back.

So he had decided to go it alone.

'How d'you know that Sabine Monette swapped the chains?'

'We have photographs,' Gerrit paused, 'and some tape.'

You tape your customers?

'You shocked? After what she did you're fucking right I tape the customers!' Gerrit retorted. 'I could have set the police on her, but that would have been a bit much. I mean, no one wants to lose a good customer. Even ones that help themselves.'

'And besides, she's worth a fortune.'

'The chain wasn't too shabby either,' Gerrit replied miserably, picking up the mister and spraying the plant again. 'Anything connected to Hieronymus Bosch is worth money. Big money. When the old fool who asked me to sell it for him came back with its provenance I nearly had another seizure.' Gerrit picked at one of the leaves, examining it through the bottom of his bifocals. 'I pay that thieving florist a fortune for these plants. For that money he should come in and spray them himself. When I complained that I had greenfly, he told me it didn't come from his shop, and that "the plant must have picked it up in the gallery". "In the gallery?" I said. "I'm in Chelsea, not fucking Borneo."'

Philip kept his patience. 'So where's the chain now?'

'How the hell do I know? Sabine Monette told Honthorst that she didn't have it any more.'

'So who has?'

'Now, think about it, Philip. If I knew, would I tell you?'

'Only if you wanted me to auction it for you.'

'I could sell it privately.'

'But I have the expertise. Remember, antique gold is my speciality. I have a list of clients who would kill to get their hands on that.' Philip paused, picking his way forward. 'Mind you, it's only a chain. I mean, its connection to Bosch—'.

'He *owned* it.'

'– puts up the value, but it *is* only a chain.' He let the words hang, but Gerrit said nothing. If he knew there was

79

more to the object, he wasn't going to confide. 'You said you had documents to prove its provenance?'

'Yes. And no, you're not going to see them.'

Piqued, Philip continued. 'Well, they're not much use anyway, are they? I mean, without the chain the papers are worthless.' He moved to the door, then turned. 'I suppose this is one sale you'll have to put down as a loss.'

Fifteen

Mark Spencer was watching Honor carefully. She was taking notes, her dark hair smooth, her eyes looking down. He could see the gap in her blouse, giving just a hint of cleavage, and imagined touching her. He wondered if she was seeing anyone. Certainly no one had come to the offices, but then again, Honor was a private person. Not for the first time he toyed with the idea of ringing her home phone number. It couldn't be difficult to find – all he had to do was to look in the Personnel files. He wouldn't say anything, just see if anyone other than Honor picked up. See if there was a man living there. Or another woman. After all, if Ms Laverne were gay he should find out now – no point wasting time.

Honor cleared her throat suddenly, catching him looking at her. To his chagrin, Mark coloured up. Who was he kidding? he thought. Honor was pleasant, but she didn't really like him. But then again, she didn't know him. Didn't appreciate that looks faded and what really mattered was ambition. And he had ambition – and a sickening, penetrating curiosity which had served him well in his criminal cases. His skill might be average, but he had a gift for unearthing secrets.

The meeting drew to its close and Honor left hurriedly. But she didn't go straight back to her office, instead she made for the lavatory, locked the door and sat down on the toilet seat, trying to fathom what she had heard only an hour before. Eloise Devereux, for once abrupt, shock making her curt. And then tears following.

'I'm so sorry about Claude's death,' Honor said over the phone line. 'I never got to know him well, but I know Nicholas was very fond of him.'

'So was I,' Eloise had replied, her tone fading. Honor imagined that she would live in this way for the foreseeable future. Strong one moment, weak the next. Lifted by forgetfulness, buckled by memory. 'It was such a terrible way to die.'

And then Eloise had told her. Claude Devereux's manner of death had been suspicious, and the police were involved.

'Suspicious?' Honor had queried. 'In what way?'

'Claude was stabbed, but the killer had set fire to his body to try to cover his tracks . . . the pathologist took a while to determine the cause of death . . . Claude was burnt alive. He was still alive.'

The words had reverberated in Honor's brain. Another murder. Another victim of fire.

'Why would anyone want to kill him? Did he have any enemies?'

'He was a landscape gardener,' Eloise had replied, almost laughing at the absurdity. 'No one kills gardeners. Everyone liked him, got on with him. Claude was kind, considerate . . . But that didn't stop someone killing him, did it?' She had grabbed at a breath as though simply living was an effort. 'It's only been two days. Two days, and it feels like he's been gone for a lifetime.'

Honor had made a mental note to ring the French police and find out what she could about the case – or whatever they would tell her. The rest she would search for herself. The internet would have the death listed, and it would have been reported in the French newspapers. Moments later she had ended the phone conversation with Eloise Devereux, but she couldn't stop thinking about the death of her husband.

Getting to her feet, Honor left the cloakroom, bumping into Mark Spencer as she did so. She had the unpleasant feeling that he had been waiting for her.

'What d'you want, Mark?'

'You all right?'

She frowned. 'What?'

'You looked pale in the meeting,' he smarmed. 'I was just wondering if you were OK.'

'I'm fine.'

'Well, if there's anything worrying you, you can always talk to me. You know, if you're unsure about anything.' He was flustered. 'Like I say, if there's anything I can do—'

'Actually there is,' Honor replied. 'At the next meeting, stop trying to look down the front of my blouse.'

Sixteen

Lloyds Bank, Chelsea, London

Hurrying out of the rain, Nicholas walked into the bank and requested his safe deposit box. A few moments later, the manager showed him into a side room and then left him alone. After he had locked the door, Nicholas sat down at the table and drew the steel box towards him. Inserting the key he carried on a chain round his neck, he unlocked it and took out twenty-eight small envelopes, each barely two inches square.

They were numbered 1 to 28.

He stared at them for a long time, remembering the moment he had discovered the first one. How he had drawn the tiny piece of paper out of the crack in the gold connector and smoothed it down, intrigued by the faint writing in a Gothic script. In a language he couldn't decipher at first. All he had recognised had been the name Hieronymus Bosch, and the date 1470. With intricate care he had levered open the joins of all the other connectors, finding – as he had expected and hoped – twenty-seven further tiny pieces of paper with writing on them. In the same hand and apparently in the same language.

So Sabine Monette had – on a whim – stolen a chain that turned out to be holding a secret. It hadn't taken a genius to work out that anything concealed so carefully must be important. The question had been simple – what did the writing say? Without telling Sabine anything about his discovery, Nicholas had set about getting the words translated.

His instinct prompted him to secrecy. He knew from the reactions of Gerrit der Keyser and Philip Preston that the chain was valuable, so how much more valuable would the writing turn out to be?

Using a different name, he had gone online and sought help from three different university scholars, one in Cambridge, one in Holland and a third in Boston. His cover story had been simple: he was a journalist trying to translate some old copy from a late Middle Ages ledger for an article he was writing. And so, gradually, Nicholas had begun to translate the papers, alternating the three scholars so that no one would ever possess the full meaning.

And then the name *Hieronymus Bosch* had come up and the questions began. As with the others, Nicholas had asked the British expert Sidney Elliott for secrecy, but his trip to Cambridge had been an uneasy one. Elliott was well into his fifties, a hunched intellectual with a stammer, wearing bad clothes and working in a makeshift laboratory. Although an expert in his field, his early promise had nosedived because of family problems and his ambition had all but petered out – until Nicholas Laverne had shown him one of the Bosch pieces.

Bending down to look at it, Elliott had made a low sound in his throat, then glanced up at Nicholas.

'Wh-wh-where did you get this?'

'I'm afraid that's confidential information. As I say, I'm a journalist and I need to speak to you in complete confidence.'

Elliott had sat down, rubbed his left eye and finished off the cold cup of coffee on his laboratory table. He didn't offer Nicholas a coffee, hot *or* cold. His hands were blue-veined, his wrists big-boned, his shoulders broad. In his youth he would have been impressive, intimidating even.

Uncomfortable in the chilly temperature of the laboratory, Nicholas had pushed him. 'I need the writing translated—'

'Wh . . . wh . . . what language is it in?'

'I don't know – that's your speciality.'

Elliott had nodded, sliding off his stool and reaching for a magnifying glass. He moved surprisingly quickly, regaining his seat and bending over the paper again. He had said nothing, giving Nicholas time to look around. Having seen better days, the laboratory was ramshackle, a broken window boarded up, the overhead strip lights glowing with a greenish hue and humming with age. Off the laboratory, Nicholas had noticed a small office with a glass door and a print of a painting by Dürer on the wall.

Elliott had made another sound in his throat, but had said nothing as he scrutinised the writing.

'I need to have it authenticated and dated,' Nicholas had told him. 'And we should keep this quiet.'

They had both been looking at the piece of paper on the table between them. Paper 2 out of the 28 Nicholas had found.

Finally, Elliott had straightened up and put down the magnifying glass.

'It's D-D-Dutch – old Dutch, educated Dutch. In the Middle Ages, the main language spoken in B-B-Brabant was medieval Dutch, called Dietsch or Thiois. In the southern part of the Duchy, Latin d-d-dialects were spoken.'

'What does it mean?'

He had touched it with his forefinger, prodding it in a tentative manner. 'It means *"The B-B-Brotherhood of Our Lady. Bought and b-b-bribed."*' The historian had then glanced back at Nicholas, his curiosity piqued. 'What a curious thing to write. I wonder what it m-m-means. I wonder who wrote it. Someone educated, naturally. That long ago m-m-most people couldn't read or write. So we're looking at a cultured m-m-man.' He flipped the paper over with his finger. 'I'd guess it's from the Middle Ages b-b-because of the style of writing and the type of paper. But I'm just going on a hunch and decades of experience.' He had smiled, the sarcasm withering. 'I'd have to have it p-p-properly authenticated to prove I'm right.'

'Without anyone else being involved?'

'*Is* there anyone else involved, M-M-Mr Laverne?'

'I've spoken to two other experts,' Nicholas admitted, 'but I heard you were the best.'

'No, you just want three opinions to see if they all tally,' Elliott said bluntly. 'How m-m-many pieces of paper are there?'

'Not many,' Nicholas had lied.

'I imagine you've let everyone s-s-see the same piece?'

'No, the others have seen copies of this piece. You're the only one who's seen and handled the original.'

Elliott had nodded, looking back at the specimen as Nicholas thought of the other papers – and their meaning. The meaning that had curdled inside him. Mouldered like bad food, gumming the vessels of his heart and leaching oxygen from his brain. That he – of all people – should be the one to find the testament. That an excommunicated priest should uncover a conspiracy that would tarnish the Church and stun the art world. Not that he cared about the latter. Nicholas Laverne wasn't interested in Hieronymus Bosch as an artist, he was interested in Bosch as a victim. As the casualty of a conspiracy shocking in its cruelty.

'Won't you confide?' Elliott had asked, turning on his stool to look at Nicholas. 'I can sense there's m-m-more to this than you're letting on.'

'I can't tell you any more yet.'

Elliott had made the same low sound in his throat. 'Why all the secrecy?'

'It's for an article—'

'About wh-wh-what?'

'I can't say.'

'Must be important, or you'd t-t-tell me.'

'Nothing important.'

'Bullshit.'

Taken aback, Nicholas had reached for the paper. But Elliott had grabbed his wrist. 'I haven't had m-m-many adventures in my life, Mr Laverne. Far fewer than most men. If there's an adventure in the offing, I w-w-want in on it.'

Angered, Nicholas had shaken off his grip. 'It's just words.'

'Oh, Mr L-L-Laverne, words are the most dangerous commodity on earth.'

When Nicholas had left Cambridge that night, he had been uneasy. Sidney Elliott had unsettled him. He had the feeling that the academic had seen something that had triggered his interest and stirred his curiosity. The very thing Nicholas had wanted to avoid. So when the tests results came back and proved that the paper and the ink dated from the fifteenth century, Nicholas had been satisfied but abrupt.

'Thank you, Mr Elliott. I'll settle your fee—'

'Tell me wh-wh-what the paper is and that'll be fee enough.' The academic had paused on the phone for an instant, his tone wheedling. 'I can be useful to you. I know m-m-many people who deal in artefacts like antique writings.' His tone shifted, becoming almost belligerent. 'You n-n-need an expert. A novice like yourself will only come unstuck.'

'*Unstuck?* How?'

'Take my offer of help, Mr Laverne, or f-f-find out the hard way.'

Reluctant to involve Sidney Elliott any further, Nicholas had pieced together the twenty-eight pieces of writing himself, together with their translations. The other two experts had also authenticated and dated the papers. They were all genuine. Luckily Nicholas had only let Elliott see one piece of writing. He had then put them in the order in which they had been numbered and had taken them to the bank for safe keeping. Where they had stayed, hidden, until now.

Rousing himself, Nicholas took out his mobile and photographed every paper. Then he returned the originals to the security box and handed it back to the bank manager. When he left the building there was a downpour, the sky watermarked, a ridiculous rainbow touting its promise of luck.

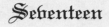

Seventeen

Huddled in his armchair, Father Michael waved away the daily woman who came in to clean and make his meals. He was old, tired and uneasy, and hearing the sound of the radio coming from the kitchen he wondered how something that used to be so comforting could now be so intrusive.

The memory of the previous night made him shudder. The man had seemed to come into the church from nowhere, sliding into the pew next to him and crossing himself. Surprised, Father Michael had glanced at him as he knelt, his profile fixed, his eyes closed. And suddenly he had felt a terrible unease. Without wanting to make it too apparent that he was moving away, the old priest had waited for a couple of seconds and then begun to slide along the pew. But he had only moved a little when the stranger's hand reached out and gripped his wrist.

'A moment,' the man had said, still staring ahead at the altar. 'I haven't finished praying.'

Father Michael had remained where he was, the stranger still holding on to his arm as he prayed, lips moving silently.

Finally he had released his grip and slid back into the pew. Without looking at the old priest, he began talking again.

'You know Nicholas Laverne.'

There was a moment's hesitation, Father Michael being uncertain how to respond.

'You *do* know Nicholas Laverne,' the big man had repeated, still staring ahead. And that had been the most chilling aspect of him – his refusal to make eye contact. 'I've seen him come here, so you must know him. He was a priest here once, under your guidance.'

'Yes,' Father Michael had agreed reluctantly. 'I know Nicholas Laverne.'

'He was thrown out of the Church.'

'He was excommunicated, yes.'

'And yet he came back to visit you after so long. Why was that?'

'He can come back to see me at any time he wants. Nicholas has not been banished from here.' Afraid, the old priest had stared at the stranger's profile. 'Who are you?'

Carel Honthorst ignored him. 'Why did Nicholas Laverne come here, Father?'

'I don't have to talk to you. You have no right to question me.'

'And yet I am,' Honthorst had replied, turning his head slowly. In the dim light his eyes had fixed on an area just above the priest's head. 'These are simple questions, Father. Nothing to worry you.' He had paused, then changed the subject. 'You know Holland?'

'A little.'

'Hieronymus Bosch was a great painter.' His head had turned away again and he was staring up at the stained-glass window. 'People copied him all the time. They say he was good at Hell.' Honthorst had paused, then tapped the old priest's knee, a gesture that was at once both familiar and threatening. 'Tell me what Nicholas Laverne told you.'

'We talked about the old days—'

'I don't think so,' the Dutchman had retorted, glancing at his watch. 'I don't have much time, so we must hurry our conversation. What did Nicholas Laverne tell you?' His large hands were resting on the back of the pew in front and a sigh escaped him. 'Tell me, or I will hurt you.'

Shaken, Father Michael had glanced around him. There had been no obvious escape route, and he was an old man who would have been easily out run. But despite his feelings of antagonism towards Nicholas Laverne, he hadn't wanted to betray him.

'Nicholas and I talked about old times. Nothing more.'

Honthorst's fist slammed into the priest's stomach with all the force of a lump hammer. Buckling over, Father Michael had then felt the Dutchman tenderly straighten him up against the back of the pew, smoothing down his vestments. Then he had picked up the priest's rosary and held it in front of Father Michael's face.

'Tell me, or I'll make you eat every one of these *beads* . . .' His fingers had closed over the attached crucifix. 'And then I'll ram this down your throat.'

Terrified, Father Michael blurted out: 'He was asking about The Brotherhood of Mary.'

'And?'

'He had a chain.'

'He had a chain,' Honthorst had repeated. 'Now we're getting somewhere. What did he tell you about the chain?'

'He said he found it.'

In one quick movement Honthorst had grabbed the priest's face, forcing open his mouth. 'You have one last chance, Father. Tell me what Nicholas Laverne told you. Tell me everything.'

And now the old priest was sitting huddled in his armchair wondering what he had set in motion.

Eighteen

George V Hotel, Paris

As ever, it was horses for courses. And Nicholas Laverne was a carthorse up against a steeplechaser. Philip Preston had hoped that Nicholas would return – with the chain *and* the story that went with it. But another day had passed, people were beginning to talk, and Philip had decided to act. His conversation with Gerrit der Keyser had been illuminating. If der Keyser had called in a heavy, it meant that he was desperate.

It would have been much easier if Nicholas Laverne had left a phone number or an address where he could be contacted, but there was no way Philip could get in touch. So there was only one alternative – skip Laverne and go straight for Sabine Monette.

Which was why Philip Preston was on his way up to the suite in the George V Hotel where Sabine Monette was staying. He had rehearsed his speech to an oily perfection. He would convince Sabine – whom he had known for many years – that he was the person to handle an artefact that had once belonged to Hieronymus Bosch. Philip didn't know the exact nature of the Frenchwoman's connection to Nicholas Laverne, only that she had stolen the chain and had perhaps hired Laverne as her agent. Why Laverne, he wasn't sure. Why a rich Frenchwoman would hire an ex-priest for the task was beyond the limits of his imagination. But whatever the reason Philip was more than ready to usurp the one-time cleric.

He paused outside the door of the suite. Having arranged an appointment to see Sabine Monette, Philip had arrived early, only to be told by Reception that Madame had dismissed her maid in order to rest. She was not to be disturbed until 1 p.m. . . . Philip looked at his watch, then smiled at a passing chambermaid, walked to the end of the corridor and looked out into the dank streets. More rain, he thought, just like London. The minutes crawled past and he counted them down impatiently. Finally he glanced at his watch – 1 p.m. Walking back to the door of the suite, he knocked. There was no reply. He knocked again. Perhaps Madame Monette had grown deaf, or was still taking her rest. Philip waited for another couple of minutes, then knocked a third time.

Again, no reply.

He rapped a little louder on the door.

No reply.

He tried the handle.

To his amazement, the door was unlocked. Unwilling

to catch his client unawares, Philip called out, 'Madame Monette? It's Philip – Philip Preston.'

He moved into the suite. The French windows were open, the white drapes spotted by rain, an overturned side table almost tripping him up. Bending down to pick it up, Philip's glance moved through the open door into the bedroom beyond. And then he saw her.

She was oddly positioned, obviously arranged, propped up on pillows like a courtesan awaiting her lover. But her head was caved in, the right side pulped, the features gone. Her false teeth lay beside her left hand, knocked out of her mouth in the struggle – Sabine Monette finally showing her age. In a cruel touch, her dress had been pulled up and two initials carved crudely into the flesh of her stomach – H and B. And on the coverlet beside Sabine Monette, pressed into the pooling of blood, was the blurred outline of a Christian cross.

Backing away, Philip tried not to vomit. He had never seen a dead body before and was shaking, the smell of blood making him retch. His impulse was to run, but instead he looked around him. Afterwards he would wonder *what* he had been looking for. The chain? There was no chain in the suite. So why had he hesitated? Philip Preston hadn't known, but before he left, something had caught his eye. Something half hidden under a cabinet. Something he took without thinking.

Sabine Monette's mobile phone.

Nineteen

Even though he had reported Sabine Monette's murder, Philip Preston was treated with suspicion, questioned repeatedly about why he had come to Paris. He had regained his composure, his fluent French an asset as he reiterated his account.

'I came to see Madame Monette about auctioning some of her belongings . . . She had been a client of mine for some years . . . No, I don't know what she wished to sell – that was why I came to Paris to talk to her . . . Check with Reception, they will tell you when I arrived . . . My own hotel will confirm that I was there all morning . . . I had no reason to harm Madame. Indeed, I had not seen her for several months . . .'

Finally the French police released Philip after he had given a statement, his composure hardly that of a man who had just butchered a woman. And besides, the killing had been a particularly brutal one and Philip Preston didn't have a mark on him. Whoever had killed Sabine Monette would have had her blood on them and would have been unlikely to report her murder. Reluctantly, after taking his details, the French police released the English auctioneer.

Philip headed back to his hotel room. He had only been in for a few moments before the phone rang.

'Where were you?'

He frowned at the sound of his wife's voice. 'I was just about to call you, Gayle.'

'I rang and rang. They said you were out.'

'I was . . . seeing a client.'

'A woman?'

'Gayle,' he said wearily, 'it was business.' He knew at once that he couldn't tell her about the murder of Sabine Monette. It would only throw her further off balance. 'I'll call you back later, darling—'

'But aren't you coming home?'

'Yes,' he said hastily. 'Of course I am. I'll be back this afternoon. I'll catch the Eurostar.'

'I miss you when you're away.'

'I miss you too.'

'I love you,' she said achingly. 'D'you love me?'

Preoccupied, Philip reached into his pocket and pulled out Sabine Monette's mobile; staring at it. But he wasn't thinking about the Frenchwoman or his wife – he was thinking about his mistress, Kim Fields. Mistress, hoping to be wife. In time. When he could work up enough courage to tell Gayle she'd been ousted.

'Do you love me?' she repeated.

'Of course, darling,' he replied. 'As much as I've ever done.'

Putting down the phone, Philip continued to think of Kim. He needed more money. Much more. Because Gayle's lawyer would screw him in a divorce. And Kim wasn't the kind of woman to stay around if he were poor . . . Philip frowned. He didn't like confrontation. His speciality was guile. He could slide in and out of situations, wheedle his way around. Sleight of mind and sleight of heart.

Flicking on Sabine Monette's stolen mobile, Philip grimaced as he noticed a blood speck and rubbed it on the coverlet of the hotel bed. Running down the list of her contacts, he paused as he read Nicholas Laverne's mobile number, followed by those of Gerrit der Keyser and Hiram Kaminski. So did the kindly Mr Kaminski know about the Bosch chain too? If so, he would definitely want it. An expert on the late Middle Ages, Kaminski was venerated for his knowledge and liked for his honesty. It wouldn't be Kaminski's way to play hardball. Not like Gerrit der Keyser.

Three of them already in the running. And how long before the infamous Conrad Voygel joined the race?

Philip continued to look through Sabine's contacts. He felt sick about her death. Not because he had been particularly fond of her, but because her murder looked bad for him. If he had had any doubts about the motive, the initials H B slashed into her skin would have removed them. This was about the chain. And something else. *What the chain had held*. Wasn't that what Nicholas Laverne had said? Before he'd been spooked and left . . .

Philip sat on the edge of his hotel bed, thinking back.

Nicholas had been ready to confide until Carel Honthorst walked in. Obviously Nicholas hadn't believed Philip's pretence at ignorance. He had seen Honthorst at the auction house and it had thrown a scare into him. Quickly, Philip glanced over at the hotel door, checking it was locked. His recollection of the Dutchman had been brief, but he knew enough about him to be worried. Gerrit der Keyser might pretend that Honthorst had only threatened Sabine Monette, but now she was dead.

Slowly Philip ran through the messages on Sabine Monette's phone. One was from her maid, another from her hairdresser, and a third from Nicholas Laverne.

Hello, Sabine.

I'm pleased you're at the George V. Keep yourself safe. Don't talk to anyone and I'll be with you soon. Meanwhile, here are some photographs to look at. These are photos of the 28 papers I found. And their explanation. They are authentic. I've had three specialists working on then. When you receive these, buy a new mobile phone and download them on to that. Then delete them off this mobile and dump it. This is important. We are on to something which will discredit the Catholic Church and the art world. But you must be careful, Sabine, and discreet. Do not let down your guard.

With affection,

Nicholas

Papers, photographs, explanations. Something that would discredit the Catholic Church and the art world. What a messy can of worms . . . Philip's hands were shaking as he opened the attachments, images of pieces of paper covered in Gothic handwriting. Scribbled, scrawled in faint script, some letters and words missing, the paper foxed, spotted with damp. But legible. Not to him – but they would be decipherable to the specialists Nicholas Laverne had employed.

He scrolled down the entries, pausing when he came to the translations reproduced underneath the originals.

Paper 1

Hieronymus Bosch, of 's-hertogen, endured much suffering, like Our Lord.

Philip stared at the words. Were these words *really* about Hieronymus Bosch? Why the suffering? *What* suffering?

Paper 2

The Brotherhood of Our Lady.
Bought and bribed.

Paper 3

Hidden away. Worked from dawn until t . . . (letters missing) *light fades. His father puts the swan to death.*

His father puts the swan to death . . . What did that mean? Philip wondered. He realised that the translations were contemporary to the time, the late Middle Ages, and would be accurate to the originals, but they were hard to decipher.

He read on.

Paper 4
Paid for Hell . . . (missing word) *living there. Demons and chimeras for sole company.*

Paper 5
The Brotherhood h . . . (missing letters) *commissioned an Altarpiece. They ask to terrorise the congregation.*

Paper 6
Hieronymus sickens with fever. From Holland comes the . . . (missing word) *of plague. Father has taken to locking the door.*

Philip paused, shocked by what he was reading. The plague had swept across Europe and killed many, but what did the words mean – *Father has taken to locking the door?* Did they refer to plague victims? Or one victim in particular, Bosch himself?

Paper 7
Jan van Aken, died this day

October 11th 14—Prayers said for his soul, that
He might enter Heaven. What justice . . . ? (missing words)

Paper 8
Hieronymus told me of his dreams; of frightful ogres,
men w . . . (missing letters) *fishes heads and naked lovers*
burning.

So Bosch *dreamed* his monsters, Philip thought. They came
to him at night . . . He could imagine how the art world
would salivate over the news – a precious insight into the
macabre world of Hieronymus Bosch.

Paper 9
From his window he regards St John's.
A spire . . . . . . (missing word) *to prick the Devil.*

Paper 10
His brother, Goossen, sits outside his door at night.
No one comes, or calls Hieronymus.

Paper 11
The Zoete Lieve Vrouw, in St John's church.
The Virgin who works miracles. Pray for our Child, our
lost boy.

Our lost boy . . . Was Hieronymus a victim of plague? Had
he faced death? Philip paused. The artist was in his sixties

when he died, so he must have recovered. Well done, *The Zoete Lieve Vrouw*, Philip thought wryly, thinking of how the statue was supposed to work miracles.

Paper 12

God's men are liars. The clergy barters worse than do the cloth merchants.

Paper 13

Antonius seeks more favour from the Brotherhood. Money fattens him . . . (missing words) . . . *silence.*

Philip paused. He felt a tremor go through him – a mixing of excitement and fear.

Paper 14

They work him like there is so little time. When he sleeps, 'tis fitful, dreaming of the dead.

Paper 15

Both of them deserve . . . (two missing words?) *. . . favour meant for another.*

Again Philip paused, glancing up at the hotel door. Footsteps passed, then silence. He turned back to the image on the phone.

Paper 16
Days pass, crouched like a spider, locked
... summer and winter bring no release.

Paper 17
The widower, Antonius, takes a whore ...
(missing word) *with money and promise of land.*

Paper 18
Commissions flow like communion wine into ...
(missing word) *the coffers of Bosch, the dupe*
of Brotherhood.

Paper 19
Inside himself, working the Devil out. The Church
asks Satan to deliver them in paint.

Confused, Philip re-read the last piece. *The Church asks Satan to deliver them in paint.* But if that were supposed to imply that Bosch was hired to save the congregation's souls, why was he placed in the guise of Satan? Philip looked at his watch, careful of the time, not wanting to miss his flight but reluctant to stop reading. What he was looking at was incendiary.

Paper 20
Forgeries passed without question, entries to ... (missing word) *record of the Brotherhood tell the*
fate of a ghost.

Paper 21

*1479 – the whore is taken as the spectre's bride.
They sleep in winding sheets.*

Paper 22

Antonius died this year 1480. His placing in . . . (missing word) *Brotherhood passed down to son.
Secret buried under the Catholic stone.*

Philip frowned, unable to make sense of what he was reading. He realised that the Church was being criticised, but didn't understand why. The pieces were little more than riddles.

A knock on the door interrupted him. He opened it half an inch and looked out to see a bellboy standing in the corridor outside.

'Excuse me, sir, I'm just reminding you that you have to leave the room in the next half an hour.' He tried to peer round the door but Philip blocked his view. 'And a message came for you.'

'The phone didn't ring.'

'It was a hand-delivered message to Reception, Mr Preston,' the bellboy replied, passing a note through the gap in the door.

Snatching it, Philip opened the folded paper. It was blank.

'Is this some kind of joke?'

'What?'

'It's blank. There's nothing on it.'

'What?' the bellboy said again, confused.

'There's nothing on the note!' Philip snapped, passing it back to the bellboy and closing the door.

Irritated, he picked up the mobile phone again. But seconds later there was another knock on the door. Philip opened it and glowered at the bellboy.

'Now what?'

'The manager told me to tell you that he was sorry about the mix-up, but there had been a message left for you. I know you said the paper was blank, but the manager said there was a verbal message, sir.'

Philip sighed. 'Which was?'

'Just one word. Bosch.' The bellboy looked embarrassed. 'I think that's how it was pronounced—'

'Who gave you the message?'

'The gentleman spoke to the manager over the phone.'

'Did they leave a name?'

'No, sir, and no contact number,' the bellboy replied. 'The manager told me to tell you that they said they would be in touch.'

Philip nodded abruptly and closed the door again. Now he knew he was being watched. He thought of Carel Honthorst and began to sweat, then turned back to the phone, his hands shaking.

Paper 23

Hieronymus Bosch is famous to the world . . . (missing word)

108

such fortune do his paintings bring to Church and family alike.

Paper 24
The Brotherhood will brook no argument. Bosch is the tool to buckle sinners. His works show Hell and Heaven as must be seen. They say God would forgive.

God would forgive . . . what? Philip wondered. What had Bosch done to need forgiveness? And secrecy.

Paper 25
Goossen, the brother, grows older, rearing
against . . . (missing word) the name not his.
Threatened by clergy, he mourns the man who was.
The one he seeks to emulate.

Paper 26
Family and riches, church and choir,
The lie that corrupts the Catholic spire.

Paper 27
Hieronymus the recluse, keeps . . . (missing word)
his rooms. Unseen amongst gargoyles and
the dead men. Rich in his winding sheet, under
the maggot church.

And then the last piece of writing.

Paper 28

In this place or abroad, none know
Hieronymus Bosch is but a dead man.
Died in the year of our Lord and his mother,
Our Lady. 1473

Philip gripped the phone.

Then he re-read the entry.

1473. Hieronymus Bosch died in 1473!

It wasn't possible. What little anyone knew of the artist for certain was his death date – 1516. But now he was reading evidence that Bosch had died in 1473 and that his family and the Catholic Church had kept his death a secret.

Philip took in a long, slow breath. No wonder everyone was so keen to get hold of the chain, so eager to be the possessor of such devastating information. There had been a conspiracy, a cover-up, dating back to the Middle Ages. The Bosch family and the Church had banded together, pretending that Hieronymus was still alive. The reason was obvious – money.

'Christ,' Philip said out loud. He could imagine how the art world would take the news, how the prices of Bosch's works might plummet if it was discovered others had faked him, passing off their works as those of the dead Master. It would be a catastrophe. Philip paused, his thoughts leap

110

frogging. How much would someone pay for such news? How much would they pay for the chain? The papers? Jesus, if he got his hands on them he was made.

He had to admire the plot. Of course the Bosch family could have pulled it off. All of them were painters: the grandfather, the father and the brothers. When Antonius died, the writings stated clearly that his son took over. One? Or all of them? How easy to perpetuate the fraud with the collusion of the Catholic Church. The Church, which was rich and powerful. The Church, which wanted to keep its congregation under control.

Bosch's visions of Heaven and Hell had done just that. Goodness rewarded in *The Garden of Earthly Delights*, evil punished by the obscenities of Hell. When the papers were written the world was still in the grip of the Middle Ages; it was to be a while before civilisation saw the light of reason. The rich and oppressive Catholic Church wielded absolute power, the means to control the people secured by the imagination of Brabant's visionary, Hieronymus Bosch. It had been his images of Hell and damnation, his painted tortures and distortions, which had frightened the congregation into pious submission. In a time when superstition was rife, when the world was still believed to be flat, when dragons and chimeras haunted the minds of men, there was a terrible power in paint.

For the wicked, Bosch promised a torment of legless creatures swallowing the damned whole, of tortoises with Death's heads and winged demons with tiger's claws. He painted ships on fire, the naked and the doomed screaming as devils dragged them into the darkness and the lost chasms of Hell. He created men seduced by pigs; bodies impaled, halved and devoured by alligators; men with arrows in their anuses; women ridden by demons. Bodies distorted, abused, bleeding, violated – and the message was there for everyone to see. Even if the congregation could not read or write the paintings told them – this is the result of sin. This is the reward for the wicked.

For the virtuous, Bosch painted a Heaven of plenty and beauty. But only for the good.

It was a message the Catholic Church had preached for centuries, and it found its perfect expression in Hieronymus Bosch. Paint and panel managed to do what popes and soldiers could not – they forced obedience by the use of fear.

Philip paused, thinking of what he had just learnt. In reality, Hieronymus Bosch had only lived for *twenty-three years*. Long enough to become famous, his visions and images immediately recognisable – and easy to reproduce. Hieronymus Bosch had created a template for his family to follow. God only knows how many paintings he had done while he was alive or how many sketches and drawings had been created by him – all ready for his avaricious family to draw upon. With the collusion of the Church, all they had had to do was to secure, and fulfil, the endless commissions.

Work for a dead man.

Paid for by a deceitful clergy.

Hieronymus Bosch was to have no headstone, no mourning. His death was never to be acknowledged; his marriage a sham. And then Philip realised something else: the only documents known to the world concerning Hieronymus Bosch were the entries in the account books of The Brotherhood of Mary. Entries that were obviously false, recording a life made up, created to keep a corpse alive. And with those entries came the counterfeit commissions. The man had died long ago, but the name had been made to work on.

Getting to his feet, Philip hid Sabine Monette's mobile at the bottom of his suitcase and grabbed his coat. He understood why the world would want a chain that had belonged to Hieronymus Bosch, but how much more would the Catholic Church want the secret suppressed?

He would have to be very careful to profit from this, Philip thought. He was in trouble, and he knew it. No wonder Sabine Monette had been killed. There were a few collectors and dealers ruthless enough to employ any means to secure something priceless – and scandalous. The chain wasn't just an object of beauty, it was a revelation. And it might well prove to be his way to a cushy life . . . Philip paused, his fear giving way to greed. This could be a way to dump Gayle and marry his mistress. A way to flaunt his success to his peers and relish the fortune that was sure to be his.

Or it might mean his destruction. Only this time it would

be *his* body in a hotel room, the notorious initials H B carved into *his* dying flesh.

Bloody hell, Philip thought despairingly. Why, in God's name, had he taken Sabine Monette's phone?

Twenty

Church of St Stephen, Fulham, London

'I thought I'd find you here.'

Nicholas turned, surprised to find Eloise Devereux standing in the doorway of the vestry. She was bundled up against the cold in a tailored coat, her blonde hair tucked under a black hat. Elegant, groomed as always, although her eyes were swollen from crying. 'I have to talk to you about Claude.'

Closing the vestry door so that Father Michael wouldn't overhear them, Nicholas showed Eloise into the church, and settled into one of the back pews. She hesitated, then sat down next to him, pulling off her gloves, revealing her right hand bandaged to the wrist. Quickly she pulled down her sleeve to cover it.

'Claude was killed—'

'What?' He wanted to reach out to her but resisted. They had been friends, but only because of Claude. And at times

Nicholas had noticed envy on Eloise's part: a jealousy for a history that had not included her.

'He was murdered two days ago.'

'I didn't know . . .' He stared at her. 'You said he was killed. Why?'

'You know why,' Eloise said quietly, her skin bloodless in the cold church. A shiver ran through her and her lips parted for an instant, then closed again.

'I *don't* know, Eloise–'

'Hieronymus Bosch . . . Don't deny it, Nicholas. I don't blame you for anything. I didn't know anything about the chain until yesterday when I went through Claude's papers. His *will* . . .' Her English accent was perfect, polished. 'He was too young to make a will. You're supposed to do that when you're old. But he made one, in great detail. He took care with it, almost as though he knew that it would be needed.' She stopped, stared at her hands, at her wedding band. 'That Bosch painting originally belonged to Claude's father, Raoul.'

The news surprised him. 'Raoul Devereux owned the painting?'

'Until it was stolen from his gallery. The following year he died, and the Bosch was never seen again. But apparently it re-emerged in England, and was bought by an elderly man. The same man who gave it to Gerrit der Keyser to sell for him . . .'

The name went like a bolt into his spine, but Nicholas said nothing.

'. . . The person who bought it was Sabine Monette. Of course you know that. But although the painting was valuable there was more to it. A secret, hidden in the chain by which it was hung. Apparently every connector between the links had a piece of paper in it. A note. Twenty-eight in all, which made up a testimony. Did Sabine know that? Did she read it?' Her eyes turned on Nicholas. 'She was murdered. Like Claude. But then you know that too – you and Sabine were close. So now tell me, Nicholas, why have my husband and your friend – who both knew about the Bosch secret – been killed?'

'I didn't know that Claude was privy to any of this. We never discussed it—'

She was composed, but brusque. 'Where's the chain?'

'I don't know—'

'Liar,' she said softly. 'You can't protect me, I don't want you to. You aren't my husband or a member of my family. I'm not your responsibility, Nicholas – I am my own person. I mean to find out who killed my husband, and why. Claude said the notes told of a conspiracy, but he didn't say what it was.'

'I'm sorry he told you any of it—'

'You have no right to judge my husband!'

'He was also my friend, and as such I can judge him,' Nicholas replied, glancing up at the altar. 'Have you still got the letter he wrote?'

'Of course.'

'Then destroy it. And forget what you read—'

117

'How very presumptuous of you,' Eloise responded. 'You can't tell me what to do. I want to know more, not less. What did the papers say?'

'I don't know.'

A soft sound escaped her lips as Eloise rose to her feet and looked around her. 'Strange that you should come back here. I thought you weren't allowed to enter a church again.'

'Excommunication doesn't mean I'm banned from the Church. It's a penalty, dished out in the hope I'll repent.'

She raised her eyebrows. 'So it's reversible? Not much of a punishment.'

'It is to a priest. I can't receive the Eucharist and I won't get a Catholic burial. Unless I repent, of course.' He held her gaze, feeling the animosity. 'Which I won't. I despise the Catholic Church. I'm not here for forgiveness, but for another reason entirely.'

'What reason?' she asked, without turning to look at him. 'I believe there was a murder here recently—'

'How did you hear that?'

'I come from a wealthy family. The only child of an over-indulgent mother and a rich – if absent – father. I married Claude for love – money didn't matter to me then. But now I recognise its value. You see, now I can find out anything I want, because I can buy information. Money is a wonderful lubricant. It oils people's memories.'

He was surprised by her. The Eloise he remembered had been a reserved woman, discreet, without particular opinions. The wife of his best friend, the woman who had made

118

Claude happy. Nothing more. But the person Nicholas was now listening to was altogether different. He didn't know this woman.

'The man who was murdered here was a vagrant,' Nicholas explained. 'His death isn't related to what we're talking about.'

She turned, walked back to him and looked down into his face.

'What *are* we talking about, Nicholas? Two murders, an ancient mystery, something so dangerous that you're here babysitting an old priest.' She nodded. 'I told you, I can find out a lot of things when I want to. And I *will* find out who killed my husband and Sabine Monette.'

Nicholas stared at her, trying to work out what she was offering.

'Where's the chain?'

He shook his head. 'I don't know.'

She walked to the door and paused. 'I'll come back and we can talk again. In the meantime, think about what I've said. I can help you – so we might as well work together.'

'I'm not putting you in danger.'

'It's too late for that,' she said shortly. 'It's spreading, Nicholas. The secret's leaked out and it's claimed two lives already. Trust me or there'll be more. And next time it might be someone *you* love.'

Twenty-One

Philip Preston's Auction House, Chelsea, London

There was an auction already in progress. Philip was on the rostrum and a large video screen was throwing up magnified images of the lots so that the audience could see – in glaring close-up – exactly what they were bidding for. Of course most dealers attended the previews and picked over the goods before the auction, making a note of lot numbers and the estimate of how much each piece was expected to reach. But there were always latecomers, and the inevitable opportunists.

Positioned at the back of the hall, Gerrit der Keyser spotted Hiram Kaminski and beckoned for him to approach. He scuttled over, peeling off a pair of pigskin gloves and laying his hat on his lap. He was, as ever, prim, his feet crossed at the ankles.

'I heard about Sabine Monette,' Hiram whispered, shocked. 'What a terrible way to die. I read that she'd been murdered.' He paused, then asked, 'Hadn't she just bought a painting off you?'

'Shit!' Gerrit said feigning irritation. 'So the secret's out, is it? Yeah, the old bat bought a small Bosch picture – and stole a chain off me.' He watched as Hiram's eyes widened. Nice man, Gerrit thought. Good dealer. Honest and trusting. Poor fool. 'She nicked the fucking chain off the back of the painting. Thought I wouldn't notice—'

'Why?'

'Why what?'

'Why did she steal the chain?' Hiram asked, his tone perplexed. 'Sabine Monette was a rich woman. So why would she need to steal? And besides, she'd bought the painting so the chain was hers by rights anyway.'

Damn it, Gerrit thought, Hiram Kaminski wasn't quite the innocent he seemed.

'She had dementia,' Gerrit lied, tapping his forehead. 'Early onset Alzheimer's. I mean, I wouldn't have pressed charges, I just wanted to get the chain back. But apparently she'd lost it – her mind *and* the chain – so I let the matter rest.' He touched Hiram's sleeve. 'Don't repeat a word of this, hey? I mean, I don't want to look like a mug.'

Hiram might have seemed guileless, but he wasn't that big a fool. Piecing together what his wife had told him and this last bit of information from Gerrit der Keyser, he asked, 'Was the chain valuable?'

'It was old—'

'Original to the painting?'

Gerrit shrugged, lying deftly. 'I suppose so.'

121

'So it dated from Hieronymus Bosch's time!' Hiram said crossly. 'I have to say, Gerrit, rivalry or not, everyone in London knows that I'm an expert on the late Middle Ages. You could have contacted me – I might have wanted to buy it.' He was flushed with annoyance, overheated in a worsted suit. 'Bosch is one of my favourite artists and any artefact which had belonged to him would have been of tremendous interest to me.'

'But you couldn't have afforded it,' Gerrit replied regretfully. 'I got a tremendous price from Sabine Monette—'

'Probably took advantage of her dementia,' Hiram snorted, watching as Philip Preston started the bidding on a small Turner sketch. Automatically, he dropped his voice. 'You shouldn't have sold it to her if you knew she wasn't *all there*. And besides, how d'you know I couldn't have afforded it?'

'People talk. And let's face it, your gallery's not been doing too well in the recession, has it?' Gerrit needled him. 'Not that you're one of the unscrupulous dealers, Hiram – we all know you're a decent man. But decent men aren't usually rich men.'

'You still could have asked me,' Hiram replied, smarting, reverting to a whisper. 'You could have given me the opportunity to put in a bid. You didn't even let me look at it. As a scholar I'd have relished the chance to study the chain.'

Gerrit sighed. 'Sabine Monette wanted a quick sale.'

'How convenient,' Hiram replied, uncharacteristically caustic. 'So where's the painting and the chain now?'

'The painting's still at her French estate, I suppose. As for the chain, who knows? Like I say, she lost it.' Gerrit shrugged, wondering himself just where the chain had got to and if it was, as he suspected, now with Nicholas Laverne. 'I suppose it's now a lost cause.'

Hiram gave him a cold look. 'Somebody cheated you and you're going to let it go?'

'I have no choice. Sabine Monette is dead.'

'Murdered,' Hiram said, feeling his way along. Gerrit der Keyser had infuriated him. He had never trusted the dealer; he was suspicious of his methods and still stinging from his patronising comments. A kindly man, Hiram was unusually abrasive. 'Why would anyone kill Sabine Monette? It makes no sense. Unless . . .'

'Unless what?'

'Unless,' Hiram whispered, leaning closer towards Gerrit der Keyser, 'they're killing everyone who knows about the chain.'

Twenty-Two

It was drizzling when Nicholas hurried towards Philip Preston's business premises. His coat soaked, he entered the auction room just as Philip handed the proceedings over to his assistant and left the hall.

Ducking round the back of the building, Nicholas took the fire escape steps to Preston's office and walked in, unannounced, to find the auctioneer kissing his secretary. Embarrassed Philip jumped back and the woman left the room hurriedly.

'Couldn't you have knocked?' Philip asked, wiping lipstick off his mouth with his handkerchief and glowering at Nicholas.

He was unmoved. 'Aren't you a bit old for that?'

'I wasn't the one who took a vow of chastity,' Philip replied. 'Where have you been anyway? I'd given up on you, thought you weren't coming back.'

'Sabine Monette was murdered.'

'I know, I found her,' Philip replied, smoothing his white hair with his hands. 'Don't look at me like that!'

'*You* found her? How did you find her?'

'I was going to have a chat with her—'

'You were trying to cut me out, you mean,' Nicholas retorted bitterly. 'Did you find out anything useful, Philip?'

He was about to lie, then thought better of it.

'I know what your big secret is. I took Sabine's phone, saw the Bosch papers that you'd sent to her.' He shrugged, feigning nonchalance. 'Quite a revelation, I must say. The art world won't like it, Bosch dying in his twenties – it means that all the paintings after 1473 were fakes.'

'Not entirely. They were done by members of the Bosch family.'

'But not Hieronymus, which is where the value lies. No one wants the also-rans.' Philip reached into his middle desk drawer and waved Sabine Monette's mobile in his hand. 'Thing is, I don't know what to do with this information. Not yet, anyway. I suppose you want to expose the part the Catholic Church played in the fraud, hang them out to dry. Certainly won't look good for them, covering up a man's death and raking in money for all those years. Then again, we have to think of the art world too, don't we?'

'Do we?'

'If we expose this subterfuge, the value of Bosch's works will take a beating. A lot of galleries and collectors around the world will have egg on their faces when this comes out. *If* it comes out.' Philip paused, pushing the mobile into his back pocket. 'Of course it doesn't have to. I know of interested parties who would pay well to keep it suppressed.'

'You're crooked.'

Philip shrugged. 'No, I just know how to be flexible. This is a business that requires a lot of gymnastics.'

'The truth *will* come out, Philip. You can't stop it. Remember, you've just seen copies of the papers, but I have the originals—'

'And the chain?'

He nodded. 'And the chain.'

'I wouldn't brag about that,' Philip replied. 'Sabine Monette was murdered. Like I say, I saw the body. There were details that didn't make it into the French press and certainly not to the UK papers. Details which link her to the Bosch matter.'

Nicholas was wondering what Philip Preston wanted. He was also thinking about Eloise Devereux. It was obvious that she was determined to find her husband's killer, and was asking for his help. Maybe he was honour bound to give it.

But helping Philip Preston was another matter.

'You saw Sabine's body?'

Philip nodded. 'I did . . . I'm sorry. I know you cared for her.'

'Did she suffer?'

'Yes, I think she did,' Philip replied honestly. 'There were initials cut into her stomach: H and B.'

Nicholas flinched. 'But her mobile wasn't taken?'

'It had fallen under a cabinet. Not easy to see, especially if someone was interrupted and had to leave quickly.' He paused, then hurried on. 'What did the phone matter anyway? They knew she had the chain – at least, she *did* have it – so they must have realised she knew about the secret . . .' He stopped short. '*Do* they know about the secret or do they just want the chain?'

'Gerrit der Keyser handled the painting and the chain so he must be involved in some way.'

'Keyser would certainly want it,' Philip said thoughtfully, 'and he's not squeamish. But then again, others would be after it too, like Hiram Kaminski and a few more I can think of. Have you heard of Conrad Voygel?'

'Everyone has. The IT giant.'

Philip nodded. 'He's a big collector too – artefacts and silver. I've sold to him on and off for a long time but never dealt with him face to face. Voygel has runners, minions who do the deals for him. No one's ever done business with him directly. He's not a man to pin down. To be honest, I've often wondered if he even exists. I mean, the photographs that occasionally crop up in the papers could be of anyone.'

'Isn't that a bit far-fetched?'

Philip raised his eyebrows. 'Why? They kept the dead Hieronymus Bosch alive for decades, so nothing surprises me any more.' He paused, thinking. 'Voygel has a bad reputation. Capable of anything, they say. But who knows – maybe that's just good PR. What I do know for a fact is that he has enough money to buy – and enough power to silence – anyone.'

'And Gerrit der Keyser has Carel Honthorst working for him, the man you denied knowing.'

'I didn't know whose side I was on then. I didn't want to show my hand.' Philip shrugged. 'And now I've got in too deep. Serves me right for being greedy.'

'You know you're not safe? Two people who knew the secret have already been killed. I'm pretty sure I've been followed—'

Philip slumped into his chair. 'And I got a warning when I was in Paris. Some note with nothing written on it, and then someone left a message which was just one word – *Bosch*. And I don't think they were talking about a bloody washing machine . . . I should never have got involved.'

Nicholas had little sympathy. 'Too late now. You're a marked man, like me. Like Eloise Devereux—'

Philip's eyebrows rose. 'Who?'

'Someone else who knows about the secret. Someone I have to try and protect.' Nicholas paused, considering his next words. 'We have to help each other. If we don't, we'll get picked off one by one. Whoever's doing this *must* know the secret – the chain's worth a fortune, but not worth killing for.'

Philip laughed, amused. 'You have no idea about the art world, have you?'

'That's why I came to you. I need someone with the knowledge I don't have.'

'Strange, isn't it, the ways things work out?'

Nicholas stared at him. 'What d'you mean?'

'I remember my father doing business with your parents and your uncle. Then I traded with Henry. But you – you were never in the picture, if you'll forgive the pun.' He sighed. 'It just seems odd, that's all, that it's you that's ended up with a priceless artefact. The one person who has no interest in Bosch.'

'Just the part religion played in all of this,' Nicholas replied. 'Remember, I *do* know all about the Church.'

'Well, let me educate you about the art world. In this business there are a number of factions: criminals, buyers and sellers, and a few dealers who employ any means to get what they want. You think the chain's not enough to create havoc? Let me tell you something: people kill for a thousand pounds so a prize like that would be well worth murdering for. The piece belonged to Hieronymus Bosch, I could auction it for a fortune tomorrow. As for the secret – what wouldn't an interested party do to keep that quiet?' He glanced at Nicholas. 'Don't tell me you're going to take the Catholic Church on again?'

'They were complicit in a deception—'

'How you love your conspiracies,' Philip said slyly. 'But no one listened before, so why should they this time?'

'This time I have proof.'

'That's lucky,' Philip replied. 'Last time your proof hanged himself.'

Stung, Nicholas stared at the auctioneer; at the lush white hair, the brilliant, calculating eyes.

'If I agree to help you,' Philip said evenly, 'I want a reward.'

'And there was I thinking you just wanted to live.'

Philip ignored the comment. He was concentrating on the money – enough money to change his life, enough to leave his wife well looked after and finally escape. Go abroad with his mistress, Kim Fields. Enough money to indulge himself.

Still watching him, Nicholas rose to his feet and walked to the door. There he beckoned for Philip to follow him. Exposed in the daylight, standing in the open doorway at the top of the fire escape steps, Nicholas handed Philip a package.

'What the hell—'

Nicholas cut him off, whispering. 'Tuck it into your jacket and smile at me.'

He did as he was told, muttering under his breath, 'What are you doing?'

Nicholas smiled back at him, as though they were friends talking. 'If anyone's watching us they'll assume I've just given you the chain. Keep smiling!' Nicholas hissed at the auctioneer. 'That's it. You almost look like a happy man.' He turned and glanced up at the sky. 'It's stopped raining.'

Unnerved, Philip kept smiling, talking through clenched teeth. 'You bastard, you set me up—'

'You set yourself up when you went to Paris and tried to cut me out,' Nicholas replied coldly. 'Question is, what are you going to do now?'

There was a momentary pause before Philip responded.

'OK . . . I'll help you find out who's behind all this. But in return I want the chain.'

'You can have the bloody thing,' Nicholas replied, making a public show of shaking hands with the auctioneer. 'We have a deal, Philip. You go after the art world, I go after the Church.'

Twenty-Three

Kim Fields was lying with her head on Philip's lap, her hair dangling over his expensive pinstriped trousers. In the three years since she had come to England from Poland she had worked her way up from secretarial temping to a life of subsidised insolence and the promise of future matrimonial security. No need for Philip to know that she passed half of the money he gave her to relatives back home. No need to tell him that her family's future depended on her getting her lover to commit. After all, in law the wife was due half of her husband's property; a mistress was due *nic*, i.e. nothing.

But she had to admit that it was taking longer than she had expected to prise Philip away from his hysterical wife. Her sensual persuasion would pay off, she reassured herself – unless the philandering auctioneer left her after eighteen months of hard labour, and found someone else.

Originally Kim had come to work for Philip in the auction house, but soon her talent in bed superseded her talent in the business and within six months she had been ensconced in a flat in Bloomsbury, living above a PR agent and next to a solicitors' office. This meant that it was quiet at night when Philip usually visited. But lately his visits had been less frequent and Kim was worried that his interest had waned.

But it hadn't, and now he was stroking her hair and explaining. 'Gayle's getting worse, she's unbalanced. Says it's because of the menopause.' He wrinkled his nose at the word, at the dropped flag of desire. 'She hears voices and see things, you know. Like her dead father and people from the past, old friends we used to have. *I see dead people*,' he mimicked, taking the line from the film *The Sixth Sense*.

Kim laughed, teeth blazing white against her pearly complexion. 'I feel sorry for her.'

'You should feel sorry for me,' Philip replied, leaning down to kiss her and then realising that his back wouldn't bend that far. Deftly, Kim rose up to kiss him, her hand around his neck. You had to make allowances, she told her friends. When men get older they aren't so supple.

'I feel sorry for you every day, darling,' she murmured. 'I want you to be happy – that's why you have to leave her. I don't want to be cruel, but your wife's a very sick woman and you have a life of your own. There's nothing more you can do to help her, you've taken her to see so many doctors already. You're such a good man – she doesn't realise how lucky she is.' Gently Kim stroked the back of his neck, her copper-coloured eyes fixed on his. Exotic, almost as striking as Gayle had once been. 'I know you have to do it in your own time, but sweetheart, it's so hard on you and Gayle's not going to get any better, is she?'

He could feel an erection coming on and wanted to stop talking about his wife, wanted to stop Kim pressurising him and wanted, above all, to get into the bedroom, which was costing him nine hundred pounds a month.

'Darling—'

'I love you so much,' Kim interrupted. 'We can sort this out and be together—'

He kissed her eagerly, his hand moving under her skirt as Kim tilted her head back so that he could nuzzle her throat. He liked that, she told friends. It turned him on. Over his shoulder Kim glanced at her watch as she began to move against his crotch, increasing the rhythm and moaning. In twenty minutes she had an appointment across town and she couldn't be late.

That was the good thing about sex with older men. It never took long.

Twenty-Four

Church of St Stephen, Fulham, London

They were having choir practice, twelve children of assorted sizes entering by the side door and then filing neatly into the wooden pews beside the altar. At the back of the church sat Father Michael, watching in silence, glad of the company although the children were scared of his dour, cadaverous figure. Pulling a black cardigan over his vestments, the old priest noticed the flutter of the incense in the burner and the soft footfall of someone approaching.

He flinched, but it was only the music teacher passing, walking up to the children and placing his score on the lectern. He tapped the wood twice, then once more, and the children fell silent as the organist made his first faltering steps into the chords of Bach. The old priest didn't move or turn. In the church, with people around him, he was safe. No violent Dutchman to question him; no furtive footfalls in locked quarters. In amongst the simmer of incense and the dry scent of old hymn sheets he was protected. He was secure. He was safe.

From everything but his memory.

Twenty-Five

On the other side of Chelsea, Nicholas waited in a shadowed doorway. He had been there for over an hour, watching the back entrance to Philip Preston's auction house. He could see the half-hearted moonlight strike the side of the fire escape steps and dribble listlessly over the office windows. He could hear various cars drive past or park, and the sound of an argument coming from a nearby street. But nothing made him move. Even the cold, pressing against him, unwelcome as a leper, didn't force him to desert his post.

And while Nicholas waited he thought of his sister, Honor. Maybe, finally, he would contact her. She had come to the forefront of his mind because Eloise had mentioned her, and suddenly Nicholas had felt an urgency to see his sibling again. But he had checked the impulse. He had had his chance and left it too late. Why get in touch when he was in trouble? When any involvement with him might be catastrophic?

Nicholas knew he had been a poor brother, difficult to know, harder to love. He had deliberately cut his sister out.

137

They were only a few years apart and should have been close. They could have made a family – but he had smashed any chance of that, alienating himself from everyone until he had decided to change his life while he still could.

For a time he was God's child, all passion turned into a religious passion. He found celibacy easy after having been promiscuous, and poverty appealing when it came with a home and three meals a day. He even conquered obedience, becaming an honest priest and a stable man. But the glimmer of anarchy within him didn't stay dormant forever. And when his disgrace came it was absolute – but contained. He kept his family out of it and instead went away. Went to ground. Which was why he knew the right thing to do for his sister was to stay away from her, even more so now.

Hidden in the doorway, his face chilled, he felt a wind start up. Across the road he could see the metal fire escape and the monotonous green blinking of the alarm. If anyone broke in the beady emerald light would snap into life, turn red as the flash of a fox's eye, its electric scream activated, and alerting the police.

Nicholas stared at the light and thought of Father Michael. Nervy, mumbling under his breath, the priest was plainly cowed by something and resentful of Nicholas's presence. He was angry at having to be grateful to a man he had failed. So many failures, Nicholas thought, so many secrets, so much guilt . . . His attention was suddenly caught by a movement to his left as someone entered the alleyway and walked towards the fire escape. Pressing further back into the shadows, Nicholas watched a hulking figure climb up the metal steps and peer into the office window. Honthorst, Carel Honthorst. He moved quietly for such a big man, and worked quickly. To Nicholas's surprise, the alarm was disabled in seconds, with only a short screech. Had he managed to prevent the warning going through to the police? Moments later, Honthorst was inside.

The light flicked on. Nicholas could see the Dutchman walk past the window, then heard the sound of shuffling. Barely half a minute had passed before he left, moving down the fire escape and walking past Nicholas's hiding place.

Suddenly he stopped in his tracks, his shadow vast behind him. Pausing only feet from Nicholas, the Dutchman raised his head and closed his eyes, sniffing the air like a dog.

Then he turned and headed straight for where Nicholas was hiding.

's-Hertogenbosch, Brabant, 1470

Stepping over a pile of pig manure in the town centre, Hieronymus held on to the panel under his arm and coughed. The winter was promising to be foul, the last week full of black moonless nights. He would have liked to be alone but he was always accompanied by a member of the family, this time, the bent rod of his grandfather.

As he moved towards the cloth market, Hieronymus nodded to an affiliate of the Brotherhood of Our Lady. The man, a merchant, was a high-ranking member of The Swan Bethren, that intimate circle of the elite within the Brotherhood. Stout, his belly hanging over his belt, his leggings splattered with mud, the merchant stepped through the muck. His fur-trimmed cloak swung awkwardly from one shoulder, an elaborate velvet cap topping his unprepossessing face.

Hieronymus wondered what the merchant would say if he knew he had been sketched, his image put aside to serve as a fat demon in a painting of Hell. Hieronymus liked to steal images, sitting in his studio at the top of the house and watching the market-

'The Temptation of St Anthony' [detail]
After Hieronymus Bosch

place with its press of people. From his eyrie he caught sight of pickpockets and whores baring their breasts to attract trade. They wore woollen chemises tied at the neck, easy to undo.

And then there were the dealers, the merchants who had profited from the flourishing wool and textile industries of Brabant, the dukes of Brabant depending on the wealth created to finance their wars and extravagant lifestyles. The towns were rich, fat on trade, and with that trade – alongside discoveries by seafarers and scientists – came the sobering influence of religion.

Hieronymus paused to watch a dog barking loudly at a penned pig as a boy poked it with a stick. For a moment he was tempted to draw the boy, but he moved on towards the church. His success had overwhelmed him; not yet twenty, he was pointed out at the market, hailed on the street. His father and brothers would have adored such attention but for Hieronymus, shy, crippled by night terrors and afraid of the world around him, it was torment. He felt at peace only in the privacy of his studio, paintbrush in hand.

Antonius might brag of his son in public, but in private he was a critical, belittling tyrant, his hatred of Hieronymus stemming from the death of his wife during the birth of this, their last child. Indeed, if the boy had not turned out to be so gifted he might well have been shipped off to a cousin in the country, forgotten and unmourned.

But for all Antonius's dislike of his son, Hieronymus's talent protected him. Its early flowering appeared like an orchid in a dunghill, provoking awe. As the boy's promise developed into an outstanding talent, Antonius touted him about the Brotherhood like a prize ram with a fleece that could be stripped and woven into

142

gold. In the runt of the family, the ambitious and pious Antonius saw his own reputation advancing, his family coffers swelling.

It was fortunate that his son had such nightmares, dreams of Hell and damnation which Antonius's treatment had exacerbated over the years. His criticism and judgemental attitude had cowed the boy; buckled the genius into a haunted wrath. But the mistreatment had also resulted in a vision, which the Church recognised and devoured. Hieronymus's paintings portrayed everyday life at a time when religion wielded a moral cosh to keep people in line. Urged on by the Church and his father, he was corralled into depicting themes of temptation, sin and punishment. The Devil that the priests thundered about lived in his paintings and their message was simple: a good life leads to Heaven, a sinful one to Hell.

But the hallucinations and night terrors Hieronymus suffered from affected his health. When the plague came to Europe, he was protected, the studio door locked and visitors turned away. His family monitored his sleeping, his eating, his walks in the walled garden. If their breadwinner sickened or died, so would their fortunes. And so the Church and his own family pressed him into work, into the endless service of his terrifying visions.

And then, one day in May of 1473, Hieronymus Bosch escaped.

Twenty-Six

Eloise Devereux stood for a moment outside the gallery in Chelsea, then opened the door and walked in. Her attractive presence soon caught the attention of Miriam der Keyser. A thin woman with a whining voice, she patrolled her husband's gallery like a jailer, his every conversation with a woman supervised.

'Can I help you?' Miriam asked peevishly.

'Is your husband here? I'd like to speak to Mr der Keyser.'

Miriam's mouth opened, but before she could speak Gerrit materialised at the back of the gallery. 'Can I be of assistance?' he asked, darting his wife a dismissive look.

'I'd like to talk to you in private,' Eloise continued. 'It's a confidential matter.'

'My husband's busy—' Miriam tried to interrupt but Gerrit brushed past her and led Eloise into his office. Once inside, he made sure the door was closed and Miriam on the outside.

'How can I help?'

He was all servile charm, using the gallant persona

reserved for his customers. And she was quite a customer, he thought, watching as Eloise sat down and crossed her legs.

'You're doing well,' she remarked coolly. 'I liked the David Teniers in the window. I know how much you admire that artist.'

His collar felt suddenly tight, an unpleasant sensation rising in him. Gerrit didn't recognise the woman, but she was talking to him as though they were old acquaintances.

'Do I know you?'

She ignored the question, glancing around the office, Her hair swept up in a chignon, her cream coat cut to perfection, elegance exuded from her. Gerrit fiddled with his over-large cuffs then reached into his desk drawer and took out a bottle of pills. Without a word, he swallowed several with a glass of water, Eloise watching him.

'You're ill, but I suspected as much. You've lost a lot of weight – you used to be a stocky man.' She paused, putting her head to one side. 'You don't know who I am, do you?'

He shook his head. 'No, I don't. Who are you?'

'We'll come to that later,' she replied. 'I have some business to discuss first: a chain which once belonged to Hieronymus Bosch.' Gerrit's eyes flickered. Eloise noted the reaction and smiled. 'I can imagine how much you must want to get it back. It was unusual for you to be slow and lose it. But then again, illness slows everyone down.'

'OK, what the fuck's going on?' Gerrit asked, all politeness abandoned.

145

'I know you're looking for the chain.' Her eyes held his gaze. 'How *hard* are you looking?'

'Sabine Monette stole it off a painting—'

'And now Sabine Monette is dead,' Eloise replied. 'Are the two connected?'

'She died in Paris, in the George the Fifth Hotel. Some fucking lunatic killed her—'

'Why did he kill her? Her money wasn't taken.'

'How come you know so much about it?' Gerrit asked, his eyes narrowing. 'This has nothing to do with me—'

'It has everything to do with you. You wanted that chain, you threatened Sabine Monette—'

'I did not!'

She waved aside his protestations. 'All right, you sent some thug to threaten her. Either way, she ended up dead. Murdered.'

Gerrit rose to his feet. 'I don't have to talk to you.'

'You're right, you don't. But if you want to get the chain back, maybe you should,' she replied. 'Maybe I can get it for you.'

He was all attention now, regaining his seat and running his tongue over his bottom lip. 'Why would you?'

'I have my reasons.'

'Which are?'

'Nothing to do with you,' she replied coolly. 'Do you want the chain back?'

'How much?'

146

'It's not about money, Mr de Keyser, it's much more valuable than that. This is about a debt. One you owe someone I cared about . . . Let me tell you something. My husband, my *dead* husband, had a friend who was in trouble. That friend went to work for an elderly lady in France, Sabine Monette. I knew about it because I was close to Sabine and she confided in me. I thought the relationship would be good for both of them. And it was.'

'What the hell—'

'Hear me out – it's in your interests,' she admonished him. 'You had an affair with Sabine Monette many years ago. It was brief and unhappy, or so she told me.' Eloise was perfectly poised. 'I suppose I should mention that I inherited a large fortune when I reached eighteen.'

'Lucky you. Want to buy some pictures?'

She smiled with chilling coldness. 'I am here to sell, not buy.'

'Sell what?'

'Not so fast, Mr der Keyser. You have to hear the rest of the story first. The rich have the money to be discreet; privilege brings protection. When you left Sabine so ruthlessly, her family married her off within weeks. She put the whole business behind her and, to all intents and purposes, forgot about it.'

'It was a long time ago. I doubt she pined for me.'

'She never mentioned you.'

His voice was suspicious. 'What's your name?'

'All in good time, Mr der Keyser . . . What would you do to own the chain?' He said nothing. 'And the secret it holds.'

'What secret?' he said, trying to sound casual but but failing.

'You know well enough.'

'I don't know the whole story. Just the rumour of a conspiracy. You've heard of it too, obviously,' he replied, piqued. 'I thought I was the only one.'

'No, you didn't. You *hoped* you were the only one. But then you found out that others knew, like Sabine and my husband, both of whom are now dead. But you must know that.'

'I know about Sabine, but not about your husband.'

'Even though the Bosch painting and chain once belonged to his father, Raoul Devereux?'

He looked rattled, thrown off balance. 'I didn't know anything about that . . . Anyway, so what? It's just coincidence.'

'No, it's murder,' she corrected him.

'And you think I'm responsible?'

'I don't know, but if you are, I'll see you punished.'

Gerrit smiled sourly and leaned forward across the desk. 'You come here and all but accuse me of murder. Why would you do that?' he sneered. 'I've never killed anyone but if I *was* violent, what would stop me coming after you?'

'You still don't understand, do you?'

He was getting angry and veins stood out on his thin neck. 'I should have you thrown out of here—'

148

'But you won't because you want the chain. You would do business with the Devil for that chain – for what it held, for what it means.'

'If I'm so dangerous,' Gerrit snapped, 'why help me?'

'Because I want to see if it *is* you. If you killed them. And in order to do that I'm prepared to help you, to get close to you, to be with you – until I'm sure of your innocence, or guilt.'

He was unnerved, but continued. 'If I'm so dangerous, why aren't you afraid?'

'You won't hurt me.' She smiled coldly. 'No father would kill their own daughter.'

Nicholas knows he is dreaming, but can't wake himself. Instead he follows the same familiar route between the yew trees towards the outhouse in the church grounds. But this time it's daylight and the dead boy is alive, leaning against the wall of the building, talking to a lad of his own age.

They see him and their bodies tense as Nicholas approaches. He knows the boys, both trainee priests from the seminary, sent from Dublin to study for the priesthood in London. Their families read the letters they send, never knowing each line is censored, believing in a false happiness. Nicholas sees the boys and calls out to them.

Patrick turns his head towards Nicholas and his left eye is puffy; there is bruising along his chin and the knuckles of both hands are bloodied. Nicholas asks what has happened. Are you OK? Is everything all right? Are you being treated well at St Barnabas's? . . . Same questions, same answers, as always. Fine, all fine. Couldn't be better . . . He knows they're lying, and watches them flinch as a voice calls their names.

Their reaction is always the same in the dream, as it was in life. They turn and move away between the yew trees passing Nicholas.

And in the doorway of the church, waiting for them, stand two priests: Father Dominic and Father Luke. The first is sleek as a wild mink, the latter standing, arms akimbo, in the fading light.

I want a word with you, Nicholas says to them. What about? About the boys . . . Father Dominic shrugs and moves away. Father Luke, his defiant arms out of proportion with his short legs and narrow trunk, stands looking at Nicholas as though he doesn't have time to chat. As though he wants him off the premises. Go back to your own church, St Stephen's, he says. Mind your own business or I'll take it up with Father Michael.

And Nicholas – as always, as ever – walks away. He'll come back, he tells himself. Check on the boys. He pushes out of his mind Patrick Gerin's bruises and puffy eye and goes back to St Stephen's, passing between the yew trees that never change.

Twenty-Seven

Honthorst was just about to reach the doorway where Nicholas was hiding when his name was called. He hesitated, then turned and walked back on to the street. Nicholas waited for a few moments, praying he wouldn't return, then moved out into the alleyway.

He was breathing rapidly, unnerved, as he walked into the high street. But there was no sign of the Dutchman, only a couple standing at a bus stop, smoking. Nicholas walked quickly back to St Stephen's church and hurried up the gravel path towards the side door. He expected at any moment to be attacked, and his hand shook as he unlocked the entrance and went in. Bolting the door behind him, he moved into the vestry. A small saucepan of milk was simmering on the gas cooker and a half-eaten sandwich lay on the table.

The triumph Nicholas had expected to feel was lacking. Yes, the Dutchman had broken into the auction house believing he would find the chain, which proved that Nicholas and Philip Preston were being watched, but that was all.

Honthorst had come away empty-handed, with only the realisation that he had been duped. He would have been angry. A violent man who used brutal tactics would resent being played for a fool.

And if he hadn't been distracted, Honthorst would have caught him.

With growing unease, Nicholas realised the danger of his situation and the ruthlessness of his opponents. And those were just the ones he knew about. Members of the art world had come out into the open, but what of the Church? What would the Catholic Church do when it realised that Father Daniel – aka Nicholas Laverne – was privy to information which could expose them for the liars they were? He had been a sacred thorn in their side ten years earlier, but they had thought him powerless after his excommunication. Maybe this time they would rely on no one taking him seriously, letting his name damn him in advance.

But if not, Nicholas thought, what would they do? He was a man on his own, without protectors, without confidantes, without power. Alone, he was challenging an institution that had obliterated rivals and crushed nations. What chance did he have? he wondered bleakly. What *wouldn't* the Church do to silence its most troublesome priest?

Twenty-Eight

There is an area of London in Kensington called Palace Gardens. The houses there are prestigious, many of them embassies or subdivided into sumptuous apartments. Only a few remain as private residences, with their own gated entrances and security guards. In one of these lives Conrad Voygel, with his wife and daughter. This Voygel travels a great deal, always leaving and arriving home at night, the windows of his car tinted so that he can see out but no one can see in.

His activities amuse his wife, Angela, who mocks his secrecy and pathological need for privacy. But he explains that it is to keep his family safe, and she believes him. After all, their little daughter would make a perfect kidnap victim. Since their marriage Conrad has also told his wife that there is another reason for his reserve: his employees do not know what their boss looks like, so he can move around his businesses unknown, eavesdropping on gossip, complaints and intimations of mutiny. But Angela knows otherwise.

His shyness is his most endearing trait. Some years ago Conrad suffered from cancer and half his face was surgically removed to halt the spread of the disease. It was rebuilt, and when the scars healed he looked like any other man, apart from a certain stiffness in his left cheek. But he is still conscious of his appearance and finds being in company difficult.

His wife pursues her own interests without needing to involve Conrad. They are not a social couple and have no close mutual friends, although Angela plays tennis and golf with her cronies. An ex-athlete, at forty-one her build is boyish and fit, hair streaked at Michael Clark's, her clothes from Armani. Even during her pregnancy with Cleo she was active, an outdoors girl, beautiful in a vitamin-pumped way. She trusts her husband, and Conrad, in his turn, is devoted to her.

They met when she was thirty and he was thirty-seven. She knows nothing of his previous life except what he tells her and that, she presumes, is the truth. If she pressed him for details he would avoid giving answers, other than the ones he has already confided. Conrad has no family, no siblings – Angela and their daughter are all he has. He protects them fiercely, loves them absolutely, and controls them as he controls every aspect of his life.

'I'll call you later,' Conrad said as Angela leant down towards the car window. 'Take care.' His gaze moved towards the house, his thoughts with his daughter. 'We should sort out which school she's going to when I get back. It's long overdue. We have to choose one or the other—'

'We will,' Angela said patiently, 'when you get back.'

His hand reached for hers. 'Do you want it?'

'Want what?'

'The Bosch chain,' Conrad said, looking intently at his wife. 'If you want it, I'll get if for you. An early birthday present.'

He had told her about the chain, about the rumour he had heard and was investigating. If it were true and there was some kind of conspiracy concerning the artist, Conrad wanted in on it. His many connections had already paid off: Sidney Elliott had informed him at Nicholas Laverne's visit. In fact, it had been Conrad who had tried to pressurise Nicholas, via Elliott; Conrad who had offered a substantial reward if the historian could obtain all of the pieces of Bosch's testament.

But despite Elliott's best efforts, Nicholas had been resistant. Not that Elliott hadn't promised Conrad that he would pursue the matter. A bitter middle-aged man cheated out of great career, Elliott was desperate. He was a man Conrad Voygel both disliked and suspected.

'G-g-give me time. I can find out m-more,' Elliott had promised him.

'D'you know the names of the other experts Laverne spoke to?'

'No, but I c-c-can find out.' Elliott replied. 'It's a small field of expertise; everyone kn-kn-knows of everyone else.'

'So find out who he spoke to, and what they know.'

Conrad Voygel's passion for collecting was twofold: he saw it as an investment as well as a means of owning objects envied and desired by others. His paintings and objets d'art served to prick the egos of lesser men; his collection was divided between his homes and galleries in California and Chicago. In the previous ten years Conrad had managed to infiltrate the art world via his hired scouts. Anything rare, or of value, came under his scrutiny. Bidding through agents, he could obtain pieces worldwide. Without putting his name to the bid, Conrad could avoid the inevitable bumping up of the prices that would have followed knowledge of his involvement. It was only later that the auction house or gallery discovered that he was the buyer.

Conrad smiled at his wife. The Bosch chain would be a birthday present for her – that much was true – but the driving force behind its acquisition would be the besting of his rivals. Conrad thought of the venal Gerrit der Keyser, the genial Hiram Kaminski and the slippery Philip Preston. And then he thought of Nicholas Laverne, the man in possession of the chain.

The ex-priest was out of his depth. Floundering like a seal in shallow water, unable to risk the beach, and yet fearful of drowning . . . Conrad had heard about the deaths of Sabine Monette and Claude Devereux – in fact, he had done business a few times with Raoul Devereux in the past – and the murders had piqued his interest. Where another man might be scared off, Conrad was intrigued. Naturally

157

he had presumed that the killings were connected and was interested to learn of Philip Preston's sudden closeness to Nicholas Laverne. So they were working together, were they? Poor Laverne, he thought. What chance did a sparrow have flying among hawks? Perhaps the ex-priest had no real understanding of the odds he was up against. The art world was no place for the vulnerable.

Especially when he was the biggest predator of all.

Twenty-Nine

Hiram Kaminski stared at his wife. 'Are you joking?' he said at last. '*Thomas Littlejohn?*' Hands on hips, Miriam watched the response from her shocked husband.

She continued. 'It was in the paper this morning, just a paragraph on the fourth page. I could have overlooked it, but it caught my eye – "Victim of Church Murder identified as Art Dealer". They managed to put a name to him because of a metal pin in his spine. They're all numbered, apparently. Thomas Littlejohn–'

'Had a bad back,' Hiram said, nodding. 'I remember. He suffered terribly after a fall on holiday. He was in hospital for a long time – used to joke that the doctors had pinned him back together.' He frowned. 'But why would a man like that end up murdered outside a church? They said the victim was a vagrant but Thomas was a successful man. It makes no sense.' He shook his head, baffled. 'Everyone wondered where he'd got to. No one had heard from him for a couple of years, ever since he sold up the gallery–'

'And left his wife and children,' Judith said disapprovingly. 'He just upped and left. Disappeared. Cruel to do that and leave your family wondering what happened to you.'

'But that's the point! Thomas wasn't like that. He was a responsible man, an honest man. He loved his family . . . And now he's been murdered, burnt alive. Dear God!' He paused, his wife watching him curiously.

'What is it?'

'Nothing, nothing—'

'Tell me!' she demanded.

'A long time ago – must be fifteen years now – he came to see me. He wanted my advice about something.'

'What?'

'I never saw it. I never even thought about it till now—'

'*What was it?*'

'A chain. Thomas Littlejohn wanted my opinion on a chain.' Hiram shook his head. 'I told him I wasn't interested, but when I thought about it later, I got back in touch with him.'

Judith was holding her breath. 'And?'

'He denied ever saying anything about a chain. We were very busy at the time, you remember? It was Helen's wedding coming up and I just thought I'd made a mistake. God knows, there's enough jewellery and artefacts constantly doing the rounds and Thomas wasn't a man to lie.' Hiram turned to his wife, his voice dropping. '*But what if it was the Bosch chain? What if Thomas Littlejohn was murdered because he was* involved? What if whoever killed him is the same person who killed Sabine Monette and Claude Devereux?'

'All of whom knew about the Bosch chain.'

'God!' Hiram began to shake. 'We know about it too.'

Judith placed her hand over his mouth. 'Say nothing. If anyone asks, we know nothing—'

He pushed her hand aside. 'But I was talking about it to Gerrit der Keyser at Philip Preston's place.'

'Did anyone overhear you?'

'No. People were concentrating on the auction.'

'Have you spoken to anyone else about it?'

'No!'

Judith nodded. 'Then listen to me, my dear, and listen carefully. No one has approached us about the Bosch chain. We know nothing about it. We have heard nothing about it. We don't want to know, because it's not relevant to us. We sell paintings here – we don't want to know about gold work.'

'But everyone knows I'm an authority on the late Middle Ages—'

'On the *paintings*, not any chain. You understand, Hiram? Forget what I said before; this whole business is now off limits to us.' She kept her eyes fixed on his. 'That chain is deadly – keep away from it. Let the big boys fight it out, not us. If there's going to be another victim, let it be Philip Preston or Gerrit der Keyser. But not us.'

Then she moved to the gallery door and locked it, pulling down the blind.

Thirty

Church of St Stephen, Fulham, London

Leaning on a stick, Father Michael watched Nicholas as he moved around the kitchen.

'Where's the chain?' the priest suddenly asked.

Nicholas turned, surprised. 'Why d'you want to know?'

'Where is it?'

'I'm not telling you,' Nicholas said simply. 'But it's not here, it's safe. I don't have it with me.' He made tea and passed a cup to the old priest.

Father Michael pushed it away. 'The man who was killed here just before you turned up was an art dealer called Thomas Littlejohn. Did you know him?'

'No.'

'His death's connected to the chain, isn't it?'

'Might be.'

'"*Might be*,"' the priest repeated, hostile. 'Of course it is! You said the chain held something – what was it?'

'You didn't want to know then so why d'you want to know now?'

'Because you're here, in my church—'

'*Your church?*' Nicholas countered. 'How pompous of you, Father. You work and live here – it's not yours. Surely your faith taught you that much—'

'Don't talk to me about faith! You hate the Church—'

'With good reason,' Nicholas snapped, leaning towards the old priest. 'You knew what was going on and you wouldn't help me. You knew those boys were being bullied—'

'I don't want to talk about it!'

'You never did!' Nicholas hurled back. 'He hanged himself, Father. A trainee priest, bullied relentlessly. Beaten, starved, locked up at St Barnabas's. Patrick Gerin was his name, remember? I bet you don't. I bet no one remembers his name. And after he killed himself, the two priests who drove him to it carried on as though nothing had happened.'

'He wasn't sexually assaulted!'

'Is that some kind of excuse?' Nicholas roared. 'Patrick Gerin was tormented, like the other boy he told me about. Tortured and starved. He was made to sleep naked in a cupboard in the church outhouse. He was covered in rat bites – I saw them. Patrick Gerin weighed less than six stone when he killed himself . . . And you knew the church well. You knew the priests at St Barnabas. You knew Father Dominic and Father Luke, but you said nothing when I told you about it. And those bastards were never punished. You knew about it—'

'It should have been dealt with within the Church. You went to the press!'

'And I'd do again. Even though it cost me my livelihood and my reputation. You can all call me a liar and cut me out of your religion, but what I did was right. And I know that, and I live with that every day. My only regret is that I didn't act sooner. That's what haunts me: not being the whistle-blower, being too late. The Catholic Church is corrupt. It always has been and always will be as long as its members turn a blind eye to what's going on.' Nicholas shook his head as he looked at the old priest. 'Jesus, how do you live with yourself?'

'I pray for forgiveness,' Father Michael replied, then looked at Nicholas. 'You said that this chain held papers, a secret about Bosch which was hidden to protect the Catholic Church . . . *What was the secret?*'

'Why would I tell you, Father?'

'Because I'm already involved. When you came here you involved me. I've already been threatened, and a man was killed outside my church. I know this place is watched. I know why you're living here – but you can only protect me so far. And who protects you?'

'Not the Church,' Nicholas said coldly.

'If you set out to expose another scandal no one will believe what you say. They won't take you seriously. You're a maverick, Nicholas. Let me help. I was silent once but I won't be this time,' the old priest pleaded. 'You have to tell me what the secret is.'

'And risk your life?'

'You're risking your own.' Father Michael paused. 'Listen. Hear that?' A noise sounded outside, footsteps on the gravel. 'They walk up and down a few times, then leave. It happens every night. And someone rings the rectory phone at two or three in the morning. When I pick up no one answers, but I can hear breathing down the line . . . I see shadows too. But then again, those could be old ghosts – Patrick Gerin for one.'

'Your mind's playing tricks on you.'

'About Patrick Gerin, yes. But I'm no fool, Nicholas – that Dutchman was no figment of my imagination.' He struggled with the next words. 'I gave you up when he threatened me. I told him you had the chain.'

Nicholas shrugged. 'So what? Everyone knows I have it.'

'They'll kill you for it!' Father Michael said desperately. 'Give it to them, whoever wants it – give it to them. You said the secret had been hidden for centuries so why expose it now? If it's so dangerous, why risk yourself? If there's a fortune involved, people will do anything to get hold of it. As for scandal, men have died for less.' He sighed and leant back in his seat. 'They won't let you get away with it.'

'Who won't? The art world or the Church?'

'Both.'

A moment spiralled between them. Father Michael was the first to speak. 'You're living on borrowed time, Nicholas. You want to expose what you know, I understand that, but no one will listen. You lost your credibility ten years ago.

You lost when the Church threw you out and called you a madman. You can't do this alone because no one will believe you.' He paused, left hand gripping the head of his walking stick. 'But they *will* believe me.'

Book Three

In the first known account of Bosch's painting, the Spaniard Felipe de Guevara described him as 'the inventor of monsters and chimeras'.

Thirty-One

Screaming, the man slumped forward against the church door. He was doubled over in pain, gasping for air, his coat shredded and wet with blood, his shoes missing. As he moved the hammer came down again and struck the back of his head, blood filling his mouth as he bit down on his tongue. Helpless, he threw up his arms, trying to fend off the blows, but instead he heard the crack of the hammer as it shattered his left arm at the elbow.

Pain seared into him, his legs giving way and his eyes blinded with blood, as he felt hands ripping aside his clothes, pulling his shirt open. Dazed, he began to slide into unconsciousness, then screamed as he felt the knife plunge into his upper chest and rip down his sternum. He grabbed for the weapon, the fingers of his right hand closing over the blade, his thumb severed as his attacker pulled the knife out of his grasp.

The victim was pleading but the words were blurred, incoherent through the blood that filled his mouth. Urine leaked out of him, his bowels loosening as the blows increased. Only yards away taxis moved down the road towards Harrods, where window decorations looking sullenly out of their glass cases, and the townhouses next to the Oratory remained glacially impervious.

He had stopped screaming now and was gurgling instead, trying to draw his knees up but lacking the strength to do anything but shake. Slowly the knife moved down to his stomach, then it was jerked upwards in an arc.

The last thing the man felt was the blade ripping across his throat and severing his windpipe, his heart pumping blood uselessly out of the gaping wound. And in those seconds the attacker carved two initials into his victim's stomach – H and B.

Then he straightened up, took off his coat and stuffed it into a plastic bag, along with his gloves and the knife. Walking briskly he moved towards South Kensington and finally hailed a cab on Sloane Street. When he left the taxi he tipped the driver generously.

It was only when he finished work that night that the driver discovered the plastic bag on the back seat – and called the police.

Thirty-Two

As he walked around the back of St Stephen's, Nicholas heard his name called. Startled, and expecting an attack, he spun round to find two police officers approaching.

'Are you Nicholas Laverne?'

He nodded.

'You live here?'

'For the moment,' Nicholas replied. 'What's all this about?'

The older officer took over. 'You knew a man called Father Luke, who used to be attached to St Barnabas's church—'

'Used to be?'

'He was found murdered in the early hours of this morning outside the Brompton Oratory,' the officer continued. 'When we talked to his fellow priests they told us about your run-in with Father Luke. Apparently you accused him of torture. You went to the press with it, caused quite a stink. Got yourself excommunicated for your trouble.'

'What I said is on the record, I don't deny it.' Nicholas's heart was speeding up. 'But I haven't seen or spoken to Father Luke for many years—'

'They said you phoned him the other night.'

'*What?*'

'One of the priests said that you rang him last Sunday and said you had unfinished business. Perhaps you'd like to come to the station and talk.'

Spooked, Nicholas looked around him, but there was no sign of Father Michael, no one to whom he could signal for help. He guessed at once what had happened: he was being set up, taken out of the running by a trumped-up accusation. And worse, he was being framed for murder. The old priest was right – they were making sure everything Nicholas Laverne said would be automatically discredited.

'I'm not going anywhere,' Nicholas replied. 'I never contacted Father Luke. It wasn't me.'

'We'll talk that about at the station,' the officer replied as the younger man moved closer to Nicholas. 'Come with us, sir.'

Thirty-Three

It was Eloise who called her, and Honor made a hurried exit from work and met her in a cafe round the corner. The Frenchwoman was sitting by a window, her expression composed as she watched Honor Laverne enter. She examined the lawyer steadily – the small-framed figure, the straight back. Not tall, but she carried herself like an athlete, her hair densely, silkily black.

'Sorry, I got away as soon as I could,' Honor said, sliding into a seat opposite Eloise. 'Is there any news about Claude's murder?'

'No, but there's been another killing—'

'*What?*'

'In the early hours of this morning. A priest was murdered outside the Brompton Oratory.' She could sense Honor's shock and continued. 'It wasn't your brother, but he's involved.'

'What are you talking about?'

Eloise leaned foward, her voice lowered. 'You didn't know that Nicholas was back in London?'

'No. I haven't heard from him for years . . .' She eyed the Frenchwoman. 'Have you seen him?'

She nodded. 'Yesterday, and I'll be meeting up with him again – if the police let him go.'

'Police?' Honor echoed, then dropped her voice, watching as Eloise stirred some sweetener into her black coffee.

'What I'm about to tell you is in confidence. You're a lawyer – you should know how to keep secrets. Nicholas returned to this country a few weeks ago. He told Claude where he was going and why. Claude . . .' Her voice caught on her dead husband's name . . . 'didn't tell me the whole story at the time. You have to remember that the three of us were close. We had mutual friends too, one of whom was murdered in Paris only days ago.'

Honor was watching her, unnerved. 'What's this got to do with my brother?'

'Have you heard of Hieronymus Bosch?'

'The painter,' Honor replied, baffled. 'So?'

Eloise glanced around to check that no one was listening. But there were only a couple of men in a booth at the back of the cafe, and a bored waitress preparing food behind the counter.

'Claude's father, Raoul Devereux . . . He was your brother's mentor, wasn't he? Helped him in his career.'

'He was very good to Henry.' Honor agreed. 'He believed in him. We all did.' She changed the subject rapidly. 'What about Bosch?'

'Raoul Devereux had a small Bosch painting stolen, which finally turned up in London, in the gallery of Gerrit der Keyser. From there it was purchased by Sabine Monette.' Eloise paused, then added, 'She was the woman who befriended Nicholas.'

'I never knew her name. But I knew about her – that Nicholas worked for her. Why didn't you ever tell me what she was called?'

'You never asked,' Eloise said simply. 'And Nicholas didn't want information passed on. You have to admit, Honor, you and I weren't friends. We spoke now and again, but we were never close. I had to respect your brother's wishes.'

Honor nodded. 'Yes, you did . . . Go on.'

'With the Bosch painting was a chain. It contained slips of paper that told of a subterfuge concerning the painter. I don't know the details, only that the secret would shake the art market and shame the Catholic Church. Your brother wants to expose the deception. He has the chain and the papers.' Eloise paused, her tone expressionless as she fiddled with the right cuff of her sleeve. 'My husband and Sabine Monette knew about the secret. They are now dead.'

Honor took in a breath.

'You don't think Nicholas had anything to do with their deaths?'

'No, of course not. But someone's trying to spin a web around your brother.' Eloise hesitated, waiting until the waitress passed by their table and returned to her post behind the counter. 'Just after Nicholas came back to London, a man was killed outside St Stephen's church – your brother's old church. That man was identified yesterday as Thomas Littlejohn.'

'I don't know him.'

'He was an art dealer.' Eloise nodded, seeing the understanding in Honor's eyes. 'Yes, all three victims were connected to the art world. I don't know if Thomas Littlejohn knew about Bosch, but I'm pretty sure he must have. And I think that was the reason he was killed.'

'But why would anyone suspect my brother of the killings?'

'No one *would* have suspected Nicholas – before this morning.'

Honor knew she wasn't going to like the next words. 'What happened?'

'Father Luke, of St Barnabas's church, was murdered. He was one of the priests your brother exposed ten years ago. Apparently Nicholas contacted him and threatened him. There is a witness to the call—'

'It could have been anyone!' Honor snapped. 'Anyone could have said they were my brother.'

'Just what I thought,' Eloise replied smoothly. 'But then again, at the moment your brother is probably safer at the police station than anywhere else. He's in trouble. You do understand that, don't you?'

Honor studied the woman across the table, her dark eyes meeting the Frenchwoman's blue gaze. Grief was leaching out of Eloise, but her self-control was unsettling. It surprised Honor to realise how much she disliked Eloise Devereux.

'Why are you telling me all this?'

'We want the same result – justice,' Eloise replied. 'You want your brother to be vindicated; I want my husband to be revenged. You know the law. You have contacts, I imagine. And your brother needs you. He will confide in you–'

'No, he won't.'

'Yes, he will, when he realises that not only his life but *yours* might be in danger.'

The hairs stood up on the back of Honor's neck. 'Are you trying to use me?'

'Yes, but in return you can use me. I have means, and I will use everything I own to find my husband's killer. The Bosch secret involves the Church *and* the art world. Your brother might discover something of interest to me and I might discover something of interest to him. Why not pool our resources? Besides, your brother's no killer. He loved Claude and Sabine. And he's not stupid enough to go after the priest.'

Honor considered what she'd heard. 'Maybe they killed the priest to remind everyone of Nicholas's past. Make him look like a lunatic–'

'I agree,' Eloise replied. 'Whoever's planning it wants to make him powerless. And they will, if he's left out there alone. Nicholas is reckless – he needs you. You have to force him to confide, and you can only do that if you're under threat.'

The Frenchwoman's callousness shocked her, but Honor wasn't going to back off. Instead, after a long moment, she put out her hand. Surprised, Eloise hesitated, then shook it.

Thirty-Four

Philip Preston was trying to calm his wife, Gayle, who was sobbing hysterically. Her instability, only controlled by strong medication, was escalating. When he was there Philip made sure she took her pills, but when he was away she forgot. Or did she do it deliberately? he wondered. Make herself clinging and helpless, tying him to her with emotional bladderwrack.

'Calm down, darling,' he said through gritted teeth. 'You're getting yourself all worked up.'

She put her arms around his neck. She smelt as though she needed a bath. Once so beautiful, so sculpturally perfect, Gayle was now bloated; her limbs the colour of a sea slug. Drink and medication had driven a stake into the heart of her appeal, and now she provoked little more than pity.

And to think, Philip mused, that once every man who saw her wanted her. Like Gerrit der Keyser – and others. He remembered Henry Laverne suddenly; felt the quick breeze of envy trickle over him. Philip knew that Henry had been Gayle's one true love. Recently, babbling and full of booze, she had been talking about all her old boyfriends, reminding herself of her spent power. Philip no longer resented such outpourings. It was a kind of revenge that she had managed to age herself out of his jealousy.

But lately Gayle had increased her drinking and with it, the inevitable outbursts. And she was having one now. 'You don't love me. You want me to die.'

'Gayle, why on earth would I want you to die?'

'So you can marry someone young and pretty,' she said, burping, her breath acid as she flopped into a chair. But then she smiled and some shadow of that punchy beauty came back and caught him unawares. 'I'm going to get better, you know. And go on a diet. The doctor wants me to talk to a new therapist. I think it'll work.' She reached for his flies and Philip winced. 'You still want me, don't you?'

How could he say no? Say 'I want Kim Fields, my mistress' instead. Say 'You disgust me, with your greedy little fingers probing my genitals and your tongue stuffed in my mouth. But he couldn't say it. Instead he let Gayle make a kind of shabby love to him, all the time thinking of Kim.

The escape route was in front of him – the Bosch chain, weaving its gilded links to freedom. Nicholas Laverne could bring Hell down on the Catholic Church, but Philip just wanted the sale. He had worked hard for a long time, cheated a few, certainly kept ahead by guile, but he was getting older – and he felt it. He wasn't sleeping well, his knees ached and a sudden desperation was afflicting him.

The slick charm he had employed for years was moth-ridden and forced, and his libido was flagging.

The money raised by the sale would mean freedom – the ability to leave his wife with a clear conscience while hiring a companion to keep her company and divvy out her drugs . . . Philip could feel his wife's lips on his stomach and tensed, trying to fight an impulse to push her away . . . He would sell the Bosch chain and then run. Take Kim with him. Get the hell away from London. Yes, it was dangerous, reckless, but it was worth the risk.

Philip thought of Carel Honthorst and cringed. Honthorst, der Keyser, Conrad Voygel – all of them breathing down his neck, and God only knows who else. He was gambling, and he knew it. Not just with his business, but with his life.

Thirty-Five

Inside the police station the old priest waited, sitting on a hard seat, his hands folded over the handle of his cane. Worry had thinned him, flesh falling off his bones overnight. Before he had been a welcoming presence, but now Father Michael looked cadaverous, hungry. Circumstances had worked on his gut, his body a living testament to his guilt.

Seeing Nicholas, he rose unsteadily to his feet, nodded, then followed him out of the door. Once outside, Nicholas turned to him.

'What did you say to them?'

'That you were at the rectory all night. I said I couldn't sleep and that we played chess into the early hours.' He moved on, tapping the way before him with his cane like a blind man.

'And they believed you?'

'I told you, I'm very plausible.'

'You lied, Father. That's a sin,' Nicholas said, hunching down into his coat as the wind blew up. 'Why did you do it?'

'Because I said I would help you and I will. Besides, you didn't kill Father Luke. You had no reason to.' The old priest paused at the end of the street and a car drew up beside them.

Surprised, Nicholas looked inside to find Honor leaning over and opening the door. 'Get in.'

Seeing Nicholas hesitate, Father Michael pushed him in the small of the back. 'She's your sister – talk to her.'

Sliding into the passenger seat, Nicholas watched as Father Michael moved off. Without speaking, Honor started up the engine and drove towards Clapham. Once there, she parked by the Common and turned to her brother.

'You look terrible.'

'I don't sleep well and it's getting worse,' Nicholas admitted. 'But you look prosperous.'

His smile jolted her, taking her back to the boy he had once been and the childhood they had spent together. For an instant she wanted to freeze-frame the image, to deny history, wipe out the memory of the events that had estranged them.

But when Nicholas spoke again the image shattered. 'What d'you want?'

'*What do I want?* Why should I want anything from you? You're the one who didn't keep in touch. You're the one who rejected me.' Her temper made her skin pale, white-hot against the black hair. 'I thought you might have changed.'

'No.'

His indifference astounded her. 'I've been looking for you for years.'

'Well, now you've found me, so what?'

Angry, she drove her hands deep into her coat pockets, her fists clenched. 'You're in trouble. Father Michael didn't have to tell me that – Eloise did.'

'Eloise Devereux has spoken to you? That's interesting. Did she tell you what this so-called trouble was?'

'She told me about the murders. Sabine Monette and her husband. And the first victim. Did you know Thomas Littlejohn?'

Nicholas said nothing, just reached for the door handle.

'Stop it!' Honor shouted. 'I can't do this any more. I can't. I don't want anything from you. Why won't you let me help you?'

'I don't need help.'

'Eloise Devereux's trying to help you and so is Father Michael. Why can't you take help from your own sister?' She gripped his arm, but he shook her off.

'I don't want you involved. It's not safe—'

'It's too late now,' Honor said emphatically. 'I am involved. I know what's going on, Nicholas. I know about the Bosch chain and the scandal.'

'You can't—'

'But I do,' Honor replied in a soft voice. 'You're in it up to your neck, aren't you?' He said nothing so she continued. 'Well, take my advice and be very careful of Eloise Devereux. She's out for blood, and God help anyone who gets in her way. Luckily she's on our side – for the moment.'

Nicholas looked at her, surprised. 'You don't trust her?'

'No. Eloise Devereux thinks she's played me, and I'm letting her believe that, but I've got the measure of her.' Honor stared out of the car window. 'We need to work together, Nicholas, or we're both in trouble. I don't want to see you dead, and I sure as hell don't want to die either . . .'

He winced at the thought.

'So let's work out a plan of action, shall we?' She glanced at her watch. 'I've got an hour for lunch – that should be more than enough for you to tell me everything.'

Thirty-Six

Weighing the chain on his jeweller's scales, Philip Preston glanced up at Nicholas. 'And the papers?'

'Are staying with me. They're locked away – no one can get at them. Remember our agreement, Philip? You go after the art world, I go after the Church.'

'I heard about the death of the priest yesterday. I also heard that the police interviewed you.'

'First strike to the Church,' Nicholas said bluntly. 'I was waiting for it to start.'

'Have they asked you about the Bosch papers?'

'No one's contacted me directly – that's not how they work,' Nicholas replied. 'It's all done at arm's length. The death of Father Luke was supposed to discredit me and it might well have done if my old mentor hadn't given me an alibi. Father Michael is beyond doubt, although he might have risked himself by standing up for me.'

Nicholas stopped talking. Suddenly he could feel his head spinning. He could see Philip in front of him, but the auctioneer was talking and he couldn't hear a word. A terrifying second passed, then another. Finally regaining control, he sat down.

'Are you all right?' Philip asked, bemused.

Nicholas nodded. 'I was just dizzy, that's all.'

'You don't look well.' Philip moved over to a cabinet and poured a brandy, passing it to Nicholas.

To Philip's surprise, he downed it in one. Thoughtful, he regarded Nicholas. The slim frame was beginning to fill out again, the jaw almost pugnacious, a blaze back in the eyes. A fanatic? Who knew?

'You think the Church would murder Father Luke to frame you?'

The dizziness had passed and Nicholas was fully in control again. 'Maybe it wasn't the Church; maybe it came from your patch. Someone in the art world, making it *look* like the Church was involved.' He paused for an instant. God, he was tired, his mind sluggish. 'You're taking a big risk – publicly announcing that you've got the chain and putting it up for sale is inviting trouble. There's a whole week until the auction – couldn't you make it sooner?'

'I need some time to whip up the buyers. A week will bring out all the big hitters—'

'It might bring out something else,' Nicholas replied. 'Are you sure you want to do this?'

Philip thought of his wife. 'Yes, I'm sure.'

'Have you said anything about the secret?'

'Not a word,' Philip replied. 'You?'

'No, I haven't told anyone. But that doesn't mean we're the only people who know.'

'Sabine Monette and Claude Devereux are dead—'

'So is Thomas Littlejohn.'

Shaken, Philip stared at him. '*Thomas Littlejohn is dead?*'

'Murdered. It turns out that he was the first victim. The man burned outside St Stephen's church.'

'I knew him well; we were friends a while back. I always wondered what happened to Thomas.' Philip was flustered, caught off-guard. 'This isn't good for me. This isn't good for me at all.'

'It wasn't too good for him either,' Nicholas replied, wondering just how far he could trust the auctioneer. 'You know about the murder outside the Brompton Oratory, but did you know that Father Luke had the initials H B carved into his stomach? Just like Sabine.'

Philip's expression was unreadable. 'I heard.'

'Word travels fast,' Nicholas replied. 'Unless you already knew about the murder of Father Luke. Unless you were involved.' He probed his way carefully. 'I've been thinking – you've been in from the start. You found Sabine and you're one of the few who knows about the secret. One of the few who's not dead.'

'Oh, grow up!' Philip said dismissively. 'I've lived and prospered by being sly; I've no appetite for violence. Especially when it's inflicted on me.' He paused, genuinely irritated. '*You* brought *me* into this. Without you I wouldn't be looking over my shoulder all the time and wondering if I might be the next victim.'

'So why don't you take the chain out of the sale? Say you're donating it to a museum?'

'You think I'd give it up?' He laughed, almost a bark. 'No, I'm not backing out now.' Philip gestured towards the door. 'I've hired security. Men who look like they could spit holes in walls. That should stop Carel Honthorst sniffing around.'

'You think it's just Honthorst you have to stop?' Nicholas asked, thinking of the unexpected phone call he had received from Sidney Elliott, the academic nervy and bullish by turns. He had told Nicholas he had a buyer who would pay over the odds for the chain. Unimpressed, Nicholas had put the phone down on him, but he had called back five times. And each time Nicholas's answer had been no.

'Whatever happens, it's all out in the open now,' Philip said. He had moved into his en suite washroom and was combing his white hair as he admired himself in the mirror. A moment later Nicholas could hear him peeing. 'Whoever wants the chain can bid for it at the auction—'

'*If* it gets to auction. It's sitting here like a stick of dynamite ready to go off.' He paused, studying the auctioneer as he re-entered the room.

'D'you believe in God?' Philip asked.

Surprised, Nicholas shook his head. 'Not any more. How about you?'

'No. There's no divine power we can appeal to. No moral Court of Justice.' Philip shrugged fatalistically. 'I'm scared, I admit it, but I'm not backing down. There's only two ways this can go – I'll either come out with a fortune or in a box.'

Thirty-Seven

Two days passed. In London the art world was buzzing with the news of Philip Preston's auction of the Bosch chain. Meanwhile the police continued their investigations into the two murders outside London churches. The initials carved on Father Luke confused them. Admittedly both of the victims had been killed on sacred ground, but otherwise the deaths were dissimilar. Thomas Little-john had been burnt alive, Father Luke stabbed. And only Father Luke had the initials on his body. They knew nothing of the deaths of Claude Devereux and Sabine Monette in France – they had no reason to connect the four killings.

Initially the police had hoped they might have a suspect in Nicholas Laverne, and although his alibi had cleared him his background incited interest. This was the priest who had been the infamous whistle-blower. The priest who had been excommunicated. The priest who might well have a score to settle. So the police kept their eye on Nicholas Laverne, and waited.

The art world waited too. Gerrit der Keyser sent for Carel Honthorst, and in his Chicago office Conrad Voygel made a call to Sidney Elliott in Cambridge. The academic was brooding, angered by Nicholas's resistance, eager to prove his worth to Voygel.

'He w-w-won't budge. The chain's g-g-going to auction.'

'I know, and that isn't what I wanted,' Voygel replied pleasantly. 'Thank you for your help, Mr Elliott, but I'm going to bring someone else in—'

'No!' Elliott interrupted. He was talking to one of the richest men on the planet, a man who could change his life. He wasn't prepared to lose his chance. 'I'll work on Laverne. G-g-give me a bit more time.'

'The auction's in five days,' Voygel reminded him. 'I'll give you two.

Like a cat finding its way into a dovecote, news of the upcoming auction ruffled feathers across the globe and Hiram Kaminski was summoned back urgently from Amsterdam.

He had hardly made it through the door of the gallery when his wife caught his arm and steered him into the back office.

'This came for you,' Judith said, slapping a large envelope on to his desk.

'You've opened it!' Hiram replied, picking it up and looking disapprovingly at his wife. 'It was addressed to me—'

'Read it, and then you'll wish it wasn't.'

193

Sitting on the sofa in his office, Judith watched as her husband slid out some papers and sat down at his desk. It took him a couple of moments to find his reading glasses, then he glanced at the first page. And the signature. Thomas Littlejohn. It was dated a month earlier.

'When did this arrive?'

'Last night,' Judith replied. 'The builders who have been working next door for the last three months finally finished and were packing up. They found the letter and realised that it had been delivered to number one-hundred and eighty-nine instead of number one-hundred and eighty-eight.' She folded her arms, her face set. 'Go on, read it!'

'But why would Thomas Littlejohn write me a letter?' Hiram wondered out loud, turning back to the pages.

Dear Hiram,

Of all the dealers in London I judge you to be the most honest. It is that, together with your learning and interest in the late Middle Ages, that determined that I send this vital information to you.

I know you – like many others, especially my family – will have wondered where I have been for the past eighteen months. To put it simply, I was hiding. I wanted to protect those I loved and keeping my distance was the only way I could ensure their safety. I have been threatened and followed for many years – because of what I know.

Unnerved, Hiram glanced up at his wife. Judith remained stony-faced.

> *... A while ago I was given sight of a valuable chain, supposedly once the property of Hieronymus Bosch. That in itself would have been remarkable, but it was what the chain held that proved to be disastrous. Within the links of the chain were papers that told the story of a deception.*
>
> *A fraud concerning Bosch. Proof that he had died in <u>1473</u>, not 1516 as previously believed.*
>
> *The fraud was perpetrated by the artist's own family with the collusion of the Catholic Church ...*

Hiram paused, his head thumping. He didn't want to read any more, but he had no choice. Judith had been right to try and protect them, but it was too late. A letter from a dead man had put them both right back in the centre of the volcano.

> *... I don't have to tell you what this means. It would jeopardise the art world and the Catholic Church. Some people would do anything to expose this scandal. Others would do more to conceal it.*
>
> *Although the chain and the papers are not in my possession, I know about them, and that has forced me to live like a fugitive.*
>
> *Reassurances that I would not reveal the secret have*

proved worthless. <u>I know</u> – *and that in itself has damned me.*

Be wary of Gerrit der Keyser and Conrad Voygel, but be careful around Philip Preston too. All three men are cunning and greedy. Der Keyser would use the secret to further his own ends, blackmail people to keep it secret. How many museums and collectors would hate to see their Bosch masterpieces exposed as fakes? As for Conrad Voygel, he would do anything within his means to get his hands on such a prize, another trinket for a trickster. And Philip Preston? He would want the chain for its value, but he might sell on the secret to other interested parties for a finder's fee.

Of course that depends on who is the strongest of them all. Which one proves to have the biggest bite. Which one will remain standing after a bout that could see some – or all of them – ruined or dead.

No one is to be trusted, Hiram, and remember also that the Church is involved. And the Church has tremendous power. Few would dare to take it on. Some have in the past, to their cost.

There is one more piece of the puzzle I should tell you about. There is a clue in one of Hieronymus Bosch's paintings, The Garden Of Earthly Delights. The figure in the right-hand panel of Hell – the image that has become known as the Tree Man. This is, in fact, a portrait of Hieronymus Bosch himself. A young man, crippled, impotent, helpless.

'The Garden of Earthly Delights' [Panel of Hell]
After Hieronymus Bosch

Of course it could not be a self-portrait as it was cre-ated after his death, but whichever member of his family painted it meant it to stand as a testament to his suffe-ring.

Do I have to tell you what you are up against, old friend? I am genuinely sorry to have to share this with you, but I need a witness in case anything should happen to me. Someone else has to share this information. I am returning to London soon and will contact you. I have heard that the chain has recently been found. No doubt before long it will be doing the rounds. We must stop this.

Don't think of going to the police. I did a while ago and was treated as a lunatic. They do not know or understand the machinations of the art world, but you and I do.

Until we meet again,

With gratitude,

Thomas Littlejohn

Without saying a word, Hiram took off his glasses and stared at his wife.

'You know what he's done, don't you?' she asked, her face ashen. 'That bastard's just signed our death warrants.'

Thirty-Eight

Even though it was bitterly cold, Carel Honthorst was sweating as he heaved himself up the steps to Philip Preston's office and walked in unannounced. Feigning nonchalance, Philip looked up from his desk.

'What do you want?'

'Mr der Keyser wants to see you.'

'When did the accident happen?'

Honthorst frowned. 'What accident?'

'The one that took away the use of his legs,' Philip replied smartly. 'If Gerrit wants to talk to me, he knows where I am.' He rose to his feet, pausing beside the Dutchman and staring at his shiny face. The sweat was affecting his concealer and his pores gaped like craters. 'Why don't you use fake tan? It would be more convincing.'

Honthorst blinked slowly. 'Mr der Keyser wants you to come to his office.'

'Like I said—' Philip stopped abruptly as Honthorst caught hold of his arm and twisted it up behind his back. The pain made him gasp, Honthorst jerking his wrist with

199

every word he spoke. 'Mr der Keyser wants to talk to you. Now.'

When they arrived at the gallery, der Keyser was standing outside, admiring his window display: three paintings by a follower of Van Dyke, one of a child with a dog. Maudlin. As he spotted Philip, Gerrit smiled and walked in. A moment later Philip followed, shoved inside by Honthorst who then stood on guard at the door.

Straightening his tie, Philip's expression was outraged. 'I don't like—'

'Being fucked about?' Gerrit said. 'Me neither. But there you go, people fuck you about the whole time. Only the other day we were talking about some chain and some ex-priest, and all along you knew where it was. *My chain*.'

'Sabine Monette's actually,' Philip replied, watching as Gerrit began tending a potted palm. 'And before that it was stolen from Raoul Devereux's gallery years ago.'

'I bought it in good faith! If it was stolen, I didn't know about it.'

'Come off it – you wouldn't have cared,' Philip replied, pointing to the Dutchman outside. 'Call him off. I have to get back to the office, I've got a big auction coming up—'

'With my fucking chain in it!'

Playing for time, Philip sat down and crossed his legs.

Surprised by the show of nonchalance, Gerrit kept tweaking at his plant, clipping off the brown, dry edges of the leaves with a pair of nail scissors. 'I want it back.'

'So buy it at the auction.'

'I'm not fucking buying it, you smarmy prick!' Gerrit roared. 'It's mine.'

'No, it belonged to Sabine Monette. You sold it to her with the Bosch painting—'

'She stole it. I have the bitch on tape.'

'You have her taking the chain off the painting you had just *sold* to her,' Philip replied, his tone oily. 'I've had it checked out. Any court in the land will tell you that possession is nine tenths of the law. The fact that you missed out on something because you were too slow doesn't count.'

'You smug bastard, I should kick you in the bollocks,' Gerrit replied, slamming down the scissors he was holding.

'If you want the chain back you can bid for it at the auction. Oh, come off it, Gerrit – you can't start going around saying that you were cheated, not without everyone starting to look at where the painting came from. How it was stolen from Raoul Devereux's gallery all those years ago, then turned up in the Cotswolds, and then found its way to you.' He shook his head. 'You can't afford to have people questioning how you obtained the picture and its scandalous chain—'

'That chain is mine by rights!'

'That's debatable. Like I say, if you want it, bid for it. Of course, I can't rely on your being successful – there might be a few other interested parties.' Philip continued, feeling his way along, wondering just how much Gerrit der Keyser knew. 'But then again, it *is* only a chain. Even if it belonged to Hieronymus Bosch, it is only a chain—'

'A very *valuable* chain.'

'So perhaps you and I could have a private sale.'

'Perhaps I could have your head nailed to the door.'

Philip shrugged. 'You lost, Gerrit. It's snakes and ladders and this time you failed. Next time you'll be luckier. By the way, I could have you done for breaking and entering.' He jerked his head to where Honthorst was standing. 'Tiny Tim out there burgled my office.'

'What he does in his spare time has nothing to do with me.'

'He works for you – you're responsible.'

Gerrit pulled a face. 'If it rains outside my gallery is it my fault you get pissed on when you walk out?'

Smiling, Philip walked to the door. 'After all, Gerrit, it's only a chain. You've never been interested in gold before.'

A moment fluttered between them, buoyed up by their combined malice.

'A chain's a chain,' Gerrit agreed. 'Paper's paper. Words are words. But if you put all three together, you could make quite a fucking story out of it.' He put his head to one side like a scrawny crow, cupping his hand around his left ear. 'Hear that? That click?'

Philip frowned. 'What?'

'I think that's the sound of your number coming up.'

And here I am again, between the yew trees.

Nicholas turns over in bed, straining to lift eyelids that won't open, that won't let his body admit he is dreaming. His arms shift like broken windmill sails against the sheets. He is walking in his sleep and now it is dark again. *Here I go, here I go . . .*

The outhouse is covered in ivy; Nicholas doesn't remember that; but knows that nature will have moved on, his own past ageing. He calls out, waits for Patrick Gerin and his friend to appear, to leave the back door of the church and move to the outhouse where the ivy grows.

But no one comes. And in the dream the ivy slinks over the broken roof and through the windows of the outhouse. As he watches, it slithers under the padlocked cupboard door and then stops. A moon, white as cut paper, grins like an imbecile through the grappling yews.

I know this part, he thinks. I know this – it's always the same . . . Nicholas reaches out, grasps the handle, feels the door open and then sees the boy. He is mewling, on his last, damp breath, under the dust, puffy from beatings, naked as a lamb, ivy twisting and curling around his cold limbs.

Thirty-Nine

Exhausted from lack of sleep, Nicholas nursed the coffee he was holding and studied his sister. He had to admit that he was impressed by her. Over the years they had been estranged he had thought of Honor often, remembering her the last time they had spoken, when she had tucked the money into his pocket without his knowing. Money that had saved him when he was on his uppers in Liverpool. He had lost count of the times he had started to write to her, or picked up the phone to call. But he had always bottled out.

He had tried to convince himself that he was being thoughtful. Later, after his disgrace, that had been the truth. But there had been thousands of times before when he could have bridged that chasm between them. It would have taken so little to bring him back home. Even less to stay in the wilderness.

And now Honor was sitting in the kitchen of St Stephen's Rectory eating a chicken sandwich. Honor, her hair black as molasses, her eyes alert.

'So,' she asked, after swallowing a mouthful. 'if the chain's now with Philip Preston, you should be safe.'

'I still know about the Bosch conspiracy. I know about the Church and what they did—'

'Let it drop! You could move back to France, show them you've walked away, that you're not going to do anything about it. They'll leave you alone if you back off,' Honor said impatiently. 'You're just looking for trouble if you pursue this. Let someone else do it.'

'No!' he snapped. 'The chain came to me – it's my responsibility.' He reached out to touch her hand and then drew back, folding his arms. 'Do you ever think about our childhood?' he asked suddenly.

She nodded, taking another bite of the sandwich.

'Did you think you'd go into the law then?' he continued.

'Did you . . .' she swallowed . . . 'think you'd go into the Church?' When he didn't reply, she went on. 'We couldn't understand it, you know. You being a priest. We weren't even Catholic. Everyone thought you were joking.'

'Everyone always thought I was joking.' Nicholas replied, changing the subject. 'Eloise Devereux shouldn't have told you about Bosch—'

'Yes, she should,' Honor replied, finishing the sandwich getting up to make some tea for both of them. 'She doesn't know the whole story though. Not what the secret is. Neither do I.' Honor turned back to her brother. 'You avoided telling me yesterday – are you going to tell me today?'

'No.'

'I think you should,' she said matter-of-factly. 'So what was it? Were the paintings faked?'

He winced.

'Of course . . . It had to be something like that. But there's more, isn't there? I know. I can see it in your face. What else?'

Again he hesitated.

'Oh, come on, Nicholas, you have to tell me. I know too much to be innocent, and too little to be of any bloody good.'

'I've told you, it's dangerous.'

'And I've told you, it's too late to think about that. I've crossed over to your side now. All you have to do is to trust me.' She took his hand, gripping it tightly. 'Poor lost boy, hey? Henry was always so organised, I was always so confident, you – you were always such an outlaw.'

He laughed, embarrassed.

'All the girls fancied you, even when you came back from London that time with filthy hair and stinking. Yeah, you did stink. Uncle David was horrified – took to his rooms and turned the volume up on that old record player.'

'And refused to talk to me for a week.' Nicholas remarked. 'Does the record player still work?'

'Oh, yes,' Honor said. Then, changing the subject, 'How many women have you slept with?'

'What kind of a question is that?'

'I have a theory, you see. You were so randy when you were young, I reckoned that either you'd had too much sex or it had put you off completely. That's why you could take a vow of chastity.'

He glanced at her left hand. 'You aren't married.'

'I was,' Honor said, shrugging. 'Didn't last. And now I'm single at thirty-six, with no kids. Never wanted them, never will . . . Don't run off again, please. You're the only family I've got. There are only two of us left, Nicholas. We need each other. I have to get back to work now.' Standing up she walked to the door and turned. 'Oh, I nearly forgot. Someone left a note for you on my car.'

She rummaged in her bag and passed him the piece of folded paper.

And then she watched as he read it and the colour left his face.

Forty

It was early, hardly light, when Nicholas awoke. For once he hadn't dreamed, and now he was desperate to urinate. Moving into the bathroom he relieved himself, his hand resting on the wall over the cistern as a sudden wave of nausea came over him. Surprised, he waited for the feeling to pass, then walked out into the corridor. Even with the door of Father Michael's room closed he could hear the snoring. He paused for a moment, listening to the old priest giving an abrupt snort and then rolling over in bed. The springs creaked and protested, but a moment later the snoring began again.

Back in his room, Nicholas got into bed then paused, listening. He could hear footsteps on the gravel outside. Who would be walking around the church at four thirty in the morning? Flicking off his bedside light, he moved to the window and looked out. The gravel path was empty, the street lamp illuminating parked cars but nothing else. Certainly no figure moving around.

Surprised, he returned to bed. Lying down, he felt something – a sharp object digging into his back. He snapped on the light and stared at the wooden crucifix lying in the centre of his bed. It hadn't been there before he went to the toilet. Someone had come into his room and placed it there . . . Gingerly, Nicholas picked up the crucifix, then dropped it, standing up and backing away from the bed.

It was not an ordinary crucifix. It was one he knew. But he hadn't seen it for a long time.

It was the one Nicholas had been given by his sister years earlier, when he had first become a priest. Grabbing the phone, he punched out Honor's number.

There was no answer.

Forty-One

Troubled by the events of the previous night, Nicholas eventually managed to contact Honor at eight o' clock. His sister was puzzled by what he told her.

'What are you talking about?' she asked. 'The crucifix *I* gave you—'

'Was in my bed last night. And I didn't put it there,' he snapped. 'Someone was in the vestry and they put it there.' His voice shook. 'I heard footsteps, and in the time it took me to have a pee someone got in and planted that crucifix in my bed.'

'Where was Father Michael?'

'Asleep. I could hear him snoring,' Nicholas retorted heatedly. 'Anyway, do you really think an old priest would play a trick like that?'

'I don't know,' Honor replied, pouring herself a coffee and sitting down in her kitchen. 'Who else could it have been? I mean, you'd have heard someone break in, wouldn't you? You're a light sleeper, Nicholas – that would have woken you.'

'Unless they were already in the house.'

She shivered. 'Are you serious?'

'They were bound to come after me sooner or later,' Nicholas replied. 'They tried to frame me for Father Luke's murder, but that didn't stick, so now they have to find another way to stop me. They can't kill me, that would be too obvious—'

'Nicholas,' Honor said softly, 'you can't *really* believe that the Catholic Church would murder you? That's crazy.'

'So now I'm going crazy?'

'I didn't say *you* were going crazy, I said the theory was crazy.' Her voice was patient. 'You're under a lot of stress. You said yourself you weren't sleeping. You could be imagining things—'

'A crucifix in my bed!' he snapped. 'Father Michael said someone had been watching the church and he's had phone calls in the middle of the night. When he answers, there's no one there. I know I'm being followed, but now they're upping the ante.' He thought for a moment, 'Maybe it was Father Dominic from St Barnabas's. Father Luke's running mate. He's scared enough—'

'You're scaring me,' Honor interrupted. 'You have to calm down, get things into prespective.'

Nicholas wasn't listening.

'It would have to be clever, nothing shocking,' he went on. 'They can't kill me outright – it would be all over the papers and people would ask questions. *Whistle-blower priest*

211

murdered would provoke some interest. Only a few people know about the Bosch deception, but someone would speak out if I were killed. The Church wants me to shut up, so they're trying to frighten me.'

'Give them the bloody papers!' Honor snapped. 'Who cares what happened to Hieronymus Bosch? No one. You're tilting at windmills again, and you're the one who'll get hurt—'

'But that's the point. It might not be just me . . . I want you to go and stay with our uncle for a while—'

'I'm not going to live with David Laverne again!' she retorted. 'And what makes you think that I'd be any safer in the country than in London? God, Nicholas, think about it. If someone wanted to harm me, they would have done so already. Besides, I don't know what the deception is, do I? You never told me – not the whole story anyway.'

'You mustn't know it. Your safety is in *not* knowing it.'

'Nicholas, please, calm down. You're letting your imagination run away with you. This is madness—'

'I don't care if you think I'm a lunatic,' Nicholas replied, his tone sharp. 'Can't you see what they're doing? They *want* you to think I'm crazy, so that they can discredit what I say. Believe me, I know what these people are capable of, and if they can't get to me they'll go for the people I love.' He cringed at the thought. 'If you won't go to the country, come here. Stay at St Stephen's with us.'

'I can't just take time off work—'

'Say you're ill,' Nicholas suggested. 'This won't go on for long, Honor. The chain's being sold at auction in a few days' time—'

'So why don't you put the papers up for auction as well?'

He was taken aback. '*What?* I don't want to raise money with them, I want to expose the Church for their part in the deception.'

'Which you would if you sold them,' Honor retorted. 'And if "they" thought the papers were going to be public knowledge there would be no point in coming after you.'

'I know what the secret is,' he said wearily. 'Whether I have the papers in my possession or not, I *know* the secret.'

'So why haven't you gone to the press with it? You did last time.'

Nicholas smiled bitterly. 'That's the point – last time I was discredited. Who would believe me this time? They won't. Unless someone respectable speaks out for me – like Father Michael. He offered, I didn't ask him to. He wants to do it, to make amends for the past.'

'*And you're going to let him?*' she asked incredulously. 'You can be a right bastard, Nicholas.'

'He wants to do it!'

'And your arriving on his doorstep with a conspiracy theory didn't force his hand?' She slammed down her coffee cup. 'You don't really care about the deception; you just want to get your own back on the Church and you're prepared to use an old man to do it.'

'*He offered.*'

'You knew he would! When you turned up out of the blue and told him about it, you knew he would have to help you. Catholic guilt and all that shit. I imagine poor Father Michael thinks he'll get a front-row seat in Paradise for doing this.' She shook her head. 'You can fool other people, Nicholas, but not me. I know you.'

'He wants to do it.'

'Even if he gets killed? You might escape, Nicholas, with your religious celebrity, but what about some old man who's on his last legs?'

Her anger shook him. Why had Eloise Devereux brought him and his sister together again? Honor would have been safer kept out of it.

'I didn't want any of this—'

'Didn't you?' Honor countered. 'Seems to me that it's offering you a very convenient way to have another go at the Church.'

'You think I was wrong to expose them?'

'Not the first time, Nicholas,' she replied. 'I admired you for that. You stood up and told the world what had been done to those boys and it cost you. I know how much. I know what it did to you, physically and mentally. But this time – this time it just looks like you're a conspiracy nut out for revenge.'

'There are papers which prove the deception!'

'And it was you that found the papers, wasn't it? I mean, Sabine took the chain off the picture, but it was *you* who found the papers hidden inside.'

'Yes, it was me. So what?'

She hesitated for a moment before continuing. 'You took them out of their hiding place . . .' she said quietly. 'Or did you put them *in*?'

Forty-Two

Honor's suspicion had shaken Nicholas. That his own sister could doubt him left him speechless as he put down the phone and cut the connection. He was still smarting when he saw Eloise later.

'Why did you tell my sister what was going on?' he asked, not even waiting for her to take a seat.

Composed, she slid into the pew beside him. 'I had to tell her that you were in trouble—'

'And put her in danger?'

'She's your sister, she's already in danger,' Eloise replied, changing tack. 'I have some news that might interest you. About Carel Honthorst—'

'So why bother with the note?'

She looked at him blankly. 'What note?'

'The one you left on Honor's car earlier. The one she gave me an hour ago.'

'I left no note.'

Suspicious, Nicholas looked at her. 'All right . . . so what have you found out about Honthorst?'

'That he was a priest in Amsterdam. One of four sons, mother dead, father also dead. Apparently he was something of a tyrant when he was alive.' She paused, thinking. 'If you were told about Honthorst in a note, that means that someone else knows, apart from us. Perhaps someone wanted to warn you.'

He passed her the note. On it was written:

The Dutchman is an ex-priest.
He is working for the Church too.
Be wary of him.

'Very melodramatic,' Eloise said, passing it back. 'Strange choice of words too. "*Be wary*" is not a normal expression – not nowadays anyway. Sounds like someone for whom English isn't their first language. Or maybe he's just an old-fashioned, educated man.'

At once Nicholas thought of Sidney Elliott, the ageing academic. Had Elliott tipped him off? Nicholas doubted it – doubted he would have come all the way from Cambridge to leave a note on a car windscreen.

'Of course,' he said tentatively, 'it could be a woman.'

Eloise turned to Nicholas, eyes steady. 'No, a woman wouldn't leave a note on a car. It's too exposed, too easy to be spotted that way. And besides, it's not how a woman writes . . . Do you know who sent it?'

'No,' he replied, pushing the thought of Elliott to the back of his mind. 'I just know that it's meant to scare me.

It means that the Church has sent Honthorst after me. It means that he's not just working for Gerrit der Keyser, he's working for both parties – der Keyser for the chain and the Church for the papers, the secret.'

'Are you going to tell me today?'

Nicholas didn't need to ask what she meant. 'No. I'll never tell you what the deception was.'

'Never is a fool's word,' she replied. 'Keep your secret if you must – all that matters to me is finding out who killed my husband. That note,' she gestured to the paper in Nicholas's hand, 'means someone else knows what's going on. I had hoped to keep this matter contained.'

'No chance. Philip Preston has the chain now. He's auctioning it. If nothing happens in the next few days, that is.'

'I heard about the sale.'

'Have you got the money to buy it?'

The corners of her mouth lifted, but it was hardly a smile. 'I could buy it, yes. But what good would that do? If someone wanted it badly enough they could outbid me, or steal it from me afterwards.' She glanced at him. 'It's not the chain I want.'

'Has anyone threatened you?'

Again the near smile.

'No, Nicholas. No one has threatened me, but I am being watched.' She shrugged as though the matter were of no importance. 'I have good protection – my chauffeur takes me everywhere and he's outside the church now. At the hotel, he sleeps in an adjoining room. As I said before, money is very useful. But you . . .' She paused, staring at Nicholas. 'Who protects you?'

'No one.'

'Aren't you afraid?'

'Yes, I'm afraid,' he admitted.

'I'm not. Everything I prized has been taken away from me. If I was killed, what would it matter? I only want to find out who killed my husband. Other than that, there is nothing else.'

'You're still a young woman – you'll think differently in time.'

'All the old platitudes! The ex-priest in you is showing, Nicholas. I thought you'd left all that behind. Claude used to tease you about it, didn't he? He was very fond of you, you know. He liked your company and thought you'd been treated badly, hounded out of London. He liked you, even loved you . . . I don't want comforting. Nothing can ever comfort me for losing Claude and—' She stopped abruptly.

'What were you going to say?'

'Nothing.'

'You were,' Nicholas pressed her. 'There was something else. Tell me.'

Getting to her feet, Eloise paused by the pew and genuflected, dipping her head towards the altar. Then, without saying another word, she walked out.

Forty-Three

Philip Preston was having his own problems and the house-keeper had called him home urgently. Gayle was drinking, babbling incoherently about being out shopping and seeing someone. When she caught sight of Philip, she leapt to her feet and clung to him.

'I went to the gym, darling,' she said, gesturing to her glass. 'I've only had one drink, honestly. I think it's those new tablets Dr Marshall gave me. They mess up my head.' She slumped on to the sofa and Philip sat beside her. She looked unexpectedly pretty – made up, her hair blow-dried, her excess weight concealed under a dark dress – and for a moment she moved him.

But only for a moment.

'The housekeeper said you were shouting and crying—'

'I was confused,' she whined. 'I tell you, it's the tablets. Or the gym. It could be the gym – all that noise and bang-ing up and down with the machines. Too loud.' She shook her head, her thick blonde hair flopping over her face. 'I'm going to change,' she said suddenly, grasping her husband's hand. 'I promise. We'll be happy again and you won't want anyone else. I'm on a diet—'

'What were you so upset about?'

'It was silly. I was confused. Like the other time, when I thought I was hearing voices and I wasn't, it was just a radio left on. At least I think it was. Anyway, it stopped after the doctor gave me that medicine.' She rubbed her temples. 'It's hormones – must be.'

He was gritting his teeth. 'Hormones?'

'But it just seemed so real. Like the past, old times. And that made me think of you and how much I loved you and didn't want to lose you. I never loved him like I loved you—'

'Who?'

'Henry.'

'Henry!' Philip said, exasperated. 'Henry's dead.'

'I know! I know!' Gayle mumbled. 'That's what confused me when I saw him. This morning, walking down Regent Street with my father.'

It was all getting too much, Philip thought, trying to soothe his wife. 'Both of them are dead, darling. Your father and Henry Laverne are dead, and have been for a while.'

She nodded. 'And Hoagy?'

'And the cat,' Philip said patiently. 'The cat's dead too.'

Forty-Four

Church of St Barnabas, Fulham, London

The passing of time had not diminished his sleekness, rather exaggerated it. Like an oil slick Father Dominic glided into the confessional booth and took his seat, laying his rosary across his lap. Hair that had once been black had faded to a reddish-brown, like an old cat that has sat too long in the sun. His stomach rumbled, reminding him he had missed lunch, as the door of the confessional opened and someone slid into the adjoining booth.

Father Dominic's stomach growled a welcome, his hand resting against his cassock. 'Bless you, my child. Have you come for me to hear your confession?'

The person nodded, hardly visible through the metal grille, the voice a low whisper.

'Bless me, Father, for I have sinned.'

'When was your last confession?'

'Many years ago.'

Father Dominic shifted his position; the bench was hard on a bony posterior. 'But you are here today and want to repent of your sins?'

Again the low whisper, impossible to tell if it was a man or a woman. 'Yes.'

'What sins have you committed, my child?'

There was a momentary pause before the person continued. 'I am guilty of anger and pride. I have been very lonely for a long time, Father. Too much alone . . .'

'Go on.'

'. . . I have slept with women, even paid for a prostitute. It was wrong, Father, but I was lonely, a long way from home, and I needed comfort.'

The same old story, the priest thought. 'Are you married?'

'No. And I have dark thoughts, terrible thoughts, Father.'

'Like what?'

'Hatred.'

'You must rid yourself of these thoughts. They are an insult to God—'

'But I can't rid myself of them,' the voice replied, 'and I have such bad dreams. Every night the dreams come. Always the same.'

Father Dominic shifted his position, and his stomach growled again. Embarrassed, he touched his belly, pressing his finger into it in the hope of stopping the noise. He would hurry this along, he thought, then eat.

'God forgives everything. I will give you a penance—'

'There's more, Father.'

There would be, the priest thought, irritated. 'Go on, my child.'

'This is my confession and as such you cannot break my confidence. What I tell you, you can tell no one else.'

Father Dominic nodded. 'I cannot break the oath of the confessional, no.'

'It would be our secret.'

'Yes. Apart from us, only God would know.'

There was a long pause. For a moment Father Dominic thought the person had left, slipped silently out of the booth, but then the voice continued.

'I let someone down. I should have helped them and I didn't. I did in the end, but by then it was too late.' The whispering paused, took in a slow breath. 'I live with that – knowing I could have saved a life and didn't.'

Wrong-footed, the priest found himself taken aback. This was not what he had expected. 'Did you take a life?'

'No. I watched someone else take a life.'

'Have you told the police about this?'

'Yes, Father, I told the police. But it was a long time ago and everyone's forgotten it now. I was punished, but that wasn't right – the real culprits got away with it . . .' Again a long pause, a blurred image behind the grille, Father Dominic straining to see who was talking. And failing.

'Did you give false witness?'

'No!' the whisperer said sharply. 'I told the truth.'

'Then God will punish the evildoers.'

'But will He, Father?'

Sudden anger in the priest's voice. 'You doubt God?'

'Why should I believe in Him when He allows such injustice?'

'It is not our place to question God!'

The whispered voice continued. 'Did Father Luke believe that too?'

A sick feeling crept over the priest, a curdling memory stirring at the back of his mind. He felt suddenly claustrophobic in the booth and attempted to loosen his white dog collar, his hand shaking. The confines of the confessional were closing in on him, the musty smell of wood and furniture polish sticking in his throat.

'Father Luke is dead.'

'I know. He was murdered outside the Brompton Oratory only the other day,' the voice replied softly. 'How does it feel to have lost your ally, Father? To know that God *does* catch up with evildoers in the end. And that next time it will be your turn—'

'Who are you?'

'You know me, Father Dominic,' the voice said, suddenly no longer a whisper but a voice the priest knew only too well.

'Laverne!'

'Yes. And before you decide to leave the confessional in a hurry, think again,' Nicholas said coldly, 'and listen to what I have to say. I know what you did. What I exposed ten years ago was the truth—'

225

'You went to the press! You attacked a priest, you abused the Eucharist. You tried to discredit the Catholic Church, of which you were a serving member.'

'You and your kind discredited the Church long before I blew the whistle. I thought I could stop what you were doing, but I left it too late. Patrick Gerin died.'

'He committed suicide!'

'He was murdered!' Nicholas retorted. 'You know it and I know it. If you didn't put the rope around his neck, you drove him to it. And no one wanted to know. Instead I was made out to be lunatic, a fantasist. Well, the Church might have gagged me once, but not this time. You're trying to keep me quiet again. Trying to stop me going public with what I know. You lied, priest. You lied to the police—'

'*What!*'

'You told them that I'd phoned Father Luke, implied that I wanted to settle an old score with him. You set me up—'

'I didn't!'

'Forgive me for not believing you.'

'A man *did* call him – I overheard the conversation,' Father Dominic blundered on, his hands pressed against the grille which separated them. 'He said it was you. Father Luke said it was you. He believed it was Nicholas Laverne.'

'It wasn't. Besides, he would have recognised my voice.'

'From so long ago? No, Father Luke was getting deaf, he had trouble with voices.' The priest was pleading, clinging to the grille. 'Believe me, he thought it was you. He was afraid, he was older, he had—'

226

'A bad conscience.'

'We didn't do anything!' Father Dominic replied. 'It was just discipline. We weren't bad priests, not like those you hear about sexually abusing boys—'

'Someone else said that. As though it lessened what you two did.' Nicholas was thinking rapidly. He could see that the priest was afraid and was telling the truth. Someone had rung St Barnabas's church, posing as him. And Father Luke would have believed them, thinking Nicholas was coming back to take his revenge. But it hadn't been him.

'It wasn't my fault!' persisted Father Dominic. 'I was only trying to help the police when I told them about the phone call. It was the natural assumption to make. You'd been our enemy once, you could be our enemy again.'

'But why now? After so long?' Nicholas asked, trying to find out what the priest knew and if he would give himself away about the Bosch secret.

'I don't know why you came back!'

'I didn't come back.'

'*Someone* came back. Someone posing as you.' Father Dominic was panicking, shaking. 'No one expected to hear from you again. We thought it was all in the past. It was old history from ten years ago. We thought it was forgotten . . .'

Nicholas slumped back on the bench. He had been sure that he had been framed by the Church, the death of Father Luke the means to silence him. After all, another scandal would be devastating to a religious order that had been tainted by recent claims of abuse. An order that had seen some of its highest members go unpunished.

But if the Church hadn't set him up, who had?

Nicholas looked back at the grille, the priest's hands still pressed against it. 'Don't lie to me—'

'I'm not lying!' the priest cried. 'I swear I'm not lying. Someone killed Father Luke, and if it wasn't you, who was it?'

Nicholas pressed his own palms against the grille, feeling the priest's flesh hot against his skin. 'Swear it! On your soul, swear that you are telling the truth. If you lie to me now I'll find out, and I'll send you to Hell personally.'

Forty-Five

Mark Spencer had to admit that Honor had pissed him off with the crack about looking down her blouse, but he wasn't deterred. He liked her too much to give up and was eager to find a way to impress her. Which had just fallen into his lap. Having overheard her phone conversation, Mark had picked up on the name Carel Honthorst, and his unrelenting curiosity had done the rest.

So now he was standing in the doorway of Honor's office, smiling as she turned round.

'Hi.'

'Hi,' she said coolly. 'D'you want something?'

'No, I'm about to help *you*,' he replied, sliding into the room and leaning against the window. The daylight didn't flatter him, the sun beaming through his thinning hair and shining on his scalp. 'I heard you mention someone called Honthorst.'

She nodded, wary. 'What about him?'

'He was an old client of ours.'

Now she was listening as Mark parted company with the window and perched on the side of her desk.

'He was up for assault eight years ago. Slashed a man's face in a pub. His father was a Dutch farmer and Honthorst was shoved into the Catholic Church to cool him down when he was a kid. He became a priest, but left soon after. Has a terribly fierce faith apparently. But he never talks about it – being godly doesn't really tally with the kind of business he moved into.'

'Which is?'

'Debt collecting.'

'Wow!' Honor said simply. 'What happened to the charge of assault?'

'Victim dropped it. I reckon he thought it wasn't worth it, that he might end up with a Stanley knife in his face if it went to court. Since then, we've heard nothing from Carel Honthorst.' Mark was happy with his performance. 'But I remember him well. Huge man. Had something wrong with his skin. Pock-marked, or burnt. He used some kind of stuff to try and cover it up, but it looked awful. Not that anyone would tell him that.' Mark paused, thinking back. 'Joking apart, he was fucking terrifying.'

So this was the man Nicholas had mentioned – the man who had followed her brother. The man who was apparently working for the art world *and* the Church.

'Do we have an address for him?'

'Why?' Mark replied. 'I've told you, he's dangerous. Besides, any address we had all those years ago probably

230

wouldn't be relevant now . . . Anyway, why d'you want to know about him?'

'Oh, it's nothing important. His name just cropped up when I was talking to a client.'

The lie caught on Mark's internal radar, like a fly frying on a butcher's light.

'Why would Carel Honthorst come up in a fraud case?'

'You tell me,' Honor said lightly, turning back to her work. 'Thanks for the information, Mark – thanks a lot.'

But her thoughts weren't on the case, instead they were on what she had said to Nicholas. It had been unforgivable, but for an instant she *had* doubted him. After all, they had lived different lives for years. What did she really know about her brother? Where he had been. What he had done. Who knew how badly exile had damaged him? He had unnerved her talking about the Church and people following him. And the crucifix . . .

That had been the real worry – Nicholas talking about a crucifix that had suddenly appeared in his bed. It wasn't possible for someone to break in, unheard, place a cross in a bed and then disappear. And Father Michael had been asleep, so it hadn't been him. But that wasn't all that was worrying Honor – it was the conversation:

'What are you talking about?' she asked. *'The crucifix I gave you—'*

'Was in my bed . . .'

But it couldn't have been, Honor thought. Because she had never bought him a crucifix . . .

So did that make her brother a liar? Or a madman?

Forty-Six

Old Bond Street, London

It was snowing unexpectedly, the white flakes coming down fast. Then, just as suddenly, the rain started, drumming like a thousand tom-toms on the windows of Old Bond Street. Locking the front door of the gallery, Hiram Kaminski turned up the central heating and moved back into his office, settling down behind his desk. Judith was away, visiting her sister in Brighton, unwilling to leave him alone until Hiram insisted.

'Get out for the day,' he had told her. 'Get some sea air – it will do you good.'

'I don't want to leave you.'

He had put his head on one side, regarding her. 'What can happen in a day? We can't allow ourselves to be frightened—'

'Thomas Littlejohn sent us those damn notes—'

'And poor Thomas is dead.' Hiram had replied. 'He can't tell anyone about us. He can't tell anyone *where* he sent the secret. Besides, the letter sat next door for three months,

232

my dear. If someone had been watching us, they would have acted long before this.' He was confident, dismissive. 'Remember what we decided? The copies of the Bosch papers have been put in the bank. No one knows about them. And no one knows where they are.'

'So who has the originals?' Judith asked smartly. 'Someone must have them.' She had crossed her arms, defiant. 'Don't talk to me as though I'm a fool, Hiram. I understand our position perfectly. Thomas Littlejohn, Claude Devereux and Sabine Monette are all dead. Murdered. That's no coincidence.'

'We don't know that it's about the secret—'

'What else could it be about? The price of plums?' she snapped, irritated.

'Philip Preston has the chain – he's putting it up for auction. Why shouldn't he have the papers too?' Hiram asked. 'He's a sly man is Philip, a born negotiator. Think of the money he could raise with that exposé. Or then again, a man like that could be persuaded to keep it suppressed – for a fee. I don't suppose the art world or the Catholic Church would like to see it splashed all over the newspapers.'

She had thought for a moment, almost convinced. 'You think we're all right?'

He had nodded. 'I think we're all right.' He had kissed her gently. 'Go to your sister's and have a day out. Please, forget all this for a few hours.'

But now Hiram was feeling lonely, rather regretting his insistence. As usual the gallery had closed at five, and although he had wanted time to work on the accounts, he was soon restless. Having bought a sandwich from a nearby cafe, he made himself a coffee and perched on the high bar stool in the back kitchen. The view was depressing, the grungy back of the opposite building a morose and uniform grey. Silently he chewed his sandwich, checking the time on his watch. Judith would be back around nine.

His coffee wasn't to his liking. Hiram preferred a finer grind, but that was his wife's department. Good thing to have, he thought – a wife. Judith could be irritating, but he loved her. Always had done. And when she gave him a daughter, Helen, he was a happy man. In fact, Hiram thought, staring out at the blank view, he had been pretty lucky.

A light came on suddenly in a window of the opposite building and he glanced up as it was opened. He couldn't see anyone, but jumped when the window was slammed shut again. The noise startled the pigeons on the rooftops, a shuffle of birds rising up towards the glowering sky.

Hiram finished his sandwich and moved back into his office. Tiredness came over him, a full stomach and the long hours making their presence felt. Yawning, he leaned back in his leather chair and, a moment later, slid into sleep.

Forty-Seven

It had stopped raining at last and the evening was dank and icily cold. Walking quickly, Sidney Elliott lit a cigarette and paused at the end of the street. It was a long time since he had been in London, his life revolving around his consultancy work for Cambridge University and his estranged family. A wife and two daughters lived in what used to be the family home, the house which had sucked money from him for over thirteen years. It didn't seem to matter that his wife had been a chemist before they had married; after the ink had dried on the licence, she had given in her notice at the laboratory and got pregnant.

The first baby was born with problems. As was the second child. Not life-threatening, just learning problems and balance troubles. Problems that had required extensive and expensive treatment. As the children had gradually recovered, the marriage had gone on a respirator. No one pulled the plug, because Sidney wanted to believe that he could regain his family, that the wasted years could be retrieved. That his spectacular career – held in abeyance because of hospital visits and menial overtime jobs – could be reignited.

As for his wife, Sara wasn't going to tell Sidney that the marriage was over and had been for many years. Her estranged husband was paying the mortgage and the medical bills. When their daughters were old enough, Sara would divorce him, But not a moment before. The day came, of course. She told him, of course. And Sidney Elliott stood looking at his wife, at this woman who had taken a machete to his career and a cleaver to his emotions, and he had wanted to kill her.

His stammering had increased from that day. His stoop intensified and he cut off all contact with Sara. Not so with his daughters, although over the following years they grew away from the round-shouldered, acerbic man who was always quizzing them about their mother.

Was she seeing anyone?

Did she go out?

Was she happy?

He made them nervous, edgy. He was demanding, imperious, then pleading. He was their father, but not a father of whom they could be proud. This man was just the pathetic remnant of their mother's machinations.

Then finally, one day at the end of a long summer, Sidney called to see his ex-wife. She was sitting in the garden, sunbathing in a spotted bikini with the radio playing beside her. Her skin was smooth, without a wrinkle, a testament to idleness and egotism. And before he could stop himself, he

236

kicked over the sun lounger she was lying on and sent her sprawling into a bed of roses and well-rotted manure. The next day Sara took out a court order forbidding Sidney from coming within a hundred yards of her.

She needn't have bothered. He never went near her again, taking some small comfort from his last image of her: scratched by thorns, compost smearing the polka-dot bikini . . .

Sidney stared down the street as he finished off his cigarette. He wasn't going to fail, not this time . . . Using his insider knowledge and contacts, he had finally discovered the identity of the other two specialists Nicholas Laverne had spoken to about the Bosch papers. The one in Holland had been unforthcoming, but the younger man in Boston, USA, had been duped by Elliott's flattering attention. After all, his achievements looked good on paper.

It had taken a while, but Elliott had gradually eased the information out of him.

'. . . Of course all of th-th-this is in confidence. Mr L-L-Laverne has asked me to act as his go-between. He's busy at the m-m-moment.'

'I'll help in any way I can. We are often entrusted with valuable and private information. I've spoken to Mr Laverne a few times,' the young man had replied. 'What d'you want to know?'

'The papers. Mr Laverne wants to ch-ch-check. H-h-how many were there in total?'

'Twenty-eight.'

'We thought so,' Elliott said, swallowing hard. Twenty-eight and he'd only been allowed to see one! 'Did you s-s-see them all? Obviously I have. B-b-but did you?'

'Only ten of them,' the American had replied, 'but you could ask the expert in Holland how many he saw. Then again, if you've seen them yourself, you don't need to—'

'I just wanted to ch-ch-check with you that w-w-we had come to the same conclusion, that was all,' Elliott had replied, taking a shot in the dark. 'Have you s-s-seen the chain?'

'The one coming up for sale in London?' the young man had replied guilelessly. 'It's wonderful, isn't it?'

Yes, it was wonderful. It was all so fucking wonderful, Elliott thought bitterly, inhaling from his cigarette and feeling a growing frustration. He needed to make that sale. He needed Conrad Voygel. The tycoon wanted the Bosch chain, but did he know about the secret? And if he didn't, how much more money could Elliott get for finding it – uncover the deception, then take it to Voygel like a sly Salome presenting the head of John the Baptist?

He glanced down the street, thinking of Thomas Little-john. A very pleasant man, a man he had met years earlier at a conference in Cambridge. A man who had hinted about some papers from the late Middle Ages that told of a deception that would cause chaos. He hadn't told Elliott what the deception was, and at the time Elliott had dismissed it because people in the art world burbled about such things regularly. There was always something sensational about to be revealed, usually a ploy to up the price on a sale.

But after Nicholas Laverne had been to see him Elliott remembered what Thomas Littlejohn had said . . . And then he remembered something else about the dealer. He hadn't attended the conference alone, but with another man. A small, rather prim little man called Hiram Kaminski.

Elliott knew of him, of course. He was an expert in the art of the late Middle Ages, renowned in his field. The perfect man to talk to about some early and valuable writings, the ideal person to offer advice. A respectable dealer, a considerable intellect – the one person Thomas Littlejohn would have taken into his confidence.

And now Elliott was standing on Old Bond Street, in the cold, staring at the door marked KAMINSKI GALLERY.

Forty-Eight

The noise shook Hiram awake and his hands gripped the arms of the leather chair as he sat up suddenly. Trying to gather his thoughts he realised he had dozed off in his office, and then noticed the sound coming from the back rooms. Wary, he got to his feet and moved towards his office door then paused, listening. Had he locked the back exit? Yes, he was sure he had. Slowly he pushed back the door then jumped, seeing a shadow move past the window.

He was tempted to call out, but stopped himself. It could be a trader or a cleaner, he thought. Someone from one of the shops or galleries working late. But he knew it wasn't. This person was moving silently now, no longer clumsy. The shadow ducked and paused by the back door as Hiram watched, holding his breath.

Then he saw the handle turn. He was immobilised by shock, his body rigid, his eyes fixed on the juddering handle. It turned to the right and stopped. It turned again and stopped again, further movement impeded by the lock. Then someone started to apply pressure to the door. An instant later Hiram heard a shoulder slamming against the wood, and yet he still couldn't move, standing transfixed in the doorway of his office.

The noise stopped as quickly as it had begun. For an instant Hiram thought it was over. He remained motionless, but feeling his legs tremble, his mouth dry as asphalt.

A moment passed.

Then another.

It was over.

It wasn't.

The next sound exploded in Hiram's ears. A heavy foot was slammed repeatedly against the base of the door, which shuddered and creaked under the onslaught.

This time whoever was outside was determined to get in.

Book Four

'A world of dreams (and) nightmares in which forms seem to flicker and change before our eyes.'

Art historian Walter Gibson

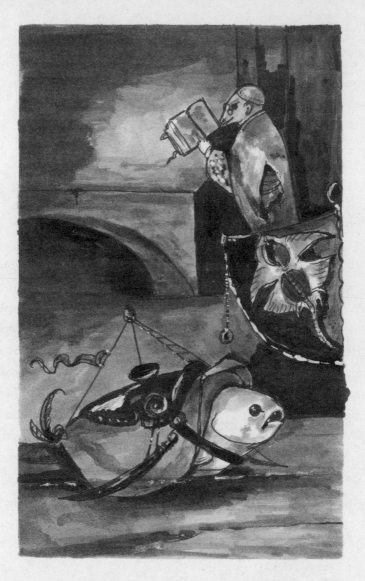

'The Temptation of St Anthony' [detail]

After Hieronymus Bosch

's-Hertogenbosch, Brabant, 1473

Hieronymus never discovered how his family found him, but someone betrayed him.

For once the studio door had not been locked. (Was it his gentle brother, Goossen?) Hieronymus had taken his chance to escape and made for Amsterdam, an overcrowded and filthy city where a stranger would be less likely to attract interest. Even a sickly, pale young man wearing clothes unsuited for the cold. All around him streets had lurched into other streets, the webbing of canals banked with markets. Congested alleyways were piled with pig manure and rotting offcuts of fish and meat, dogs scavenging alongside beggars. Men who had lost legs fighting in the wars of Brabant played hurdy-gurdies on street corners while women carried children on their shoulders as they weaved a foul pathway through the mud. It was like 's-Hertogenbosch but on a larger scale, seen through a fish-eye lens, grand and terrifying.

Hieronymus found lodgings, using the little money he had managed to steal from his father's study. Money he had earned, but never received. And in his place of safety he slept with a chair propped up against the door handle to stop anyone entering. Strange, he thought in the darkness. *I was imprisoned and now – a free man – I imprison myself. A prisoner always.*

He dreamed of his chimeras, his hands moving in sleep as though he were painting. He woke, turned on the straw mattress, felt the prickle of a flea bite and fell back to sleep.

Coughing woke him around six, because his lungs were cold and the air damp. As he had done for over three months, he coughed up phlegm and spat it into a rag, blood spotting the corners of his mouth. His forehead was tacky with sweat, his narrow chest heaving, his ribs a dull ache of pain. Then the attack subsided and he fell back into a clammy sleep.

He dreamed he was sitting by water, drawing with a stick of white chalk on an ebonised rock. He dreamed that the studio in 's-Hertogenbosch had burned to the ground, that his family had all perished, and felt no sadness. As the night turned over, he lay on the straw with the city fleas and dreamed of a boat coming for him, taking him through the canals of Amsterdam and into the sea beyond. As he rode the water, monsters followed him and he reached out his hand to touch the chimeras, the men fish and the flying ghouls. Animals with human heads told him stories, and under the lapping sea a shoal of demons drew the boat onwards.

He was crying in his sleep so loudly that it woke the man in the room next door, who called for the landlady. When she found Hieronymus he was grey, shiny with fever, his fingers still clenching a stick of white chalk.

Forty-Nine

Uncharacteristically thoughtful, Gerrit der Keyser sat in the sauna with a towel around his middle, his bifocals steamed up. He was trying to take his mind off his diet and the effects the medication was having on him. Like the puffy feet he had had to cram into his handmade shoes that morning. Feet and ankles like dimpled tripe, his silk socks tourniquets to the flesh. He had been quite good-looking once, but that was about five hundred years ago . . .

He blew his nose loudly, looking around. But he was alone, steaming, sweating, his glasses beginning to slip down his nose as he thought back. Sabine Monette – Sabine Guillaine when he first knew her – had been absurdly attractive, and clever. Much too clever for the life of a bourgeoise. It had been summer in Provence . . . Gerrit laughed aloud. Fucking summer in Provence! Christ, he sounded like a travel brochure. But it *had* been summer and it *had* been Provence and he had met this scrumptious piece of French arse and fallen in love.

Which had been easy when he had all his hair, all his heart vessels were working, and his sex drive could have powered a nuclear war . . . He could remember Sabine very well now that he allowed himself to remember. Pushing aside the grasping obsession of his work and his lascivious chasing of money, Gerrit thought nostalgically of his younger self. If they had met a little later, when he had set up the gallery and his fortunes were on an upward course, they could have made a go of it.

But then Miriam had come along and her father had offered to invest in Gerrit's new gallery, and he would have been a fool to pass up the chance. Of course in return for the money he had had to marry the girl, but Miriam had been a reasonable wife. Jealous, certainly, but blissfully stupid. If he had thought of Sabine over the years which followed Gerrit might have had a fleeting pang of regret. Now and again as he remembered the brutality of his leaving . . . he put it down to youthful callousness. At least that was what he told himself.

And then Sabine re-entered his life. She was in her forties, still glaringly handsome, and now wealthy. Apparently his leaving had not destroyed her. Neither had their furtive affair spoiled her chances of landing a good catch. To Gerrit's chagrin, Mr Monette was even richer then he was. With a better looking wife . . . A few years later Sabine contacted Gerrit and asked about a painting he had just purchased. She spoke to him over the phone as though he were a minion. Which, in a way, he was.

Rearranging the towel over his thighs, Gerrit took off his glasses and closed his eyes. He was so hot he thought he might expire, his heart pumping like over-boiling soup. But he stayed where he was, thinking of Eloise Devereux. *His daughter* . . . Why he hadn't made the connection immediately he couldn't imagine. She was so like her mother. Same elegant limbs and luminous eyes, but lacking in Sabine's sensuality and warmth. Eloise was a beautiful woman but a chilling one.

And of course it was possible. He had slept with Sabine and the timings were accurate to their affair. But he was strangely miffed by having been excluded from fatherhood. Then again, if he *had* been told that she was pregnant would he have married her? Gerrit opened his eyes wearily. He was getting old, developing that most dangerous human trait – a conscience. He had managed – profited – without one for many years. No broken sleep for Gerrit der Keyser; no fucking guilty regrets; no looking back and feeling queasy about the past.

Until now . . . Gerrit scowled into the steam, the sauna a little replica of Hell. It made him think of Hieronymus Bosch and the chain. And how Sabine had cheated him out of it. Smart move, he thought with grudging admiration. Was that her revenge? After all, she would have known it was valuable. Perhaps she had even known about the papers hidden inside it.

But *he* hadn't known about the secret then. Not until later, when the chain had left his hands and the rumours

251

began. Stories about a deception perpetrated by the Bosch family and the Brotherhood of Mary. He didn't know the whole story, but enough to realise it was explosive.

Gerrit sighed. Sabine had always been clever and finally she had bested him. But it had cost her. Murdered in a hotel room, initials carved into her stomach. Unexpectedly, Gerrit felt tears behind his eyes and blinked, shocked by emotion he hadn't experienced for a long time. He could remember the young Sabine so well, her rounded stomach warm under his lips. Not grey-skinned, aged, ripped up . . . Even in the heat, Gerrit shivered as an image of Sabine lodged in his mind – and beside it, an image of their daughter.

The beautiful, and vengeful, Eloise.

Fifty

While Gerrit was brooding in a sauna in Piccadilly, Judith Kaminski had returned to London and entered the gallery by the front. Once inside she paused, confused, hearing the battering against the back door. Dropping her handbag, she ran towards the noise, pushing Hiram aside and shouting: 'Who's there!'

The banging paused.

'Who's there?' she repeated. 'I've got a gun, I warn you, and I've called the police. They're coming.'

She could hear a muffled curse and then heavy footsteps running off, dying out in the distance. Silence fell. Neither of them moved. For several moments Judith stood rigid, facing the back door, then she slowly turned. Hiram was slumped in his chair, his mouth slack.

'I caught the earlier train . . .' she said blankly.

'Good.'

'. . . If I'd got the one I was intending to catch I wouldn't have got here for another hour.' She stopped, moved over to her husband, stroking his head as he rested it against her stomach. 'I knew I shouldn't have gone to Brighton.'

Fifty-One

The following morning Judith Kaminski made her way over to Philip Preston's auction house in Chelsea. The street was greasy with rain and her high heels caught on the edge of the pavement. Righting herself, she entered the building, spotting Philip at the back of the hall.

'Can I have a word?' she asked. Philip winched up his best smile and showed her into his office. Once inside, he slid behind his desk and watched as she took a seat. 'It's about the chain,' she explained.

'Ah.'

'Ah?' she repeated. 'I think *ah* is an understatement. My husband was threatened last night at the gallery—'

'That has nothing to do with me.'

'Oh, hear me out!' Judith replied. 'I haven't got all day so let's get down to it. You're auctioning a chain that belonged to Bosch. And what else?'

'Should there be something else?'

'You are a schmuck, Philip,' she retorted. 'You and I know there's a lot more to this than a chain. You knew Thomas

Littlejohn, didn't you?' He nodded and Judith continued. 'He knew about the chain's secret and he's dead. As are Sabine Monette and Claude Devereux – three people connected to the art world murdered. Why?'

'The chain's valuable. It belonged to Bosch—'

'Bah!' she said dismissively. 'Let's try again, shall we? What do you know? And I suggest you tell me the truth, because if you don't, my next stop is Gerrit der Keyser. Or maybe Conrad Voygel – I hear he's back in London—'

Philip put up his hands. How much to tell, how much to keep secret? Judith Kaminski had a big mouth and her husband was a leading authority on the Middle Ages. Perhaps, instead of excluding them, it might be to Philip's advantage to bring them into the fold.

'There's a rumour going around about some papers hidden in the chain—'

'Have you seen them?'

'Yes.'

Relieved, Judith blew out her cheeks. 'Well, that's a start. So you know about the Bosch secret?'

'Yes, but how d'you know?'

'Thomas Littlejohn sent us a letter. He wanted a witness in case anything happened to him.' She shrugged. 'Hiram thought that if we said nothing no one would find out what we knew. He was wrong.' She leaned towards the desk. 'I love my husband more than you can imagine, and I tell you here and now I will do *anything* to protect him. He's a good man, something of a novelty in this business, and I won't see him hurt. Do I make myself clear?'

'I don't intend to hurt your husband,' Philip said smoothly. 'You say that he's been threatened, but it wasn't by me. Oh, come on, Judith, everyone knows I'm a born coward. If I can't get what I want by stealth, I back off.'

She knew that much was true.

'Well, someone tried to break into the gallery last night. Thank God I came home early—'

'D'you know who it was?'

'No. Do you?'

Philip paused, thinking. Would Honthorst go after Hiram Kaminski? Did the Dutchman know he was privy to the secret? And if it weren't Honthorst, who else might it be? Sticky, he thought. It was all getting very sticky indeed.

'D'you know Nicholas Laverne?'

She shook her head. 'No.'

'He was the man who brought the chain to me.'

Judith narrowed her eyes. 'Why?'

'He wanted to sell it.'

'The chain? Or the papers?'

'Oh, you *have* seen them,' Philip said blandly. 'I'm so glad you weren't bluffing. There's already one liar in this room.'

Slowly, Judith began to count on her fingers. 'So you know the secret, Hiram and I know, this Nicholas Laverne knows, Thomas Littlejohn knew and so did Sabine Monette. Six people at least . . . For a secret it's pretty public. What about Gerrit der Keyser?'

'He wants the chain back, but the secret? I don't think he knows, but then again, he might. Gerrit isn't a man to show his hand.'

'What about Conrad Voygel?'

'Desperate to buy the chain. Already offered me a fortune—'

'Which you didn't take?'

'I think I can get more at the auction.'

'If you live long enough . . . Why risk it?' she asked, baffled. 'What's money worth to you? Isn't your life worth more?'

'Not the one I've got,' Philip replied curtly. 'Anyway, I've hired security.'

'I got to you easily enough.'

'You're . . .'

'A dumpy old Jewess?' She pulled a face. 'Remember, the biggest threat comes from the most unexpected place. Napoleon knew that.'

'The Russian winter finished his tactics.'

'And we have a London winter to get through,' Judith replied deftly. 'Or in this instance, three days. Have you been threatened?'

'Why d'you think I got the security?' Philip replied. 'Gerrit der Keyser has been throwing his weight around. He has a cohort – a big Dutchman. I know he sent him to talk to Sabine Monette.'

'You think he killed her?'

'He could have done, but Honthorst would be too obvious a suspect. And I don't know if Gerrit's a killer. A crook, yes. A

258

murderer, even once removed? Unlikely. But then you never know about people, do you?' Philip changed tack. 'As for Honthorst, I think he's just hired muscle. More to intimidate than anything else.'

'You think he could have been at our gallery last night?'

Philip dodged the question. 'Did you call the police?'

'I scared the man off, so why bring the police into it?'

'Why not?' Philip countered. 'But then again, they would ask questions, like *why* your husband was being threatened, and then you'd have to tell them about Thomas Littlejohn and his confession. Which would interest the police, seeing as how they're running around trying to find out who put a match to Mr Littlejohn.' He paused. 'You didn't want to get involved, did you?'

'I want to get my husband out of the mire, not drop him further in it.'

'So why come and see me?'

'Strategy.' She took out a large envelope from her handbag and passed it to him across the desk. 'That's what Thomas Littlejohn sent us. *Everything* about the chain and the secret—'

'I already know all about it.'

'Not all of it.' She pointed to the envelope. 'There's something extraordinary in there – a portrait of Hieronymus Bosch.'

'What?' Eagerly Philip rummaged through the pages until he came across the image of *The Tree Man*. Incredulous, he looked at Judith. '*This* is Hieronymus Bosch?'

259

She nodded.

'Jesus! Does anyone else know about this?'

'Apart from us, only Thomas Littlejohn. And he's dead.' She tapped the desk with her forefinger. 'You can do what you like with that. Drum up interest, the price of the flaming Bosch chain – whatever. I don't want anything. I don't want the chain. I don't want to be clever and try to sell what I know about the Bosch conspiracy. And I don't want to be paid to keep it quiet.'

'So what do you want?'

'Safety,' Judith replied. 'I don't care if there was a cover-up, I care about my family.'

Philip was eyeing her suspiciously. 'You're a dealer, Judith. Why give away something that's worth a fortune?'

'It's only worth a fortune if you live long enough to enjoy it,' she replied. 'I want you to do one thing for me. Tell everyone what you know—'

'About the deception?'

'Oh, that part's up to you! The rumour's spreading,' she said dismissively. 'God knows how many people know already. I mean the painting. The chain. Everything. Tell them about *The Tree Man* and who it really was – Bosch.'

He was finding it hard to follow her. 'And how does that help you?'

'Who'll come after us for information that's been made public? Hiram won't be the only one to know then – he'll be one of many. Safety in numbers, it's called. I want the gun pointing at someone else, Philip, not my husband.'

Fifty-Two

Church of St Stephen, Fulham, London

Watching from the back of his car, Conrad Voygel studied the church. As the windows of the car were tinted, no one could see him but he could see everything outside clearly – the church, the entrance porch where the unfortunate Thomas Littlejohn had been torched, the gravel path which led round to the back entrance, and the dark-haired man sitting talking to an old priest.

His gaze moved back to the porch, scorch marks still discernable on the stonework and the two steps up to the church door. What a way to die, Conrad thought sympathetically. What a terrible way to die.

His attention shifted towards the two men again, his focus on Nicholas Laverne. The ex-priest, the man who had gone after demons and been demonised for his pains.

Conrad tapped on the glass partition and watched as the chauffeur slid it open.

'Yes, sir?'

'I want you to deliver a message for me.' He scribbled a quick note and passed it to the chauffeur. 'You see the men sitting over there? Give this to the younger man. Don't wait for an answer, just come back to the car.'

Leaning back in his seat, Conrad watched the scenario play out. Saw the wary expression on Nicholas's face as he glanced at the note, and smiled as the old priest anxiously grabbed his arm. A moment later, the chauffeur returned to the car and Conrad signalled for him to drive on.

Fifty-Three

Nicholas was still bruised from his sister's lack of faith. Despite all the messages she had left on his phone, he had not called Honor back, so she had decided to visit St Stephen's that evening. She was just packing up when Mark Spencer entered her office with a barely disguised grin on his face. He was grinning – trying not to – but grinning none the less.

'I'm about to leave, Mark—'

'Meeting your brother?'

She turned slowly, her expression cold. 'What about my brother?'

'You kept quiet about him. Apart from the photograph, that is.' He pointed to the print on her desk. 'I thought it was your boyfriend . . . Mind you, I suppose your brother's the kind of black sheep families *do* keep quiet about.'

'I can't chat,' she said curtly. 'I have to leave—'

'Not yet. We need to talk first,' Mark replied, closing the door and sitting down. 'Don't look at me like that, I'm trying to help.'

'I bet you are,' Honor said, sitting behind her desk and flicking the phone on to voicemail. 'So, what d'you want?'

'I told you – to help. That's all I've ever wanted to do, help you. That query about Carel Honthorst – I mean, a bit obvious, wasn't it? You weren't asking about him for some fraud case, were you? So it got me thinking – you know how curious I am, my mother used to say it was freaky how I could find things out – and I dug around a little and discovered that Honthorst is working in the art world now. Then I found out about your brother—'

'Who doesn't work in the art world.'

'True, but he's been touting a chain around London, a chain which is soon to be auctioned by Philip Preston. And before you ask, Preston is a client of mine, and we had a meeting yesterday and he told me about the chain – and who had found it.' He paused and Honor said nothing. 'I asked him about this Nicholas Laverne and he didn't know much, but Google did.'

She swallowed nervously. 'And of course we all know that everything on Google is gospel.'

'Funny you should use that word, seeing as how your brother was excommunicated. Something of a whistle-blower, it said.'

'He exposed a scandal in the Catholic Church—'

'Naming two priests in particular, one of whom has just been bumped off.' Mark pulled a face. 'It's OK, I found out that the police didn't charge your brother, so he's not committed murder. Well, not this time.'

'What the hell is that supposed to mean?'

He dropped his voice conspiratorially. 'How well d'you know Nicholas Laverne?'

'He's my brother. Of course I know him.'

'So you know he was arrested in Germany for assault?' Mark asked, moving on rapidly. 'And in France for theft? I can see from your expression that you didn't know. Don't worry, I won't tell anyone. It wouldn't do your promotion prospects much good if the partners found out. I just want—'

'Get on with it!' Honor snapped, folding her arms.

Refusing to be offended, Mark continued. 'Nicholas Laverne was in a fight with another man over a woman in Munich. The man pressed charges but then backed off, saying it was a case of mistaken identity.'

'Maybe it was.'

'You don't believe that, do you? As lawyers we both know that people who go back on their stories have usually been pressurised—'

'Or thought better of what they said. Or reneged on a lie.'

Mark reached into his briefcase, opened it, and then tossed a photograph across the desk. 'Günter Reinhardt. Facial abrasions and a ruptured spleen. It was no lie, he *was* assaulted. Your brother was eighteen at the time.'

Picking up the photograph, Honor stared at the image and swallowed again as Mark slid another photograph across the desk to her. This one was of a painting, a small pastoral scene by Corot.

'This picture was stolen in France, from the Devereux Gallery. The late owner, Raoul Devereux, dropped the charges when he discovered who the thief was. Apparently your families knew each other.'

Honor said nothing, just stared at Mark Spencer and the photographs on her desk.

'Your brother was lucky. Twice he got away with it.'

'Nicholas is no thief.'

'He confessed to taking the painting.'

'*I don't believe it!*' she snapped, her face colouring. 'How old was he when this was supposed to have happened?'

'Nineteen.'

She thought back. They were still living with David Laverne in the country; Henry had moved to France, she was taking exams, and Nicholas was in that grim patch where he came and went without explanation. She had hoped that the crimes had been committed after he had been excommunicated. Then she would have some excuse for her brother's actions. That he was under stress. Unbalanced, even.

But this had happened *before* he had entered the Church. Before he left Nicholas Laverne behind and became Father Daniel.

'He was young—'

'He was a menace,' Mark said firmly. 'Apparently there were all kinds of other rumours about your brother. He was living with a woman old enough to be his mother for a while, then he dabbled in drugs—'

'No!' she said shortly.

'Yes,' Mark replied. 'It's hard to hear, I know. But you have to hear it. It's important you know what kind of a man he is before you get involved with him any further. I guessed that he'd been out of your life for a while – I remembered how you reacted to that homeless man being murdered. I'm not stupid, Honor – I kept following the clues.'

'Congratulations. What's the prize?' she asked, her tone acid.

'There's no prize for you if you stick with him. Your career will be damaged by association.' He leaned towards her. 'Look, I understand, he's your brother, but think about it carefully. What do you really know about him?' He pointed to the photographs. 'What if there's more? Worse?'

'I'm sure you'd have dug it up, Mark.'

He ignored the comment.

'I'm not telling anyone else what I've found out. I'm just trying to help you, like I say. You're clever, Honor – you could go a long way. But you need to stay in your own class, with your own type. Marry someone respectable, maybe set up your own practice one day.' He paused to let the inference sink in. 'With a clever partner – in business and in life – you could get to the top.'

She wasn't listening any more, she was thinking. Assault, drugs, theft – *was* that her brother? She could hardly deny it; what looked to be proof was lying on the desk in front of her. Where were you all those times you went missing, Nicholas? Where did you go when you came home filthy, hungry? You never said, and no one ever asked. Our uncle wasn't interested and you always joked with me. The younger sister, the baby. I was no real confidante of yours.

Pushing aside the photographs, Honor walked to the window. If she supported her brother, who was she really protecting? He wasn't a little boy, he was a man now. Should she risk her own career for someone she didn't really know? She had longed for a family, for her estranged brother to come back to her, but maybe her longing had been misplaced. Maybe what she was really chasing was security – and looking for it in the least secure of people.

However much she hated Mark Spencer for shattering her illusions, Honor had begun to have doubts. She might have tried to suppress them, but she had wondered if Nicholas were becoming paranoid. If the one-time hero were merely an obsessive fantasist. His talk of murder and the Catholic Church was extreme, and his mention of the crucifix had troubled her.

Reluctantly, she thought of what Mark had said. If Nicholas *were* a thief and a liar, was he crafty enough to have plotted the whole deception? Could he have *created* a reason to get back at the Church? He hadn't found the chain, but he had always been inventive. Could his troubled mind have devised a plan, secreting the paper slips into the chain only to discover them later, thereby giving himself another conspiracy to expose?

How much had he wanted to be a hero again?

You are my brother, Honor thought. You are Nicholas. But which Nicholas?

'Clumsy,' she said at last, turning back to Mark.

He blinked. 'Pardon?'

'Your attempt at blackmail – it's clumsy.'

'I wasn't blackmailing you, I was trying to warn you!' Mark replied, certain that she would appreciate his interference at a later date. 'Your brother kept out of your life for a long time and maybe that was a blessing. When he exposed the abuse ten years ago he was a hero—'

'He *was* brave.'

'Then,' Mark agreed. 'But now he's washed up, sinking fast. Don't let him drag you down with him.'

Fifty-Four

The rain had given way to mist, a low white ghosting which lingered over the buildings and the street as Nicholas checked his watch against the chiming of the church bell. Nine thirty. It seemed that the wind had exhausted the air itself; it hung heavy and moist, rain droplets clinging to the bare branches and the decaying iron spire. It was a night to be at home. A night to lock doors and light fires, play music and relax behind dark curtains and under the fluffing of a duvet. As Nicholas walked along he could see the misted bonnets of the cars, and knew that by dawn the moisture would be frosted. Winter had shown her hand.

So had Conrad Voygel, he thought, remembering the note he had been given. It read:

I would like to know more about the rumoured Bosch deception. I believe you know the complete story. Perhaps we could talk.
Conrad Voygel

Nicholas's first instinct had been to ignore the note, but an hour later another was delivered asking for him to wait outside the Victoria and Albert Museum at 9 p.m. that evening. He would, the note continued, be perfectly safe.

'You can't go!' Father Michael had said, shocked. 'You could be walking into a trap. Father Luke was killed outside the Brompton Oratory. That's very close to the V and A. Suspiciously so.'

'This isn't a threat,' Nicholas replied. 'If it were dangerous, there would have been no invitation, they would have just attacked me. Conrad Voygel wants to find out what I know about the deception—'

'And when you tell him? Then what?'

Nicholas didn't answer and the old priest reached for his coat. 'I'm going with you.'

'No, you're not.'

'You need a back-up.'

'I don't need you,' Nicholas replied, remembering what Honor had said to him, his conscience pricked. 'Stay here. I'll be back soon.' He moved to the door. 'And lock this when I've gone. Don't worry, I can look after myself.'

But now Nicholas was wondering about that as he moved into the underpass, walking towards the exit closest to the Victoria and Albert Museum. There was no one else in the subway, only footsteps and traffic grumbling overhead as he climbed up the exit steps on to Brompton Road. He looked around but could see no one waiting, no car parked at the kerb. Rubbing his hands together, he leaned against some railings and waited.

Ten minutes passed, Nicholas checking his watch and then feeling an unwelcome nausea come over him. God, he thought, he should never have bought a burger from a street trader. This was the second time he'd felt close to throwing up. A moment later a car drew up at the kerb and a man got out as Nicholas straightened up.

The figure walked towards him, dressed in a long coat, the collar turned up. A big man, Nicholas thought, wondering if it was Honthorst. Then he saw the stoop – Sidney Elliott.

'I thought I was meeting Conrad Voygel,' Nicholas said, turning to walk off.

Elliott ran after him. 'I'm M-M-Mr Voygel's representative.'

'His mouthpiece?'

'He wants to know about the d-d-deception. He'll pay you well.'

'Forget it,' Nicholas snapped. 'I don't want paying.'

'So why come to the m-m-meeting?'

'Conrad Voygel said he wanted to talk. I'm willing to talk to him, but no one else.'

'You should talk to m-m-me,' Elliott replied. 'Look, I can p-p-put in a good word for you with Voygel. He's a wealthy m-m-man with lots of contacts. You need to stay on his good s-s-side.'

'What is this *break* you want?' Nicholas asked him. 'You want an adventure, go bungee jumping. Your life hasn't worked out the way you want, so what? No one gets the life they expect. You've done all right,' he continued. 'Why lower yourself to be the runner for someone like Conrad Voygel?'

Angered, Elliott reached for Nicholas's sleeve and gripped it. 'Give yourself a ch-ch-chance. And me. I need a chance—'

Nicholas shook him off.

'Why w-w-won't you help me?' Elliott snarled. 'I know there are t-t-twenty-eight pieces of writing, I know it's about a d-d-deception regarding Hieronymus Bosch. Just tell me what the deception is. I can get a g-g-good deal for you—'

'I told you, I don't want the money!' Nicholas replied, suddenly feeling nauseous again and slumping on to a low wall, his focus blurring. 'Just leave me alone.'

Elliott stood over him, his gloved hands deep in his pockets, his expression curious.

'What's the m-m-matter with you?'

'Something upset my stomach,' Nicholas replied, 'probably the company I'm keeping.' He looked up at Elliott. 'The secret isn't for public consumption. Tell Voygel that. Tell him he can buy the chain, but the secret's off limits. Unless he wants to talk to me privately.'

'Mr Voygel d-d-doesn't like being disappointed, neither d-d-do I.'

'That's a shame. I hear it's good for the soul.'

'Of course,' Elliott replied, 'you're n-n-not a journalist,

are you? You're an ex-p-p-priest. You know all about the s-s-soul.' He tapped Nicholas on the shoulder. 'I heard you were living b-b-back at Saint Stephen's church—'

'So it's you, is it?' Nicholas replied, wincing as a pain ripped through his stomach. 'I knew someone was watching the place. And I heard someone walking around.' He grimaced as the pain increased. 'Was it you that broke in and planted that crucifix?'

Elliott looked baffled. 'Not m-m-me, Mr Laverne. Perhaps you sh-sh-should look a little closer to home?'

Scowling, Sidney Elliott fastened up his coat and turned away. He didn't even pause as he heard Nicholas fall off the wall and slump, unconscious, on to the winter pavement.

Fifty-Five

As Nicholas slept, Honor watched her brother, Mark Spencer biting his thumbnail as he waited in the hospital corridor outside. He should have washed his hands of her, but couldn't. He had hoped that Honor would come to her senses and avoid any further involvement with her brother, but that had been before Nicholas Laverne was found on Brompton Road with an acute case of food poisoning.

Nothing like sickness to bring people closer together, Mark thought ruefully as he wandered up and down the corridor. Still, he consoled himself, Nicholas Laverne would recover and then Honor would think over what he had told her, and with luck she would pin her colours on to his mast and not that of the ex-priest. If she didn't, Mark had a problem. He couldn't seriously consider her wife material if she stayed close to Laverne. It was irksome, but a man had to protect his career and his reputation, whatever sacrifices that entailed.

Another thought presented itself. It was Honor who had mentioned the word blackmail. He hadn't considered it, but now Mark was thinking that perhaps he *could* apply a little judicious pressure to Honor Laverne. Her brother or a partnership in the firm – it was a simple choice. Security against uncertainty. Respectability against infamy.

Still chewing his thumbnail, Mark wandered back to the ward and looked in. Honor was still sitting at her brother's bedside, Nicholas still asleep, his eyes closed against all of them.

I am back, Nicholas thinks, moving between the yew trees and seeing the outhouse before him. Only this time it is different. Strange . . . This time the outhouse roof is missing and an arrogant magpie is strutting across the exposed beams . . .

He moves inside, as always, and sees the huge cupboard. But then again, this is different. This time the cupboard door is wide open, the interior empty.

Patrick Gerin is sitting on the roof beams, watching the magpie, crooning to it under his breath. And as he sits the sun moves swiftly behind a banking of clouds and the rain begins. I remember the rain, Nicholas thinks. This part is always the same . . . Patrick is swinging his legs, thin white legs like strands of cotton, his hands grasping the roof beams, the magpie bouncing towards him.

What is this? Nicholas thinks, confused. What is this? He reaches into the pocket of his priest's robe and pulls something out. A crucifix and a piece of rope. Puzzled, he weighs both articles in his hands, one against the other, and then glances back at the crooning boy.

And the rain keeps falling through the open roof of the outhouse, on to Patrick Gerin and the magpie, as Nicholas moves forward . . . I do not remember this, he thinks. This is not the same . . . He moves lightly, quickly, under the roof beams and then grabs the boy's left foot and pulls him, screaming, down to earth.

Fifty-Six

The touch on her shoulder made Honor jump. She turned round, expecting to see Mark, but was surprised to find Eloise Devereux standing there. Putting her forefinger to her lips, Honor walked out into the corridor and Eloise followed her.

'How is he?'

'Doctor said he'll be fine. He just had a really bad case of food poisoning. Got dehydrated, but they've given him fluids and he's coming round,' Honor replied, changing the subject. 'I'm glad you came by. I wanted to have a word with you.' Catching sight of Mark out of the corner of her eye, she guided the Frenchwoman to the Waiting Room and closed the door behind them. 'How did you know Nicholas had been taken ill?'

'Father Michael told me,' Eloise replied calmly. 'What did you want to talk about?'

'Nicholas . . .' Honor paused, awkward and uncertain of how to continue. 'You had contact with him in the years we were estranged and I wondered how much you knew about him. What he'd been doing—'

'Why don't you ask him yourself?'

'He's not talking to me at the moment – we had an argument,' Honor replied, hurrying on. 'Nicholas was very close to Claude, but I never knew when they first met.'

If Eloise was surprised by the question she didn't show it, merely took off her coat and sat down on one of the hard-backed green chairs. 'In their teens, I believe.'

'How did they meet?'

'Through Henry, I suppose. Henry was mentored by Claude's father, and he spent a lot of time with Raoul. I imagine Nicholas was introduced to Claude that way.'

'So Nicholas visited France in his teens?'

'A few times. Didn't you know?'

Honor bristled. 'We didn't have a normal upbringing. Our uncle wasn't too interested in what the boys did. He couldn't handle Nicholas and so he let him run wild. What else could he have done? David Laverne was a single man with no experience of children; he couldn't cope with a difficult nephew.'

'Why was Nicholas difficult?'

'He went off the rails when our parents were killed in a car accident. Henry always said that it was Nicholas's fault—'

Eloise was taken aback. 'How was it his fault?'

'It wasn't. It was just that our parents had come back from a trip and were tired and Nicholas had missed the last train and needing to be picked up from London. My father said he'd go alone, but my mother said she'd go with him to keep him awake. They crashed on the motorway . . . Henry never forgave himself for what he'd said, and Nicholas never forgot. He started playing truant from school, acting up.' Honor paused. 'He was impossible, but eventually he'd settle down and we'd all think it was over and then he'd go off again. Even in his teens Nicholas used to disappear.'

'Difficult for you.'

'Yes, it was. I worried about him.'

'How did Henry cope with it?'

'He was older than us, so he was already pretty much sorted. He had his career mapped out. He was sensible, focused, whereas Nicholas was capricious. Women loved him and he had a way with them . . .' She thought of what Mark had told her, about her brother living with a woman old enough to be his mother.

'Was Nicholas ever involved in anything serious?'

'Like what?' Honor asked. But she spoke the words too quickly and alerted the Frenchwoman.

'Did he get into trouble?' she repeated.

'He never told me if he did,' Honor replied deftly. 'Then he suddenly seemed to settle and went into the Church. We kept in touch, but when the scandal broke he did his usual thing and disappeared.'

'Maybe he wanted to protect you.'

'Maybe. But for ten years I didn't know what he was doing, except for what Claude told me.' Honor thought about the stolen painting and the assault. 'Look, you knew my brother after he was excommunicated. What was he doing then?'

Turning away, Eloise looked through the partition window into the hospital corridor. She was thinking about how jealous she had been of the Englishman, the elusive fixture in her husband's life. And her first impression of Nicholas Laverne had stuck. He had arrived late one night, dishevelled, wearing old clothes, with a holdall flung over his shoulder. Dark-eyed, suspicious, asking for help.

'Can you put me up for a while?' he had asked Claude. 'Just for a bit.'

'Yes, yes, of course. But why didn't you return my calls? I've been trying to get hold of you ever since I heard.'

Nicholas had slumped into a seat by the fire, despondent but angry. 'They threw me out. I've nowhere else to go,' he had said, glancing at Eloise as though expecting an argument. 'Those bastards ruined my life.'

Eloise turned back to Honor. 'Your brother never confided in me. And if he confided in Claude, my husband didn't tell me. But I don't think Nicholas would have involved us in any trouble. He was secretive, but that was because he was protective of his friends. And his family.' She held Honor's gaze. 'Didn't you ever think he wanted to confide? Sometimes it seemed as though he was about to say something, then he held back.'

'He was like that when he was young. Like he was always looking for someone to trust and never found them. Perhaps your husband was the closest he came to having a confidant.'

Eloise rose to her feet. 'There's one thing that sticks in my memory. Always has. Nicholas found a place to live close to us, then began to work for Sabine Monette. He did her gardening, odd jobs and maintenance on the property.' She paused, smiling slightly. 'Nicholas was very happy then. He was fond of Sabine and enjoyed her collection—'

'*She was a collector?*' Honor asked, alerted. 'What did she collect?'

'Paintings, mostly Dutch. Sabine had natural taste, could always buy well. Her collection wasn't large but it was impressive, and she was so proud of it.' Eloise paused. 'Then she had a burglary. Someone broke in and stole a couple of her most valuable pictures . . .'

Honor held her breath. 'And?'

'Nicholas told us all about it. Said it was his fault. Sabine had been at her apartment in Paris and he had been looking after the chateau. The thief got in because Nicholas had forgotten to turn on the alarm.' She looked intently at Honor. 'Then your brother said something I'll never forget. He said it "was a true mark of friendship that Sabine never suspected him."'

Fifty-Seven

Standing in front of his cloakroom mirror, Philip held a second mirror up to look at the back of his head, at what he thought was a bald spot. He had always been vain about his hair and the innocent chance remark Gayle had made that morning had irked him. Bloody woman, he thought, comforted that he could see no thinning of his pate. Bloody stupid woman.

His vanity restored, Philip moved back into his office and studied the auction brochures that had just arrived. On the front cover was the Bosch chain and inside a description:

Extraordinary and rare object, believed to have belonged to the most important artist of the Late Middle Ages, Hieronymus Bosch. Papers claiming this provenance offered with the sale. The initials H and B are inscribed on the first links of the chain, closest to the clasp. The H is prominent, the B less so.

284

Philip liked the last line best, hoping that a relatively low estimate might encourage more bidders. After all, there were collectors who would think nothing of paying so much for a piece of such prominence. For a moment he thought of the papers and felt a pang of regret. He should have put them up for sale with the chain. They would have raised a fortune . . . But his greed had been overshadowed by his cowardice. Let Nicholas Laverne reek havoc with the Church, Philip would settle for the chain.

And although it had been difficult, Philip had managed to say silent on the subject of Bosch's *Tree Man*, a portrait of the artist himself. The temptation to brag had been almost too much to resist, but he had managed it. This was a little nugget to expose at the auction. A thunderbolt for the art world, and healthy exposure for his auction rooms. Every Arts correspondent would publicise the news and, by default, Philip Preston.

It was all going to work out perfectly. And his hired security had managed to calm his anxieties. No one could get to him with them around, not even the formidable Honthorst. In fact, he thought, perhaps the whole business had been blown out of all proportion. And then he remembered the murders . . .

Reaching into his desk drawer, Philip picked up the two plane tickets. One way. It was all organised; he had his flight booked. Immediately after the sale he was going to take Kim to his new home outside Milan, a place no one knew about apart from his lawyer. All the arrangements for Gayle's welfare, his business concerns and his divorce could be handled long distance. He wanted out of London. Permanently.

Outside, the clock struck three and Philip was surprised when the door opened and security informed him that a Mr Gerrit der Keyser wanted to talk to him.

'OK, send him in.'

He came in flushed and out of breath, luminous with fury. 'You bastard,' he began, flinging a heavy object across the desk towards Philip. 'If you're auctioning the real Bosch chain then what the fuck is this?'

Fifty-Eight

Church of St Stephen, Fulham, London

Discharging himself from hospital, Nicholas made his way back to St Stephen's, where Father Michael greeted him and ushered him inside.

'Are you all right?'

'I'm fine, fine,' Nicholas replied. 'Just food poisoning. I should watch what I eat.' He changed the subject. 'Anything happen here?'

The old priest shook his head. 'Nothing. I was worried out of my mind when you didn't come back from that meeting.'

'It wasn't Conrad Voygel after all. It was Sidney Elliott. Unbelievable. I collapsed and the bastard left me lying there.'

'At least he left you alive,' Father Michael replied. 'Honor rang again. And Philip Preston—'

'What did he want?'

'I don't know. He didn't say.' The priest replied, making them both some tea and putting the mugs on the table. 'You don't think it was deliberate, do you?'

'What?'

'You being ill. I mean, you don't think—'

'Someone poisoned me?' Nicholas laughed. 'No, I think I got felled by an under-cooked burger. This is one thing I can't blame on the Catholic Church.' He took a sip of his tea. 'Did anyone come last night?'

'I heard someone walking around. And the phone rang in the early hours. Same as usual.' He looked at Nicholas. 'When are you going to make the Bosch deception public? I've told you, I'll help you in any way I can. Whenever you want to speak out, I'll be right next to you. I promise I won't go against my conscience this time.'

Nicholas hesitated for a moment, wondering if he should say the next words, then let them come.

'Did you know what they were doing to Patrick Gerin?'

The old priest took in a breath, hobbled by regret. 'I knew about the other boy.'

'But not Patrick?'

'No. I heard rumours about David Sullivan. I even mentioned it to Father Luke and Father Dominic, but they told me he was a difficult boy. Needed discipline, they said. He was going to be a good priest; he had to be obedient.' Father Michael was stumbling on the words. 'Patrick Gerin was another matter . . . he was . . . No, I didn't know about him.' The old priest paused again, glancing up at Nicholas. 'They were just rumours – nothing concrete, just gossip. A year earlier some boy had lied about being mistreated at St Barnabas's and we thought this was just more of the same. You can't believe everything you hear.'

'But you could have looked into it.'

'Why didn't you?' Father Michael countered, catching Nicholas off guard. 'You exposed the abuse – but if you knew about it all along, why didn't you do anything earlier? Why wait until Patrick Gerin died?'

Nicholas looked away. 'I think about that every day. I dream about it. Even in my dreams it's always too late. I should have acted sooner. I failed—'

'That time, but not now,' the old priest replied. 'You still want to expose the fraud about Bosch, don't you?'

'Not until the auction. When the chain goes up for sale there will be a lot of publicity and I want to use that. The press and the internet will report the sale of the chain – and then I'll come forward with the Bosch papers. The proof of what was done to him. The proof of how the Catholic Church colluded.' He took another drink of tea, feeling the warmth spread through him. 'I failed a living boy, but I won't fail a dead man. This time I won't fail.' He glanced at the old priest, his voice firm. 'Let me do this alone.'

'No!'

'Don't jeopardise your life. It's not worth it, not worth the recriminations that would follow. You'll suffer if you support me—'

'And suffer if I don't,' Father Michael retorted. 'I'm backing you, yes, but you're the one in real danger. The Church will come after you – you know that.'

'They haven't stopped me yet.'

'Not yet, Nicholas,' the old priest said quietly. 'Not yet.'

Fifty-Nine

Philip Preston's Auction House, Chelsea, London

Philip snatched up the chain that Gerrit had flung across his desk and stared at it. Hurriedly he turned it over in his hands and then took out a magnifying glass and scrutinised the links. The same initials were there – H and B. He weighed it. Same weight as his chain. Then he moved into the next-door room and carried out the acid test. It was genuine. Gold, like the other chain. He moved back into his office, running the chain through his hands, his expression incredulous as he looked at his visitor.

'What is it?'

'A fucking chain. What did you think it was?' Gerrit replied, slamming the door of Philip's office closed. His glasses were sliding down his nose, his neck scrawny with the after-effects of illness. But his temper was still impressive. 'What are you playing at, Preston?'

Philip stared at him, the chain dangling from his fingers.

'Well, say something! Don't just stand there with your mouth open like a fucking haddock.'

It took Philip another couple of seconds to respond. Then he rushed out of his office and returned shortly afterwards holding a wooden box. Carefully, he unfastened the box and lifted the lid.

They both looked inside. At the Bosch chain.

'OK,' Gerrit said unpleasantly. 'Let me guess: they're breeding.'

'This is no joke!' Philip replied, examining the chain Gerrit had brought in. 'They're identical. But they can't be. There can't be two of them.'

'So which is the original?' Gerrit asked. 'The one Sabine Monette stole from me?'

'She bought the bloody painting with the chain!' Philip roared, losing his composure entirely. 'It was hers by rights. Stop whining like a bloody girl,' he raged, his face red against his white hair.

Gerrit was unmoved. 'Has this chain – the one in your box—'

'The *real* chain—'

'But we don't know that, do we?' Gerrit countered. 'You've always been a slippery bugger, Preston. I don't trust you, never have. If you're trying to pull a fast one—'

'Why would I cut my own throat?' Philip retorted. 'I need this sale. I don't need the art world to think I'm dealing in fakes. No one would ever trust me again.'

'No one fucking trusts you now,' Gerrit replied, staring at the chain in the box. 'Has anyone handled it apart from you?'

'No.'

'Has it ever left this place?'

'No!'

'So it's always been at the auction house?'

'Ever since Nicholas Laverne gave it to me . . .' Philip trailed off, glancing up at Gerrit. 'He couldn't have. Could he?'

'He fucking has,' Gerrit replied, looking back at the chain he had brought in. 'So if he swapped the chains and gave you a replica, that makes mine the real one.'

'Maybe he *didn't* swap the chains!' Philip replied desperately. 'Maybe he just had a copy made.'

Gerrit's tone was withering. 'So he could remember what it looked like?'

'Where did you get it?'

'Some woman dropped it off at my gallery this morning.'

'Who?'

'I don't bloody know!' Gerrit snapped. 'My secretary handled it. She didn't get a name. She didn't get any fucking fingerprints either.'

Philip looked at the chain in the box and then looked back at the one Gerrit had brought in. 'Maybe *both* of them are fakes.'

'Well, they can't both be real, can they?'

Philip's skin was now crimson, his blood pressure rising. At any other time Gerrit would have enjoyed the show, but he had been cheated too and wasn't laughing.

293

'One of them must be real—'

Gerrit nodded. '*One* of them.'

'Nicholas Laverne had the chain authenticated with the papers—' He stopped short.

Alert, Gerrit tilted his head to one side. 'Oh, don't go shy on me! I know about the papers. Don't know the details, don't care. It's the chain I want. Let some other fucker expose the fraud, I can only benefit from the publicity. And besides, seems to me that everyone who knows about the papers ends up dead.' He smiled slyly. 'Is that why you've got the security, Philip?'

'You've got Honthorst.'

'Yeah, but he doesn't work exclusively for me. Not like your fucking doorstops.' Changing tack, he gestured to the chains on the desk. 'You'll have to get them both checked out to see which one is authentic—'

Philip shrugged. 'It looks like the same gold, same weight. Of course I can get them dated, but . . .'

'Oh crap. What?'

'If both chains were made from the same metal at the same time, they would be identical.'

'Hieronymus Bosch had two chains made? Why the fuck would he do that?'

'Who said it was Bosch who had them made?' Philip countered, slumping into his office chair. 'Jesus, this is clever, very clever . . . Someone could have obtained an old antique chain. Difficult, but not impossible if you went to a specialist dealer or bought one from a sale abroad. Then

294

it could have been refashioned into two identical chains. Same links, same markings, the same in every way. The gold is antique, but the chains could have been made yesterday.'

'That makes no bleeding sense!' Gerrit snorted. 'Why make two?'

'To cause havoc,' Philip replied. 'Which it has done. To makes us all run around trying to work it out. To confuse, to deceive, to slow us up. To make fools of us. Hieronymus Bosch is world famous – everybody's interested in his story.' He remembered the scandal which had resulted in Nicholas's disgrace. 'Like I say, Bosch is important, not like the boy who was abused and hanged himself.'

Gerrit threw up his hands in despair. 'I don't know what you're talking about—'

'*Laverne!*' Philip snapped. 'Nicholas Laverne – who's had years to hone his plan. He knew that he had to come up with something to catch the world's attention, and Bosch will do that.'

'*You mean there was no deception?*'

'I don't know,' Philip said bleakly. 'Perhaps Laverne heard a rumour, some old story about the painter, and decided to embellish it – use it for his own ends. He told me that he'd spent time in the Netherlands.' Philip collapsed further into his chair. 'It's a scam. I sell the chain for a fortune and then up pops another one and my reputation's down the toilet—'

'So let's put one of the chains in the bank and forget about it,' Gerrit suggested. 'I could be encouraged to forget what I know.'

'And then you'd have that over me for ever, wouldn't you?'

'I don't see that you have a choice,' Gerrit replied.

Philip thought for a moment. 'If Nicholas Laverne organised this, he had to have a reason. Laverne isn't involved in the art world. His family was, and his uncle still buys, but not him. So why would he do it?'

Gerrit shrugged.

'Because Nicholas Laverne wants to get his own back on the Catholic Church, the institution which excommunicated him. Disgraced him, abandoned him—'

'Yeah, yeah, I get the point. Get on with it.'

'He wants revenge. So how could he get it? By uncovering another scandal, of course. But it had to be a scandal which involved the Catholic Church.' Philip paused. 'Are you following me?'

'All the way off the fucking cliff.'

'He needed something which was newsworthy, something which involved money and power. I think that's why Laverne chose the art world. Unless he has a grudge against us as well. Think about it,' Philip said, pausing for a second. 'Who found the chain?'

Gerrit kept his voice steady. 'Sabine Monette—'

'You know that Nicholas Laverne was close to Sabine Monette? He lived on her estate in France . . . You didn't know?'

'I do now.'

Philip was thinking rapidly. 'Sabine found the chain, yes. But she didn't find the papers. Laverne was the one who found those. Laverne uncovered them, hidden between the links of the chain. *Or did he?*' He stared at Gerrit. 'Perhaps he didn't find anything. Perhaps he pretended to find them. That little Bosch picture you sold to Sabine Monette – you said it had come from some old guy who wanted you to sell it on his behalf.'

'Yeah, that's right.'

'And he gave you papers which authenticated the validity of the painting, which by extension authorised the validity of the papers?'

'You've got the papers. So?'

'How can I contact him?'

'You can't. He sold up and pissed off abroad after I gave him the money from the sale of the painting. Said he wanted to retire, although he must have been fucking ninety,' Gerrit replied. 'He never left a forwarding address.'

'What was his name?'

Gerrit frowned. Illness had slowed him down and it took a moment to drag the name up from his memory. 'Guillaine . . . Oh, fuck!' he said incredulously. 'I don't believe it.'

'What?'

'. . . I never made the connection . . .'

'*What?*'

'. . . Sabine Monette's maiden name was Guillaine.'

Sixty

Rain again. Rain and more rain, leaving the capital waterlogged, the monuments spotted. Along St James's Street, people walked with their heads down, umbrellas held against the wind like a phalanx of Spartan shields. And it kept on raining as Carel Honthorst crossed over and continued to follow Nicholas. The Dutchman hated rain. He was always afraid that it would dislodge his concealer, send it sliding down into his collar like a beige tsunami. Rain made him mean.

He had despised Nicholas Laverne for a long time, ever since Laverne had gone public and exposed the abuse at St Barnabas's church. He might not be an active priest any longer, but the Dutchman held his religion in awe. To Honthorst – whose only security was the Church – any criticism was treachery. He would have stayed a priest, because he had found the religious life easy, but he hadn't found the other priests easy. He didn't find the politics comfortable either. Seeking succour and simplicity, Honthorst had run away from a tough childhood into the arms of Mother Church.

But her arms had been less loving than he had imagined and her caresses less forthcoming than he had hoped.

Never popular, Honthorst found himself pulling away from the Church, his natural viciousness re-emerging as he felt himself cheated of salvation. It was not the Church's fault, it was his. His violent nature was too engrained to forgo, his pleasure in inflicting pain too seductive to relinquish. Confession absolved him, but only for so long. The incense and the candles worked on his senses like a sedative, the red light of the incense burner the eye of a demon staring down at him in his pew. The eye seemed to say he was fooling no one, blinking in the church and puffing out little breaths of smoke like a dying cat. Honthorst would grip the altar rail and take the Sacrament, but as time passed the wafer stuck like a blister to the roof of his mouth and the wine poisoned him.

It was all his fault – he knew that. So he left his life as a priest and took up debt collecting, relishing a legal excuse for brutality. His life split like a rotten apple: on one side religion, on the other violence. And he developed a hatred of anyone who spoke out against the Church. Honthorst might not fit in, but he would brook no criticism. So when Mother Church opened up her arms to him, needing his help, Honthorst went back in.

Walking quickly, the Dutchman saw Nicholas cross over the street and began to follow him, always keeping a little distance behind. Finally he saw Nicholas enter an old building set in an alleyway off the main street. The place was haphazardly built on three floors and seemed virtually empty. Honthorst checked his watch: six thirty, well past closing time for businesses. Curious, he looked through the window and watched as Nicholas spoke to a stout middle-aged man on the ground floor. The man listened, then together they entered a cramped, old-fashioned lift.

Hurrying round to the back of the building, Honthorst took a moment to get his bearings, then clambered up the fire escape. The two men were directly in his line of sight and he drew back to avoid being seen. He could hear murmured conversation, and then watched as the middle-aged man nodded and descended in the lift again. A few moments passed, but when the man didn't return and no one else came in, Honthorst tried the window. It was unlocked. Climbing in, he moved quietly across the landing and glanced through a half-opened door.

He could see that it was some kind of sitting room, but there was a computer in there and a drawing board with sketches lying on it. A moment later Nicholas came into view, reading the paper. Honthorst sniffed the air like a gun dog. He was tired of holding back. *Frighten him*, they had said, *ratchet up the tension*, but Honthorst wanted more. And now he was in the perfect position to get it.

Slowly he pushed the door open. But Nicholas had left the room by an adjoining door and was back on the landing. Retracing his steps, Honthorst heard the sound of the lift rising upwards and then the metal grille being drawn back. In that instant he lunged forward, catching Nicholas off guard. But he recovered fast, getting into the lift and pulling the Dutchman's arm through the grille as he slammed it shut.

'What d'you want from me?' Nicholas asked as Honthorst struggled to free himself. But his sleeve had caught on the grille and that, together with Nicholas's grip, held him fast.

'Let me go!'

'You've been following me. What for?'

'I work here—'

'No, you don't. I know everyone who works here and you don't. Remember, I saw you at Philip Preston's—'

'You're breaking my arm!'

'So relax,' Nicholas said, his tone lethal. 'Who sent you?'

'No one.'

'What do they want you to do? Kill me?'

'I'm not after you. No one sent me!' Honthorst gasped, watching as Nicholas put his finger on the lift button.

'Tell me who sent you or I press this. The lift will pull your bloody arm off—'

'No one sent me!' Honthorst screamed, scrabbling to free himself.

'One last chance – who was it?'

'Go to Hell!' Honthorst shouted, trying to grab Nicholas and missing. 'I'll get you. I swear I'll kill you, you bastard—'

The lift started to descend the moment Nicholas pressed the button. The noise was deafening, but even over the machinery, he could hear the sound of the arm breaking, Honthorst screaming as his limb was torn out of its socket.

'The Temptation of St Anthony' [detail]
After Hieronymus Bosch

302

'*s*-Hertogenbosch, Brabant, 1473*

Dawn was holding back, coming slow and heavy with mist as Hieronymus turned over in his bed and slowly got to his feet. After he had been brought back to 's-Hertogenbosch he had been watched constantly, the studio door only unlocked when food was brought in. As the church clock struck nine the timid Goossen entered, carrying a tray of food.

As ever, he mumbled apologies and tried not to look at his brother.

'Ignore him, Goossen,' Antonius had said, perpetuating the lie he had preached for years. 'Don't say a word to your brother. He's possessed. We have to look after him. We have to keep him safe.'

But Goossen had never believed what his father had said. Too scared to stand up to the formidable Antonius, he had defied him in small ways. He had smuggled in treats for Hieronymus, slipping heavy Dutch fruit loaves into the basket of paint pigments. Sometimes he had even managed to secrete a little beer, but after his father had found out, the baskets were always searched.

In silence, Goossen watched his brother paint the head of a fish with a man's body.

'What is it?'

'What I dream,' Hieronymus replied, pausing.

For a moment he was tempted to ask for help, to appeal to his brother to aid him with another attempt at escape. But he remained silent. He was sick in the lungs, coughing, spitting up blood red as the cadmium paint on his palette. Blood like the red of the devils in his paintings, blood like the colour of the flames of Hell. He was tired. Too tired to plot or to escape. Too tired to live. He would have liked to talk more, but Goossen merely touched his shoulder and left. A moment later, Hieronymus heard the lock turn in the door.

Downstairs, Antonius was in his study talking to two members of the Brotherhood of Mary. A great fire had been lit in the hearth as the damp, foggy morning banked the windows. One cleric was squeezy with fat, the other narrow-shouldered, a black tadpole of a man. They were discussing a matter which was of great importance to them: the imminent death of Hieronymus. The Brotherhood had sent doctors to bleed him and try to effect some recovery, but he had been stubbornly resistant.

'We can't bleed him again,' Antonius said, tugging irritably at the trimming of his cape. His heavy legs were stretched out before him, taking in the fire's warmth. The room was panelled, hung with tapestries to flaunt Antonius's wealth and the fame of his son, and by the window stood three ceramic vases, hand thrown in Amsterdam. Luxury pleased Antonius even more than his mistress, and he was loath to relinquish it.

'When Hieronymus dies—'

304

The first cleric put up his doughy hands.

'No, we must not think it. He may yet recover,' he said, but the words were insincere, his eyes fixed greedily on Antonius. The plan had been mooted before, and now he could sense it was about to be fulfilled. Not one of the trio thought of the young man upstairs, dying in a studio without a fire.

'My son's work is priceless. To the Church and to the country.' Both clerics nodded as Antonius continued. 'Hieronymus has taught everyone about God and the Devil. His paintings have kept the population controlled . . .'

Again the clerics nodded in unison.

' . . His work must continue,' Antonius said, moving on, his voice a whisper. 'We all know I commission the paintings for the Brotherhood. What hangs in the church is organised by me. Everything is handled by me. When Hieronymus dies, no one must ever know he has gone.'

The thin cleric nodded solemnly, his priest's robe dusty. 'It is for the glory of God—'

'For the glory of God,' the other cleric echoed. 'And for His worshippers.'

'We are doing nothing wrong,' Antonius continued, relieved that his source of income would continue after the death of his irksome child. 'My son has made many drawings, which I have collected together. Ideas for paintings. Images that could only corrupt in the wrong hands. Images that must be preserved and reproduced to the glory of God.' He paused, let the inference take root. 'After my poor son's demise, his work can continue within the family. We are all painters, after all; we can recreate his vision. There are many

305

drawings, many sketches. Much to produce.' He poured the clerics some wine, smiling like a wolf. 'We do this only in the service of God . . .'

They nodded, already damned.

'. . . The Church will prosper and so will we,' Antonius continued. 'Naturally I will reward your silence in this matter, gentlemen, even though we are doing no wrong. With your help, we can make any necessary entries into the books of the Brotherhood. It should appear that Hieronymus is living a normal life. Perhaps a marriage for him in a few years' time?' The firelight caught in his eyes, flickering like the flames of Hell. 'In this way, Hieronymus will never die. He will remain the pre-eminent painter in the Netherlands, his work desired and valuable. Our city's most famous son.'

The thin cleric was suddenly dubious. 'Is this not pride?'

'Hieronymus will live on only to honour God,' Antonius persisted. 'We do this for God.'

'We do this for God,' the cleric agreed, sighing and shifting his position as though his body could not stand the weight of his deceit.

'But in pleasing God, there is no reason to punish ourselves,' Antonius continued. 'We will keep the studio busy here. My other sons, my father and I will use it after Hieronymus has gone—'

'But what of his burial?'

Antonius had already plotted a pauper's interment in a village in the north. Without a headstone. Hieronymus lying penniless amongst strangers while he made money from his corpse.

'I will organise a Christian burial for my son,' he replied, glancing at the clerics and faking sadness. 'He will be missed. But his work must appear to continue – for all our sakes.' He leaned his bulky frame towards the two clergymen. 'No one must know of his death.'

'No one will learn of it from us.'

Antonius nodded. 'It won't be long now. He's weakening every day, but still working. He works like a man possessed. Maybe he paints what he will soon see . . .'

'It's sinful to pretend a man alive when he's in his grave,' the thin cleric announced suddenly, chilled by what they had planned.

'The Church serves the country, and Hieronymus's work serves the people,' Antonius chided the man. 'How would they find their way to Heaven without being guided there? People are weak, fools, some barely more than animals. They revel in sin, in licentiousness. But when they look at my son's visions of Hell and Damnation, they are fearful and turn back to God. There's no dishonour in what we do. God will understand.' A smile came, then went. 'Order is everything, gentlemen. A little deception is nothing.'

Sixty-One

Hiram Kaminski's Gallery, Old Bond Street

The incident had unnerved Hiram. Whoever had tried to break into the gallery had failed due to Judith's intervention, but not without causing him some serious anxiety. He no longer cared about the Bosch chain, the Bosch portrait or the Bosch deception. He was scared. So when Gerrit der Keyser sauntered into the gallery, Hiram was on edge.

Wearing a raincoat that was too big for him, Gerrit nodded at the receptionist, passed three customers looking at the paintings on view, and made for Hiram's office. From where he had already been spotted.

'Hiram,' he said by way of greeting.

'Gerrit,' Hiram replied.

'Well, at least we know who the fuck we are,' Gerrit said, laughing and taking off his coat. 'It's cold out there. Must be due to hit zero tonight. I hate the cold. Didn't used to mind it when I had some weight on me, but now – starved to bleeding death – I feel it.'

'You still on a diet?'

Gerrit nodded. 'I'm about to be signed up by *Vogue* magazine.'

'What d'you want?' Hiram replied. 'I don't mean to be rude, but I'm a bit on edge at the moment—'

'Wait till you hear what I have to say.' Gerrit sat down, checked the office door was closed, and put up two fingers. 'There are two of them.'

'*What?*'

'Two chains,' Gerrit replied, 'Two fucking chains. Preston has one and someone dropped one off at my gallery. When I took it over to Preston I thought one was fake, either his or mine. But he's just rung me and told me that it's official – *there were two chains made from one antique chain.*'

'Both with initials engraved on them?' Hiram asked, incredulous.

'Exact in every bleeding detail. Same clasp, same links, same everything—'

'Wait a moment,' Hiram said. 'You said that Preston had had them authenticated—'

'I'm ahead of you there. I checked it out with the expert who examined them, just in case Slippery Phil was trying to pull a fast one. And it turns out that both are genuine. But both could genuinely have been made last week.'

Hiram studied Gerrit der Keyser. He was surprised that the dealer had come to him and been so forthcoming. It was unlike der Keyser – unless he had another reason to throw in his lot with Hiram.

'Why are you telling me this? If they are fakes, Preston could have hidden one and auctioned off the other and no one would have been any the wiser – apart from you.'

'Don't panic, I'm not losing my touch,' Gerrit replied, fingering a maidenhair fern on Hiram's desk. 'You want to give this some plant food—'

'Why are you here?'

'I want your opinion. Something I should have asked for when all this started.' He shrugged. 'I'm a fucking idiot, but there you go. You know about this chain and the deception, blah, blah, blah?'

'No, I don't—'

'Don't lie. Preston told me all about it. Said you knew.' Gerrit pulled a face as he caught Hiram's stunned expression. 'Judith told him everything. Said she wanted to keep you out of trouble and thought she could shift the pressure on to Philip Preston. She was worried after someone tried to break in here.'

'Does everyone know about that!'

'Oh, calm down,' Gerrit told him. 'No one has secrets for long in this business, you know that. It's the auction of that fucking chain in two days and every nut's coming out of the woodwork. But only me and Preston know that there are *two* chains. Both of which could be fakes—'

'I don't believe it,' Hiram said emphatically. 'Thomas Little-john tried to tell me about the Bosch chain years ago. And he sent me a letter about it. Which I only received after he was killed.' Hiram could see Gerrit's eyes widen behind his bifocals. 'Littlejohn was the best – he was an expert. If he put his name to anything, it was genuine. He wrote and told me the whole story, including the Bosch portrait—'

'*What* fucking portrait?' Gerrit snapped.

'So Philip Preston didn't tell you *everything* that Judith told him, did he?' Hiram replied, almost gleeful. '*The Tree Man* in the triptych is a portrait of Hieronymus Bosch. He didn't paint it, but it was his likeness.'

'Shit.' He glanced back at Hiram. 'You going public with this?'

'No. I don't want anything to do with it. It's bad luck, all of it. And I'd be wary of what Philip Preston's telling you. He might be right about some of it – two chains *could* have been made out of one long chain . . .' Hiram stared at his visitor. '. . . perhaps *he* had them made—'

'No way! What would be in it for him? If it comes out that there are two chains, he's going to look like a fucking laughing stock. Nah, this is one tricky bit of business Preston isn't involved in.'

Irritated, Hiram shook his head. 'If there are two chains now, they *could* have been made to look identical in every way. But the chain Thomas Littlejohn saw was genuine. He never said anything about two chains. And he wouldn't have lied – I'd stake my life on that. Thomas needed a witness because he was in danger, terrified that something would happen to him.'

'Which it did,' Gerrit said thoughtfully. 'So which chain did Littlejohn see?'

'Obviously the one with the papers in it.'

Gerrit laughed. 'I heard the rumour, but wasn't sure. And I never knew the proof was hidden in the bleeding chain. How did they do it?'

Hiram paused. Any other time he would have resisted confiding, but now he didn't care. He didn't want the chain, he wanted rid of it. And if Gerrit der Keyser wanted to go after it, that was fine by him.

'There were pieces of paper hidden in every link. Put together, they told the whole story, and the part the Church played in the deception. Nicholas Laverne found them.'

'That basket case! He broke the arm of one of my employees the other day. The man's a fucking nutter.'

'Why?'

'Why *what?*'

'Why would he break someone's arm?'

Gerrit's expression was guileless. 'There was a misunderstanding. Honthorst was just trying to put his bloody point across, and that ex-priest attacked him.'

The lie didn't ring true and Hiram stared at his visitor warily. Meanwhile Gerrit tried to make sense of what he had been told – and – failed miserably.

'Who brought the second chain to you?'

'Some woman.' Gerrit said sourly. 'And no, I don't have a bloody name. My secretary was busy – she just took the parcel and hardly glanced at the person who delivered it. Stupid cow.'

He lapsed into a disgruntled silence. His visit had not proved to be as useful as he had hoped. Certainly Hiram believed that there was a genuine conspiracy, but it was obvious that he wasn't curious to discover more, or likely to join forces. Gerrit was going to have to work it out for himself, he realised, remembering the old man who had given him the painting to sell. The man called Guillaine. Which just happened to have been Sabine's maiden name. But Sabine couldn't have been the woman who brought the chain to his gallery. Ghosts don't do deliveries.

Then a clammy feeling crept over Gerrit. Sabine was dead, that was true. But her daughter wasn't.

Sixty-Two

Church of St Stephen, Fulham, London

It was past three in the morning and Nicholas was awake
and listening. There were noises outside. He tried to sit up
but was unable to move, paralysed, his throat dry. Panicking,
he struggled to breathe, his eyes wide open, the room filled
by an ominous black shadow. The shape moved towards his
bed, its shadow crossing the window, its right arm raised as
though about to strike.

Unable to cry out, Nicholas stared blindly, his body
useless. He could feel sweat on his skin, his mouth working
soundlessly. The shadow moved towards him and bent
down. Closer, closer it came, until its face was only inches
from his, a feeling of pressure crushing his body as the
shape spread over him.

Sixty-Three

Conrad Voygel left Chicago and came back to London late. Angela was at the airport to meet his private plane, and with her, Sidney Elliott. He was sitting in the back seat of the chauffeured limousine as Angela got out to greet her husband.

'This man's been pestering me,' she whispered. 'Some man called Elliott, Sidney Elliott. He came to the tennis club and was watching me, then he called by the house.' She looked into her husband's face earnestly. 'I don't like him, Conrad. There's something wrong with him.'

'Why didn't you call security?'

'He said he was desperate to talk to you,' she replied, pulling up her coat collar against the cold night. 'I thought if I brought him with me tonight you could deal with him and then it would be over and done with. Besides, I wasn't on my own with him in the car, was I?'

Thoughtful, Conrad kissed his wife on the cheek. Then he bent down and beckoned for Elliott to leave the car and follow him. Without another word, Conrad moved towards the airport building but didn't enter. Instead he stood just outside and waited for Elliott to catch up with him.

Out of breath and jumpy, Elliott frowned against the wind which was blowing hard. 'I had to s-s-see you. You w-w-wouldn't answer my calls—'

'You had no right to involve my wife.' Conrad replied as an aeroplane started up nearby, its engines howling into the headwind. 'I want no more to do with you—'

'*I can help you!*' Elliott all but screamed. 'L-l-listen to me.' His eyes were wide, dilated. 'I've g-g-got one day left—'

'Not any more. You're fired.'

Enraged, Elliott caught hold of his arm, Conrad shaking him off and putting up his hand to his bodyguard who was about to intervene. Then he turned back to Elliott. 'Listen to me. I don't want you working for me any longer. Approach me again and I'll call the police—'

'I'll tell th-th-them about you.'

His face was expressionless. 'Tell them what?'

'You must have something to h-h-hide. All this secrecy . . .'

'I'm a private man, nothing more. I don't like people interfering. You would do well to remember that.'

But Elliott wasn't listening. 'You're a c-c-crook . . . ! You used me . . .'

'You came to me with information. You offered me a service which you could not supply.'

'I told you about the Bosch p-p-papers—'

'But you didn't get them for me, did you?' Conrad replied. 'You failed. End of story.'

'You said I h-h-had one more day!' Elliott yelled over the sound of the plane engines. 'You p-p-promised me—'

'I promised you nothing,' Conrad replied warningly. 'Contact me again and you'll regret it.'

Sixty-Four

Church of St Stephen, Fulham, London

The thud woke him. Grabbing his cane, Father Michael hurried into Nicholas's room as fast as he could, only to find him on the floor. Concerned, he reached down, but Nicholas pushed him away and clambered back on to the bed.

'What happened?'

Dazed, Nicholas shook his head. 'A nightmare,' he explained, trying to calm his own panic. 'I thought there was someone in the room, someone coming for me, but I couldn't wake myself up.' He wiped the sweat off his forehead with the back of his hand. 'Night terrors, they call them. I used to suffer from them when I was kid, but I thought I'd grown out of it. God, what the hell is happening to me?'

'Stress. You're restless and you dream a lot.' Father Michael poured some water from the carafe by the bed and passed it to Nicholas. 'You dream a lot. I often hear you cry out.' He lowered himself into the bedside chair. 'Can I help you?'

'No.'

'You can trust me if you want to talk. We're old friends, Nicholas. We've known each other for years. I know I let you down once, but that's in the past. Now I want to help you.' Father Michael's face was lean, anxious. 'What's troubling you? Is it what's happening now? Or what happened before?' When Nicholas didn't reply, he waited. The light from the bedside lamp glowed faintly, revealing a cramped room covered in striped paper from the 1960s, an electric fire secured halfway up one wall. One bar was lit, its red light eerie. 'Whatever you tell me will go no further.'

'The past is done with.'

'No, the past is never done with until we come to terms with it, Nicholas . . . Do you regret what you did?'

'No,' he said softly. 'I exposed wrong-doing.'

'You betrayed your Church, your colleagues—'

'And they betrayed Patrick Gerin and the Sullivan boy!' Nicholas turned to look at the old priest. 'A few years ago I went to Ireland to talk to David Sullivan, but he refused to see me. He wrote to me instead and said that I deserved everything that was coming to me.'

The priest was shocked. 'Why would he say that?'

'Because I failed, Father. No matter what I did, it was too late. *I* was too late . . . Mine was a pyrrhic victory.'

'Is there nothing else?'

Sighing, Nicholas closed his eyes. He was feeling drained, limp as a glove. The nightmare had disturbed him, along with his most recent dreams. Dreams that were familiar, but

319

altered. Changing, growing malignant, making him doubt himself and his memories. It seemed that all his mind's silt had been scuffed up, his thoughts polluted. I need sleep, Nicholas thought. Sleep is what I need.

'Is there nothing you want to tell me?' Father Michael urged him. 'Nothing?'

His voice was coming from a long way away. Somewhere beyond the dank bedroom and the meagre fire. Somewhere hidden beneath the old wallpaper and the water casting blurry shadows in the confines of the glass.

Sixty-Five

Honor was just coming out of the shower when the intercom buzzed. Pulling a towelling robe around her, she answered. 'Hello?'

'It's Mark . . . Mark Spencer.'

'It's past ten. What d'you want?'

'It's about your brother.'

She buzzed him up, wrapping the robe tighter around her body, her hair wet as she answered the door. 'Come in and take a seat. I'll get some clothes on.'

He was about to say don't bother for me, then thought better of it. Honor wasn't impressed by him yet. She would be in time, but not yet. His clumsy attempt at blackmail hadn't worked. It was clear that she wasn't going to desert her brother, and although Mark knew it would be wiser to walk away, he found he couldn't. His admiration for Honor was too entrenched. So instead he had decided to become her confidant and win her over that way.

As he waited for Honor to return, Mark looked around the flat. There were many rows of shelving holding hundreds of DVDs and CDs and some worn legal books. At eye level there was a photograph of a little girl. Curious, he touched it as Honor walked up behind him and tapped him on the shoulder.

He jumped, just as she had hoped he would. 'D'you want some tea?'

Flustered, Mark returned the photograph to the shelf, 'Tea? Yeah, tea would be good.'

He was disappointed to see that Honor was now in jeans and a jumper, her damp hair tucked behind her ears. But he had to admit that even without make-up, she was striking. In time they would have great-looking kids.

She was staring at him. '*Well?*'

'Pardon?'

'What did you want to tell me about my brother?'

'Oh, yes,' Mark said taking the tea she offered him. 'I found out some interesting information. I thought you should know.' He paused. 'I won't pass this on to anyone else.'

'No, that wouldn't be wise and it might be bad for your career,' she replied shortly, then softened her tone. 'What is it?'

'Nicholas Laverne was arrested in Milan for assaulting a woman nineteen years ago.' He paused, swallowed. 'He was released and deported. Rumour has it that someone paid the police off.'

Her expression was flat. 'I don't believe it.'

Mark handed her a mugshot. It was of Nicholas. Younger, dark-haired, heavier. Handsome. But calling himself Nico Lassimo.

'Anything else?' Honor asked.

'Later he worked for a woman called Sabine Monette in France—'

'I know about that.'

'She was killed. Murdered.'

Honor shifted in her seat. 'Yes, I know about that too.'

'The police have no idea who killed her.'

'It wasn't Nicholas.'

'No!' he said hurriedly. 'I wasn't suggesting that. But Madame Monette was killed in a very odd manner. I have contacts in Paris.' He waited for her to look impressed, but when she didn't he continued. 'They told me that she had been butchered and that someone had engraved the initials H and B into her flesh.'

Honor was giving nothing away. 'So?'

'Well, this is what's odd,' Mark replied, fiddling with a messy pile of notes. 'I can't stop making connections. You know, getting the pieces to fit. It's almost a hobby . . .' Honor's face was expressionless as he hurried on. 'And when I was looking at that murder of the priest again, I found out that he had had the same initials carved into his body – H and B. Someone leaked it on to the internet.'

'I told you before: the police talked to Nicholas about that, and cleared him of any involvement.'

'But did you know that the priest had been one of the men your brother accused of abuse ten years ago?'

She stood up. 'Yes. Nicholas told me about it himself. It's no secret—'

'But what about the trouble when he was twenty? Just before he entered the Church? Did he tell you about that? Or was *that* a secret?' Mark was struggling to keep his papers in order as Honor watched him intently.

'It's here – look.'

He held the paper out towards her and for a moment she hesitated, afraid of what was coming. It was a cutting from *Le Figaro*, which Mark had thoughtfully translated underneath. It read:

> Giles Rodin, 45, has been arrested and charged with forgery. It is suspected that he has been dealing in faked paintings and jewellery. A museum in Germany (name withheld) has admitted to having obtained a piece of metalwork they believed was genuine, apparently dating from the Middle Ages. Enquiries are ongoing.
>
> Rodin was arrested with his associate, Alain Belfon, 56, and Giles Fallon, 43. A younger English man, also believed to be involved, has disappeared.

'It doesn't mean it was Nicholas,' Honor said, handing the paper back to Mark.

'You said he travelled around, especially in France. He could have been visiting his brother. Henry worked in Rome and in Paris. Nicholas could have been in Paris at the time—'

'So could a lot of people! And I'm sure a lot of them were young Englishmen.'

Without saying a word, Mark handed her another clipping. It was a photograph of three men: Alain Belfon, Giles Fallon – and 'an Englishman'. He was much younger, his hair long, his smile infectious. He was different.

But he was still Nicholas.

Sixty-Six

Glancing at his watch for the third time, Hiram Kaminski moved across the communal garden and sat down on a bench. A moment later, he got up and moved to another bench. His nervousness was obvious to anyone watching, his hands constantly fiddling with his coat buttons or his shirt cuffs. The cold made his nose red, his ears scarlet as he pulled up the scarf around his neck.

He was certain that at any moment he would be attacked and everybody who passed him was scrutinised. Then the garden emptied and he was left alone, sitting on a wooden bench under a glowering sky. So when a tall man entered and moved towards him, he panicked and made a rush for the gate.

'Mr Kaminski?'

Hiram stopped short, his back to the man. Praying.

'Mr Kaminski?' Nicholas repeated as he hurried up to him. 'You wanted to talk to me?'

The dealer turned round slowly, then sighed with relief. 'Mr Laverne?'

Nicholas nodded, gesturing to a bench where they could talk. Fastidious as ever, Hiram brushed a stray leaf away before he sat down, crossing his ankles as he hunkered further into his coat.

'It's about the Bosch deception,' he began. 'I wanted to tell you that I believe in it.'

'You should,' Nicholas replied. 'It's the truth. I saw the proof. I took the papers out of the chain myself.'

'One chain?'

'There *is* only one chain.' Nicholas paused, staring at the dealer. 'There is – and has only ever been – one chain. Anyone who says otherwise is a liar.'

'Yet some people are now claiming there are *two* chains—'

'No.'

'– and that the deception is a fake, something created for malice.'

'By me?'

Hiram nodded. 'As a way of getting revenge.'

Stunned, Nicholas stared at the dealer, his voice raw. 'Have you been talking to my sister?'

'No.'

'Someone from the Church?'

'No!' Hiram replied, aghast. 'I wouldn't speak of this to anyone. I am merely passing on what I was told. Some people believe that you faked the papers and pretended to find them. That all of this is a fabrication—'

'I am not lying!'

'I know you're not – that's why I'm here,' Hiram retorted, dropping his voice as a man passed by. 'You don't know the art world as I do. I have been working in it for decades and I understand that greed makes people into monsters. Liars, cheats, even killers.' He paused, blowing on his gloved hands to warm them. 'I know the conspiracy is true because I knew it existed years ago. I had no details then, you understand, but later a colleague told me everything. Thomas Little-john sent me a letter. He needed a witness because he was scared. Somebody was after him. Somebody caught up with him . . .'

'So you know when Bosch really died?'

Hiram nodded.

'Have you seen the papers?'

'No, I just know of them,' he replied. 'Who wrote them?'

Nicholas paused for a moment before answering. 'Someone desperate to make a record. Someone who had watched what happened and been a witness to it. Perhaps one of Bosch's brothers? Certainly it was someone who couldn't live with the knowledge, but couldn't expose it either. It had to be a member of his family.' Nicholas continued, 'No one outside knew about it – except for the Brotherhood of Saint Mary.'

Hiram nodded. 'No one ever knew much about Hiero-nymus Bosch, there was so little information to go on. Now I know why.'

'They made a mock life for him.'

Hiram nodded again, 'A mock life—'

'A mock marriage. A mock death. Hieronymus Bosch was imprisoned, abused by his family and tortured by demons that never let him be.' Nicholas's voice fell. 'It was chilling. It was cruel. *And it was true.*' Nicholas stared ahead. He was stunned that people – even his own sister – doubted him. That they thought him capable of such deceit.

'You know of the portrait? I can see from your face that you don't,' Hiram said, answering himself. '*The Tree Man* is a likeness of Hieronymus Bosch. It must have been painted by a member of his family because by the time the image was created, he was already dead. It's a memento mori.' Hiram leaned closer to Nicholas. 'I know you want to expose the Church's part in this, but the whole truth about Hieronymus Bosch *must* come out. One of the greatest painters who ever lived was treated abominably. His talent was hijacked by his family. His vision was bastardised by them.' Hiram paused, taking in a breath. 'Think me an old fool – maybe I am. What's Bosch to me, after all? I'll tell you, Mr Laverne. All my life I've studied the works of the late Middle Ages. I've become an authority on the matter, and I'm proud of my reputation. Perhaps *too* proud.'

Nicholas hesitated, queasy again. His skin was waxy, sweat beaded his upper lip.

'Are you all right?' Hiram asked anxiously.

'I'm just tired. I don't sleep well . . . It's an old problem, slows me down.' His eyes seemed to glaze over for an instant and then he looked back at Hiram. 'What were you saying?'

'That I was a coward . . . Are you sure you're all right?'

Nicholas nodded, but his head felt like putty, his neck floppy. Jesus, he was tired . . .

'Yesterday I wanted to run, to forget everything I knew,' Hiram continued. 'My wife's worried. She doesn't know I'm talking to you – she wants to pretend ignorance. But today I realised that I *can't* stand by and do nothing . . . You seem to be very alone, Mr Laverne. And I wonder if you are as afraid as I am. Someone tried to break into the gallery the other night. I don't know if they wanted to harm me or scare me, but they succeeded. Have you any idea who it was?'

Recovering his senses slowly, Nicholas shrugged. 'It could be anyone. Some hired thug. There's a man called Carel Honthorst—'

'He works for Gerrit der Keyser!' Hiram said hastily. 'Gerrit told me that you'd broken his arm.'

'If I hadn't, he'd have done worse to me,' Nicholas replied. 'I don't know if it was Honthorst who came after you. He can't be the only person involved. Someone's been watching the church and following me for days.' He thought for a moment. 'D'you know a man called Sidney Elliott?'

'Only by reputation. He works in Cambridge.'

'He translated one of the Bosch papers for me and then wanted to get involved. He was desperate. When I said no, he got very angry, overreacted completely. He's working for Conrad Voygel now.'

Hiram stared across the darkening garden. 'The elusive Conrad Voygel.'

'Is he a crook?'

'The Italians have a saying – *"behind every large fortune is a small crime."* Everyone pretends not to know how Voygel made his money, but it's simple. He grabbed every opportunity that came his way and made his own luck.'

'Legally?'

'If not, no one will ever find out. Actually, I met him a few years back.'

Nicholas raised his eyebrows. 'Not many people can say that. What was he like?'

'Nondescript, like an accountant. His need for privacy isn't that remarkable really. Voygel had face cancer and lost the left side of his jaw and his nose. They were reconstructed very well, but it left him shy about his appearance. He's not Howard Hughes, he just doesn't like having his picture taken.' Hiram pursed his lips, remembering his earlier meeting. 'Gerrit der Keyser's a sly one, but I don't know how far he would go. To be honest, I don't know how far *any* of them would go.'

'Philip Preston's hired security, so he must be scared.'

'He has every reason to be. He has the chain.' Hiram glanced at Nicholas. 'D'you think it will get to auction?'

'I don't know. I don't know what – or who – will make it through the next two days.'

'The art world can be a dangerous place.'

'So can the Church,' Nicholas remarked. The drowsy sensation was threatening to overwhelm him and it took all of his concentration to continue the conversation. 'At least

331

in the art world you can see your enemies coming. With the Church, you never know who will bless you and who will damn you.'

He paused and Hiram looked at him intently. 'You're ill.'

'No, just tired.'

'Are you sure?'

Nicholas tried to nod his head, but the action was too much for him.

'You look drugged.'

Nicholas shook his head, his voice slurred. 'I don't take drugs. I had food poisoning.'

But as he said it, Hiram Kaminski's face was coming in and out of focus.

'Watch out for yourself, Mr Laverne,' he said kindly. 'No one is ever what they seem.'

Here I am, amongst the yew trees leading to the outhouse that is changing as I look at it . . . Nicholas frowns, turns in his sleep, sweat oily as his skin. Walk in, he tells himself. Walk in. Look and see. Look and see, and remember.

I can still count the bottles, beer bottles in rows along the chipped window ledge behind the broken lawnmowers that don't work and the old discarded bird's nest. This is the same as always. The bottles are where the boys left them, and where Father Dominic, sly as a stoat, found them. Taking the first bottle, greasing its neck and forcing it down Patrick Gerin's throat until he choked. He heaved, bringing up bile over the priest's shoes . . .

I didn't see it, Nicholas thought. I was only told. I explained how it was, as always, as ever. I wasn't there, just told what had happened by a boy with bruises around his mouth. He was waiting in the space between the yew trees while David Sullivan hung back under the dull arc of the oak. He says – I want to go home. Do something. Help me . . . Nicholas stirs in his sleep, sweating, turning . . . I'll talk to them, I promise. I'll talk to them . . .

333

I did talk, Nicholas thinks, eyes moving under closed lids. But I was too late. As ever, as always, too late . . . He sees the perished roof of the outhouse, the door swinging open to reveal the dark gut of the cupboard inside. And on the floor lies urine and faeces, dropped from a boy hanging.

Nicholas is walking forward. He can hear the sound of broken glass under his feet and sees Patrick Gerin look at him, pleading for help . . . He sees him, as ever, as always, only this time Nicholas turns away and locks the door behind him.

As he moves back through the yew trees they fold over his head and he begins to run. Away from the bird's nest that holds nothing and the roof that is long gone. As ever, as always, towards the grey hump of the church. Away from the bottles, the cupboard and the broken glass . . .

And away from the boy hanging.

Sixty-Seven

Eloise Devereux sat in her hotel room and stared at the papers in front of her. Her conversation with Honor had stirred her curiosity and her growing suspicions about Nicholas Laverne. In truth she had told Honor everything she knew, but as she had recounted Nicholas's history, Eloise had developed a sudden and queasy unease. Events that had not worried her before seemed strange, his reluctance to involve her less like caution and more like evasion. Her hands reached out for the report which had been brought to her that morning: the chequered past of Nicholas Laverne assembled by a private investigator, the facts and counter facts alarming.

Who had this man actually been? Eloise thought. This treasured friend of her dead husband. Claude had never told her anything about the alleged assaults, the faking or the thefts. Had he not known – or had he not believed it? Eloise leaned back on the sofa, curling her legs under her, staring at the incriminating evidence. If she were honest she had always found Nicholas evasive, but had put that down to his being the third wheel, caught between his old friend and his wife. But now she wasn't so sure.

A memory of Sabine came in that instant. *Her mother.* Not that people knew that . . . Sabine was young when she became pregnant and her parents hadn't wanted the scandal to become public, so she had given birth to Eloise in Switzerland and the baby had been adopted. It had been discreetly arranged, childless friends of Sabine's parents taking over the baby and raising her. The families never referred to it, and Sabine had married Monsieur Monette soon after.

It would have remained a secret forever, had Sabine stayed silent. But when Eloise was sixteen, she contacted her daughter and told her the truth. Relieved that she was not related to her dull adoptive parents, Eloise had soon become close to her mother. She was thrilled by their similarities and by the interests they shared. From the first, Eloise had understood why she had been adopted: the pressures of a bourgeois French family would have been impossible for a young girl to withstand. She had no grudge against her mother; Sabine's presence in her life had been merely postponed.

Few people knew the truth. Except Claude, in whom Eloise naturally confided . . . Her glance went back to the papers on the coffee table in front of her. Nicholas Laverne, suspected of involvement in fakery and theft. Surely it was no coincidence that Sabine had been robbed while he was working for her? But did it go further than that?

She remembered Claude's father, Raoul Devereux, talking about Nicholas in guarded tones. And now she knew why – Nicholas Laverne had stolen a painting from him and only the intervention of Henry had prevented his being charged. She could imagine that Claude would have supported Nicholas too, defending him, pleading with his father not to destroy his relationship with one son because of the actions of the other. Raoul had been Henry Laverne's mentor for years, had admired him and encouraged his progress. Yet all the while the shadow of Nicholas hovered in the background.

Were they always wondering when he would cause a scandal? Always wondering when the reputations of Raoul and Henry would be undermined by Nicholas's erratic behaviour? Their relief when he entered the Church must have been immense. When Nicholas Laverne was transformed into Father Daniel, ensconced far away in London: a priest bound by the strict rules of the Catholic Church.

But it hadn't lasted.

Eloise stared at the notes, her mouth tight, doubts troubling her. Claude was dead, presumably killed because of his involvement with the Bosch deception. A conspiracy that Nicholas had uncovered. History repeating itself . . . Hurriedly she snatched up the papers and sifted through them, then found what she was looking for. Nicholas and his alleged faking. *Faking art works and jewellery* . . . Eloise took in a breath.

What if the whole conspiracy was a lie? A fabrication created for revenge? Nicholas had never professed much interest in the art world, but his parents and his uncle had been minor collectors. He would have known the power of that environment: the money, the risks, the ruthlessness of dealers after the ultimate prize. Perhaps Nicholas Laverne had picked his own pack of wolves, and thrown them a sheep's carcass in the shape of the Bosch chain.

Eloise could feel her heartbeat speed up. Was she right? Certainly Nicholas must have been desperate for revenge, his accusations of clerical abuse ostracising him. Not so much a hero as a leper. Eloise didn't doubt that the allegations were true. Nicholas was always looking for some apple cart to overturn, but this time he had excelled himself.

If he had made up the deception he knew exactly what he was doing. Brutalised boys would never grip the world's attention, unlike the Bosch chain and the rumoured conspiracy.

Claude would never have gone along with the deception. He had been an honest man – even affection wouldn't have coerced him into a crime. But Sabine had been skittish at times, even daring. Had her mother known the truth? Eloise took in her breath, held it, felt the sting of tears behind her eyes. Had Nicholas and Sabine planned it together? And if they had, why was Sabine dead? Eloise got to her feet, pressing her hand against her mouth to stop herself crying out. Nicholas Laverne *couldn't* have been her mother's killer. He had been in London when Sabine was murdered.

But he could have arranged it.

Coldness overwhelmed her. Claude had been killed in France. In their house, close by Sabine's country home. The place Nicholas knew well. The police had said Claude had put up no struggle. He had no defence wounds, had not even raised his hands to protect himself. It was as though he had been shocked into inertia. It had puzzled the police, but it didn't puzzle Eloise any more.

Claude wouldn't have reacted. Because he wouldn't have expected his killer to be his closest friend.

Sixty-Eight

Disturbed by what Mark Spencer had told her, Honor called in sick and stayed at home. Her calls to St Stephen's had been answered by Father Michael, her messages taken but not returned. How could she find out what was going on if Nicholas wouldn't talk to her? Her first instinct had been to reject everything Mark had said, but on further investigation she realised that he had been telling the truth. The photographs seemed to prove what he said, as did the various and irritating pieces of information he kept texting her.

Along with the inevitable.

I just want to help. Don't worry, no one knows you're not sick. Speak later.

She wanted to text him back 'Fuck off' but couldn't, because she wasn't sure what to believe and needed time to think. Nicholas was her brother, but did she really know him? His refusal to talk to her only compounded her anger and made her wonder if it was a sign of guilt. Or maybe Nicholas was about to assume another identity.

Unsettled, Honor snatched up her coat and left the house. The freezing temperature punched the air out of her lungs and her hair was crisp with frost as she turned the corner and passed by the school. Preoccupied, she was caught off guard when a man grabbed her and dragged her into the empty playing field. Her anger overtook her fear as she fought to release his grip. Struggling, she kicked out, but the man had a firm hold of her, his left hand covering her mouth. Terrified, she tried to scream but failed, biting down into the flesh of his palm instead. As she had hoped, the man let go of her. But before she could get away, he knocked her over and she fell forward, her face pressed to the ground.

His left knee pushing into the small of her back, he spoke.

'Miss Laverne,' he said, panting, 'I want you to t-t-talk to your brother—'

She struggled to throw him off, but only managed to antagonise him further.

'Stop it!' Elliott snapped, 'I c-c-could break your back.'

Reluctantly, she stopped fighting. His weight crushed her, pushed her into the ground as he bent down, his mouth only inches from her ear.

'Tell him I w-w-want to see him t-t-tonight. Ten o'clock, S-S-Saint Martin in the Field's church, Trafalgar Square.' Elliott got to his feet and looked down at her. 'You h-h-hear me?'

It took Honor a moment to gather enough breath to answer.

'Yes,' she finally gasped. 'I h-h-hear you.'

Enraged that she was mocking him, Elliott kicked out. He put his weight behind the action as his foot slammed the remaining air out of her. Then he left Honor crying and rolling over, her legs pulled up against her stomach as his footsteps faded away.

Sixty-Nine

'You're all ready, aren't you?' Philip asked his mistress over the phone. 'We leave after the auction tomorrow. Catch the late flight – it's all arranged.' He glanced at the glazed door, at the two impressive – and comforting – outlines of the security guards. 'Don't be late. I'll meet you at the airport, like we agreed.'

Kim was ready for their escape. Had been ready for eighteen months. Once she got Philip away from London and his wife, it was all plain sailing. God, she thought, it had been hard work, but finally it was about to pay off. Good old Philip – he thought he was cunning but he wasn't that smart. Not clever enough to realise he had been played.

'I've sorted it out about Gayle . . .'

Kim wondered if he knew how little she cared about his soon-to-be-ex wife. 'Oh good.'

'. . . I've got a nurse to start tomorrow. She'll be there when I've left and I've written a letter to explain everything. I've told the doctor Gayle might need some sedation too.'

Philip paused. He was being very kind, he thought, very sensitive. 'She'll be fine, honestly.'

Kim shrugged her shoulders, changing the subject. 'Are a lot of people coming to the auction?'

'God knows,' Philip replied truthfully. 'I don't care how many come, or how many stay away. I just need one bidder. One big sale.'

He thought of the money that was nearly his and then remembered Gerrit der Keyser. Of course der Keyser would say nothing about the second chain, as long as Philip was bribing him to stay quiet about the faked deception. Philip smiled to himself. Only in the art world could someone fake a fake. And if Gerrit should suddenly have an attack of conscience, so what? Philip would be in Italy. Out of reach.

All he had to do was to get through the next day and a half – thirty-six hours and counting.

Seventy

As Nicholas walked into his sister's flat, Honor jumped up then winced, touching her ribs. In the chair beside the sofa sat the soft-fleshed Mark Spencer, embarrassed to be in the presence of the man he had been spying on.

'God, are you all right?' Nicholas asked, ignoring Mark. 'I know who did this and I'll get him for it. I knew it was Sidney Elliott as soon as you said he stammered.'

Mark was trying to make his presence felt. 'I think we should call a doctor.'

Nicholas ignored him as Honor stared at her brother earnestly.

'He wants to have a meeting with you,' she said. 'Ten o'clock tonight. St Martin in the Field's, of all places. Mad bastard.'

'This was why I didn't want you to get involved,' Nicholas said anxiously. 'You should get checked out. Let me take you to the hospital.'

Mark tried to interject. 'I will—'

345

Again, Nicholas ignored him. 'I don't want anything to happen to you—'

'Then you shouldn't have got her involved in the first place, should you?'

Slowly Nicholas turned to look at Mark Spencer. 'Who are you?'

Colouring, Mark rose to his full height of five foot eight, six inches shorter than Nicholas, his tone pompous. 'Your sister has been attacked—'

'I said, "Who are you?"'

'Mark Spencer, a colleague.' He glanced at Honor, who was rolling her eyes at him.

'Nicholas, it's OK,' she said. 'Mark's a friend.'

Friend, Mark thought bitterly. She should have said, 'Mark's been digging up all your greasy secrets, Nicholas. Because of Mark I'm finding out what you're really like.' But she didn't, because despite what he had told her, she was looking at her brother and Mark could tell – without her even saying it – that she was on Nicholas's side.

'You should call the police—'

Nicholas stared at him. 'And say what?'

'That your sister has been attacked!' Mark blustered. 'Let the police go to St Martin's tonight. Why risk yourself? Why risk her any more?'

'Nicholas has to go—'

Mark spun round to look at her. '*What?*'

'The police would only spook Elliott and he'd run. Then

what? How would they catch him after that?' She looked back at Nicholas. 'D'you know what he wants?'

'It'll be about the Bosch chain—'

'The chain!' Mark almost shrieked. 'Are you both mad? This man is violent—'

Slowly Honor rose to her feet, guiding Mark to the front door. His arm felt resistant under her touch, his hostility obvious as she spoke to him.

'Look, I'm OK. I'm just bruised. If I'd broken any bones I'd be in agony, and I'm not; I'm just shaken.' She smiled. 'I have to talk to Nicholas alone—'

'And you think you'll get a straight story out of him?' Mark asked. 'Remember what I found out—'

'I need him to explain,' she said, interrupting. 'I can't just take your word on this. I have to know what he did, and why. And *if* he did it.'

'You saw the proof—'

'I saw papers, clippings, old photographs,' she replied. 'I want to hear it from his own mouth. Good or bad, I want Nicholas to tell me.'

Exasperated, Mark opened the door to leave, then turned.

'You're a fool. You should back off from this now, before you really get hurt. Your brother stayed out of your life for years – why don't you return the compliment and stay out of his?'

'Because I'm his sister, and he's all I've got,' Honor replied crisply. 'I trust him. Nicholas will look after me.'

'Want to bet?' Mark replied, slamming the door behind him.

When Honor returned to the sitting room, Nicholas had made coffee for both of them, pushing a cup towards her as she sat down. He could see a bruise beginning on her cheek and her left eye was swollen.

'I could kill Elliott for hurting you . . . Maybe we *should* go to the police.'

Her tone was sarcastic when she answered. 'That's a good idea, Nicholas. The police have already questioned you about one murder – they can't fail to be interested in what happened to me today. Especially as you know my attacker personally.' Her tone hardened. 'Don't be stupid. The police can't get involved . . . What does this Elliott man want?'

'The chain—'

'It's all about that bloody chain!' she snapped, touching her ribs gingerly.

'But you don't believe in the chain or the conspiracy, do you? You think I faked it all,' Nicholas said, his tone cold. 'Apparently other people believe that too—'

'I didn't mean—'

'What you meant was clear enough. You even suggested that I was losing my mind. Paranoid—'

'You were talking about people being murdered! About the Church and them coming after you—'

'And now you've been attacked,' he said simply. 'Or was that was all part of my master plan? Maybe I wanted to throw suspicion off myself and hired someone to go after you—'

'I didn't say you were lying!'

'You didn't have to say it, you *thought* it,' Nicholas retorted hotly. 'My sister, the one person that I thought believed in me. Your suspicion hurt me more than you can imagine—'

'And what about you?' Honor countered, glaring at him. 'You come in and out of my life and I'm not supposed to ask any questions. Yes, you're my brother, but there are big gaps in your life that I don't know about—'

'I don't know everything about your life either!'

'But I don't have anything to hide.'

'*And I do?*' he queried, turning to leave.

Angrily she slammed the door closed, forcing him to stay.

'No! You are not walking out of here now. Not this time, Nicholas. I'm not risking my good name or my safety for half a story. I want to know what's going on.'

'I've told you the truth!' he shouted. 'You know about the chain and the deception. I'm not telling you the whole story about Bosch for a reason. What you don't know you can't give away. And what you don't know can't hurt you.'

'Are you talking about Bosch? Or yourself?'

Anger drained the colour from his face. 'What d'you mean?'

'What were you doing in Europe when you were in your teens and early twenties? All those times you went away and never explained . . .' Her tone softened. 'Tell me, Nicholas. Before you entered the Church, what were you doing?'

He said nothing, his face blank.

And it frightened her.

'I just want to help you. That's all I've ever wanted. I'm not prying into your past—'

'I suppose the little prick you had here earlier is doing that for you,' Nicholas replied, his voice hard. 'I imagine you set him a task, digging around, scraping up all the dirt he could find. Of course, you two being lawyers, you'd want to know everything.'

She was astounded by his anger. 'Nicholas, I'm not judging you—'

'You've never stopped judging me since we were children! You and Henry. You think I didn't hear you two talking? *"Poor Nicholas, he feels so guilty about our parents' death, but it wasn't really his fault—"*'

'It wasn't your fault!'

'No, but it certainly felt like it!'

She shook her head. 'You're changing the subject. I was asking about what you'd been doing in Europe—'

'And I'm not telling you!' he roared. 'What d'you really want to hear, Honor? That I fucked a lot of women? You know that. That I was irresponsible, bummed my way round? You know that too. I was a kid, dammit. Kids do stupid things.'

His rage unnerved her. Was he angry because she was prying into his life, or because she had uncovered what he had done? Honor knew that she should back off, but couldn't. Instead, like the lawyer she was, she went in for the kill.

'Who's Nico Lassimo?'

The name punched into the air between them. It left the room winded as Honor watched her brother and waited for him to speak. Explain, she willed him. Tell me that Nico Lassimo wasn't you. Deny that you were in Munich and Milan. Protest your innocence. Tell me that you were never involved in faking. Tell me it wasn't you that attacked that woman, or stole from Raoul Devereux. Tell me it was another man.

But Nicholas didn't explain. Instead he looked at his sister with sadness and a kind of resignation. 'My God,' he said finally, 'when did you stop knowing who I was?'

This is the last time I will come here, Nicholas thinks, deep in sleep, walking between the dream yew trees. This is the last time that I will see this. As ever, he hears the crunching of glass, his priest's shoes treading the broken beer bottles into a mosaic underfoot.

The old nest is still here, he thinks, as always, as ever the same. The cupboard too, and across the narrow wedge of worn grass the priests whisper, two men under the arch of the entrance, next to the message board that displays the church Bring and Buy sale . . .

But this time the man walking up the gravel path is not a congregant. Not a worshipper . . . Nicholas turns over in bed, restless, sweating in his winding sheet . . . This stranger comes armed with a lens more vicious than a sword and points it at the church, grabbing at images of the pitted stone and the yielding spire. And the name Patrick Gerin scowls over the desolate garden like a fall of dead leaves . . .

Tear it down, Nicholas thinks. Tear it down.

He knows they will. That someone – not a congregant, not a worshipper – will come in the night and light a match. They will fire up the outhouse with its cupboard, burning the old nest and the roof rafters where once a boy sat and crooned to a bird.

As ever, as always, Nicholas turns in his memory . . . And now he is walking towards the flames that someone – not a worshipper, not a congregant – lit to destroy what he saw. And what he was too late to prevent. He walks in without pausing, feels the heat. So hot, as ever, as always, the fire purifying both his dying limbs and his living mind.

And beyond this, above the memory, the dead boy, and the spiralling flames, a man cries in his sleep and wakes no one.

Seventy-One

Trafalgar Square, London

In the evening the lights illuminate the smug white patch of the square, with its morose lions and the novelty displays – the enormous ship in a bottle or the giant mutant hen, its feathers the colour of cheap toffee wrappers. Perched like ludicrous sentries on their plinths, their presence is only ever temporary, their impact negated under the daunting, old soldier gaze of the National Gallery.

Sidney Elliott sat on the steps outside St Martin in the Field's church, smoking. The bluish white of the floodlights aged him cruelly, although his size was still impressive, even seated. The bitter wind blew his grey hair across his face. He was wearing a heavy quilted jacket, his eyes fixed on Nicholas as he began to climb the steps towards him. Elliott didn't move, didn't even seem fazed by the look on Nicholas's face; he just continued to smoke.

There were enough people around to stop any attack.

Laverne could hardly start a fight in the presence of at least ten witnesses, and Elliott knew it.

'How dare you hurt my sister—'

'I h-h-had to get your interest somehow,' Elliott replied, stubbing out his cigarette and jerking his head towards the National Gallery. 'Bosch's *Crowning with Thorns* is in th-th-there. I bet *you* think of yourself as a b-b-bit of a martyr. I bet the National wouldn't thank you for exposing any s-s-scandal about one of their m-m-most famous painters.'

'What d'you want?'

'I want to know what h-h-h-happened to Bosch. I want to know what you're investigating.' He stood up, towering over Nicholas who was standing on a lower step. 'Mr Voygel n-n-needs to know.'

'What's he promised you?'

Elliott hesitated. He had been fired by Conrad Voygel, unceremoniously dumped. But if he could bring him the information he wanted, he was sure he could wheedle himself back into the tycoon's good books.

'Th-th-throw in your lot with me and we can make a fortune. Oppose m-m-me and you'll regret it.'

'You dare go near my sister again—'

'And you'll do what?' Elliott said. 'There's nothing you can say or d-d-do to make me back off. I will find out wh-wh-what I want to know, one way or another.'

'My sister doesn't know anything. Leave her out of this.'

Elliott's eyes flickered.

'You know the h-h-history of this place?' He gestured to the church behind him. 'In 2006 they found a grave, d-d-dated around 410. A Roman burial, they th-th-thought. And in the Middle Ages the b-b-building was used by the monks of Westminster Abbey.' He moved closer – so close Nicholas could catch the smell of nicotine on his breath. 'Henry the Eighth rebuilt it later, so th-th-that the victims of the plague wouldn't have to p-p-pass through Whitehall Palace—'

Impatient, Nicholas shrugged. 'What's this got to do with anything?'

'I am an academic! A l-l-learned man. Possessed of a brilliant original mind. I w-w-was the best in my year at Cambridge. I was p-p-published before I was twenty-one. Lecturing around the world at thirty. I was supposed to m-m-make a reputation, a fortune, to be one of the greats.' He paused. 'And yet here I am, fifty-n-n-nine years old, a nobody.'

'I don't care.'

'Oh, you *should* care!' Elliott snapped, 'You sh-sh-should care, Mr Laverne, because I will make you care. I g-g-give you one last chance. You have one day left before the auction and in that time you m-m- must tell me the whole secret.'

'*Or?*'

'His n-n-name was Patrick Gerin, wasn't it?' Elliott asked nonchalantly, and saw seeing Nicholas flinch. 'Yes, Patrick Gerin. He hanged h-h-himself. Or was he hanged? I don't suppose we'll ever know, w-w-will we, Mr Laverne? Or should I say Father Daniel?' he smirked, circling Nicholas. 'I kn-kn-

know why you don't go to the police. You c-c-can't risk them prying into your life too closely. You w-w-want your revenge on the Church, I understand that. But I want my revenge too – for p-p-poverty and a wasted life.' He passed Nicholas, knocking into his shoulder as he did so. '*One day*. That's all you've got left.'

'You're giving me a day to decide whether or not I'm going to tell you the secret?'

'No, Mr Laverne,' Elliott replied coldly. 'I'm g-g-giving you a day to live.'

Seventy-Two

Spooning up against her husband's back, Judith Kaminski stared at the clock by the bed: 3.45 a.m. Later that day, at 2 p.m. in Chelsea, London, Philip Preston was going to auction the Bosch chain . . . Even though he knew his wife wasn't asleep, Hiram said nothing. Instead he thought of the securely locked doors, front and back, and the burglar alarm he had set for the night. Such a long night.

Every sound outside had quickened his pulse, every noise a reminder of the previous assault. But no one came. Even the urban foxes stayed away. No overturned bins, no stalking of wild cats, nothing but a thick, unyielding and portentous silence.

Impatient, Gerrit knocked the papers he had been reading on to the floor of his study and poured himself a whisky. Then doubled it. Bugger his fucking heart, he was close to collapse anyway . . . All his searching had revealed nothing. No information about the old man Guillaine who had brought him the Bosch picture and the bloody chain.

His instincts were heightened because it was well into the night and he couldn't sleep. Of course the whole thing *could* be a set-up, Sabine plotting her revenge on him. Some old codger Guillaine relative of hers bringing the painting to Gerrit to sell – the painting that had originally been stolen from Raoul Devereux's French gallery. She could have planned it with the help of that ex-priest, Gerrit thought. Then she *could* have bought it from him, along with the fake chain, knowing she was going to be filmed taking it. What a perfect way to throw suspicion off herself.

Mind you, being murdered was an even better way . . . Gerrit thought of his conversation earlier with Carel Honthorst. He had come into the gallery with a plaster cast on his arm, his face grey under the concealer, his demeanour unnerving.

'I'm not working for you any more.'

'You're supposed to be guarding me!'

Honthorst looked at him, a slow smile hovering on his lips. 'You and I both know you don't need guarding.'

'Then bugger off! You're not much good with that fucking thing on your arm anyway,' Gerrit retorted, then frowned. 'Are you working for another dealer?'

'No. The art world isn't my only employer.'

'I know you work for the Catholic Church,' he retorted. 'I do my fucking research, Mr Honthorst. Anyone I employ is thoroughly checked out.'

'Half of the people you employ are crooks.'

'True, but they're all good ones,' Gerrit had replied, taking a wad of money from his desk and handing it to Honthorst. 'Our business dealings are to remain a secret between the two of us.'

The Dutchman had taken the money and nodded. 'I won't say anything.'

'Are you going back to Holland?'

'Not yet.'

Gerrit had frowned. 'You're taking your time with Nicholas Laverne, aren't you? I can imagine that your other *employer* might have wanted him sorted out by now.' He had caught the anger in Honthorst's eyes, but had carried on. 'Seems he bested you.' Gerrit pointed to the plaster cast. 'Hired muscle up against a fucking ex-priest – who'd have put money on the cleric?'

Honthorst had made a move towards Gerrit and the dealer put up his hands. 'Easy, boy, I'm just having a little joke with you. But be honest, you don't intend to let Laverne get away with it, do you? Unless you've been *told* to back off.'

Gerrit paused, remembering the conversation in every detail. *Had* Honthorst been forced to stay his hand? After all, the Catholic Church – for all its covert mumblings – hadn't made a move to silence Laverne. Their troublesome priest was unharmed, and tomorrow was the auction. If Laverne was going to speak up, that would be the perfect opportunity. Press coverage guaranteed . . . Gerrit finished his whisky and clicked off the light, then walked up to his bedroom. Miriam was asleep, snoring slightly with her mouth open. It was a pity they had never had children. Some buffer against old age, some offspring to keep an ego thriving in the world. Gerrit would have liked a kid . . .

And then he remembered Eloise and winced.

For the third time in an hour, Philip Preston looked out of his window to check that his security guards were still there. He had chosen to sleep in the office at the auction house, within feet of the safe in which the two chains were locked up. Philip rubbed his chin, feeling the scratch of stubble, thinking of Gayle. He would never see her again. After the auction he would leave with Kim Fields, a rich – and free – man.

But that was later. He still had the rest of the night to get through and dawn was slow in coming. He wondered if Nicholas Laverne were sleeping, or if he were awake too, knowing that within the space of twelve hours nothing would ever be the same again.

Another man was awake too. Conrad Voygel was rereading the auction house catalogue, staring at the glossy photograph of the Bosch chain and knowing that soon he would own it – if not the secret that had been hidden inside. Sidney Elliott had failed him there, but nothing would have persuaded Conrad to work with the academic any longer. He was unbalanced, aggression always just below the surface.

Not like Nicholas Laverne: his aggression was curtailed and the reason was obvious. He was playing safe, waiting for his moment. When the chain was auctioned the ex-priest would speak up and hurl himself back into notoriety again. Conrad knew the type: the righteous hero.

It would have been so much better if Laverne had stayed in France. Out of London, away from the auction. Stayed an anonymous priest, removed from a world too clever for him. Perhaps he hadn't realised how much danger he was in. The art world was watching Laverne, the Church was watching him, even the police had him under observation – and God only knows how many others. But Laverne was determined. He was vengeful, reckless and, worst of all, a zealot. The deaths of Claude Devereux, Sabine Monette, Thomas Littlejohn and the priest had not deterred him. He was ripe for martyrdom, out for justice as well as revenge, hoping to bring Hell down on the Church and, indirectly, the art world.

Within hours Nicholas Laverne would be world news, his family interrogated, his past picked over, his intentions questioned. Fêted by some, despised by others, targeted by a dangerous few, his accusations would draw interest and attention globally. Nicholas Laverne – the infamous whistle-blower who became an outcast.

And should have remained one.

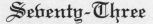

Seventy-Three

'You're awake,' Father Michael said, looking up as Nicholas entered the kitchen. 'Did you sleep?'

He shook his head. 'No, I was dreaming again. Always dreaming. I don't feel like I had any rest . . . Did you sleep?'

'Not much.'

'Did you hear anything last night?'

'Nothing, it was quiet,' Father Michael replied, putting the kettle on to boil. 'It surprised me, to be honest. Maybe they've given up. They might think that because you haven't spoken out so far, you have decided against going public.' He paused, staring at Nicholas curiously. 'Have you?'

He shook his head.

'No. Nothing would make me change my mind now.'

'I'm glad,' the old priest replied, laying out two place settings for breakfast. Two mats, two plates, two sets of cutlery, two cups and saucers. Old-fashioned, oddly comforting to Nicholas.

'I'm just going to have a quick shower. I'll only be a couple of minutes.'

'I'll have breakfast ready when you get back,' the old priest said kindly. 'We've got a big day ahead of us.'

Nicholas was halfway up the stairs when he remembered something and made his way back to the kitchen, pausing in the doorway. Obviously he hadn't heard him, because Father Michael was by the window with his profile to Nicholas, and he was putting something into a cup of tea. Nicholas could see the steam rising and then glanced at the table. There were the two placing settings, but one cup and saucer was missing. *His.*

Nicholas remembered the conversation:

'You don't think it was deliberate, do you?' Father Michael had asked.

'What?'

'You being ill. I mean, you don't think—'

'Someone poisoned me? No, this is one thing we can't blame on the Church . . .'

His heart pumping, Nicholas backed away. It made sense in an instant: the dreams, the sickness, the stomach pain, the restless, frenzied anxiety . . . But Father Michael? Of all the people after him he had never suspected the priest. Silently he climbed the stairs, making sure that the old man didn't hear him. Throwing on his clothes, he then slid open the back window and looked out. There was a flat roof about eight feet below and he jumped on to it, pausing for a moment to check that he hadn't been heard.

He could easily overpower the old priest, but not if he

had accomplices . . . A moment later Nicholas had lowered himself on to the gravel and was running as fast as his legs would carry him towards the main road.

Seventy-Four

Philip Preston's Auction House, Chelsea, London

There was half an hour to go before the auction. The turn-out was even better than Philip had expected and his palms were sweating with tension as he looked around the hall. He knew most of the faces, but others were new to him – one of them probably being a bidder on behalf of Conrad Voygel. Which one, Philip didn't know, but he was certain the IT giant wouldn't let the Bosch chain go to anyone else.

A tap on his shoulder made him jump, as Gerrit smiled up at him. 'Lovely display,' he said, jerking his head towards the raised dais, where there was a massive photograph of the chain on an easel. 'Which one is it?'

Grabbing his arm, Philip hustled him into the office and closed the door behind them. 'Keep your voice down. Someone could have heard!' He forced himself to calm down, smoothing out his waistcoat.

Gerrit began to laugh. 'You look fucking scared.'

366

'Really?' Philip asked, surprised. 'I thought I was covering it up well.'

'Honthorst thought he covered up his pockmarks well. Both of you were wrong.'

Philip smoothed his waistcoat again, nervous, edgy. 'I don't know if I'm up to all this. I keep waiting for something to happen – like the gunfight at the OK Corral.' He glanced at Gerrit. 'Nothing from Laverne?'

'Silent as the grave,' Gerrit said wryly. 'In which he might well be before long.'

'You wouldn't—'

'Kill Laverne? Don't be bleeding soft, Philip. Why should I care if the secret comes out or not? It's the bloody Church that has to worry.' Gerrit moved over to the safe and tapped it with his forefinger. 'Go on, I won't tell anyone. Which one did you pick to auction?'

'They were exactly the same. What difference does it make?' Philip replied, checking his reflection in the cloakroom mirror and then walking back over to Gerrit. 'I've been thinking: why don't we get the other one melted down?'

'You *are* a fucking amateur! When you've buggered off abroad, I'll wait for a while and then go to one of my best clients and tell them that the one you auctioned was a fake – and then I'll sell them the *real* one.'

'That makes me look good,' Philip said sarcastically.

'Oh, I'll say it was a mistake. The buyer won't give a shit – if they think they got the *genuine* article.'

'I want half of whatever you get.'

Gerrit nodded, then changed tack. 'Nicholas Laverne was clever, faking a fake. Nice touch. He would have done well in business – pity he became a fanatic.'

'He gets what he wants in the end. To crucify the Church—'

'He hasn't done it yet,' Gerrit said wryly. 'No one's the winner until they cross the finishing line.'

Seventy-Five

No one could be trusted, Nicholas thought as he ran along the road and then jumped on a bus. He could hardly believe what he had seen. His old mentor had been working against him all the time. Either from choice or pressure, Father Michael had tried to stop Nicholas – and he had nearly succeeded. Far from being idle, the Church had been working hard to silence him. They might have succeeded too if he hadn't been lucky the night he collapsed, a tourist finding him unconscious on Brompton Road.

Nicholas sat beside the bus window and rested his left temple against the steamy glass. He had mistrusted Elliott from the first and he had been right to be cautious. The academic was obviously working for the Church. Carel Honthorst wasn't the only one in their employ; it had been a two-pronged attack. If one of them didn't get him, the other would.

He glanced at his fellow passengers, all involved in their own thoughts, silent in the fuggy bus, no one meeting his eye. And then Nicholas remembered something that had happened the previous evening.

'You sleep so badly,' Father Michael had said. 'I've made you a hot drink – that should help.'

Nicholas had smiled his thanks, but when he tasted the over-sweetened drink he had winced and thrown it out of the window to avoid hurting the old man's feelings. He could imagine how surprised the priest would have been to see the empty glass the following morning and Nicholas up and about when, by rights, he should have been felled.

The treachery winded him. Father Michael had promised support, had pledged to make amends for his past negligence, while all the time attempting to wheedle confidences out of Nicholas. Where were the papers? he had asked. Are you still going to expose the conspiracy? And while he had been feigning concern, he had been reporting back to the Church. Expressing sympathy as he had drugged Nicholas's food, distorting his dreams, increasing his paranoia along with his intermittent confusion.

Then another thought occurred to Nicholas. Was it the priest who had planted the crucifix in his bed? He had heard him snoring, but he might have managed it. Unless there had been someone else in the house, someone quick. Someone who knew the layout of the rectory. Someone who had expressed doubts about Nicholas's suspicions. His sister, Honor.

He couldn't believe it. Not Honor. She was too straight. She had told him what she thought directly – she wasn't the type to sneak around. But she *had* been prying into his history, digging up the past, his litany of sins regurgitated. She knew what he had done and how suspicious it looked . . .

'Sorry, mate,' a man said, knocking into Nicholas as he sat down next to him. 'Rain again, hey? What can you do?'

Ignoring him, Nicholas kept staring out of the window. At the next stop he left the bus and watched it as it passed. But the man didn't move, just stayed in his seat as the bus moved on.

Seventy-Six

All great auctions were an event, Gerrit thought, looking around him, but this was a fucking eye-opener . . . Amused, he watched collectors, dealers and private buyers sitting on their dainty gold chairs, a few lardy arses hanging over the sides. They were trying to appear nonchalant, but the temperature in the hall was increasing with tension and that peculiar, florid heat of greed.

Philip Preston mounted the dais and checked his microphone, which hissed and clicked into the hall like a woken rattlesnake, Philip unusually awkward as he began the auction. He was leaving the Bosch chain until last, the final and tremendous lot, cleverly building up the tension. And there was plenty of that. Leaning forward, Gerrit looked along his row, surprised to see Hiram Kaminski, a dealer who had professed to want nothing to do with the chain. And yet here he was and, just behind him, the beautiful and glacial Eloise Devereux. Her manner revealed nothing but

372

her glance settled on her father for a long instant and her expression warned him that she would never stop, never give up until she had discovered who had killed her husband and her mother and punished them. And if it turned out to be Gerrit der Keyser, so be it.

Over a hundred people had gathered into the hall, security at the doors and at the front and rear of the dais. All eyes were focused on Philip Preston. No one noticed the stooping figure of Sidney Elliott in the crowd, or the ominous Carel Honthorst. No one spotted Father Dominic from St Barnabas's, or the ever-curious Mark Spencer. They were all fixated on the Bosch chain. The chain that provoked fear and desire in equal amounts. The infamous chain which had supposedly carried a secret so potent it had resulted in murder.

If there were ghosts in the hall then Sabine Monette was there alongside Claude Devereux and Thomas Littlejohn. If there *were* ghosts, the guilty spirit of Father Luke was also watching. But one person was missing; the instigator of the sale and the man who had begun the rumour of the Bosch deception.

The troubled – and troubling – Nicholas Laverne.

Seventy-Seven

Church of St Stephen, Fulham, London

Running in from the battering rain, Honor knocked on the side door of the vestry. There was no answer. Again she knocked, this time loudly, thumping the iron knocker up and down. Finally Father Michael answered her.

'Where's Nicholas?' she asked him.

But he didn't reply and he seemed ill at ease. Surprised, Honor moved past him into the hall, glancing towards the kitchen. Inside sat a man she knew. A thickset man with bad skin. A man she recognised from the photographs Mark Spencer had shown her. Carel Honthorst.

Spooked, Honor stepped back, almost losing her footing as she ran out into the street and made for her parked car. She had just clambered inside when Honthorst caught up with her and tried to wrench open the door with his uninjured hand. Horrified, Honor turned on the ignition and slammed her foot down on the accelerator. The car jerked forward, its wheels spinning, and as it knocked

Honthorst off balance Honor swerved out into the traffic, a passing taxi blaring its horn.

One hand on the wheel, Honor reached into her bag for her mobile. At the traffic lights she stopped, glanced into the rear-view mirror, and then phoned Nicholas's number.

It rang out.

'Pick up!' she said frantically. 'Pick up!'

But there was no answer and the lights changed, forcing Honor to drive on. She knew that there was only one reason for Carel Honthorst to be at St Stephen's – he was in league with Father Michael. In collusion with the Catholic Church. There was no other explanation. She thought of what Nicholas had told her. About his dreams, the night terrors, the food poisoning, the crucifix he had found in his bed, the one she had only recently remembered giving him as a new priest. All the things she had put down to imagination and paranoia. But she had been wrong. Nicholas wasn't unstable, he was in danger.

And then his words came back, haunting and damning: *'When did you stop knowing who I was?'*

Seventy-Eight

Head lowered, Nicholas kept on walking. The rain was coming down hard and he bought an umbrella from a street trader, holding it close to his head and turning up the collar of his coat in an attempt to disguise himself. He felt more alone than he had ever been, but he wasn't going to back down. Unless someone stopped him, he was going to expose the truth. Nothing else mattered to him. If it cost him his life, it was worth it. He had no family to speak of, no reputation left. No home, no friends. He was an outcast.

But he was still fighting. And all he needed was access to the internet. He cursed the fact that he had left his phone behind when he fled St Stephen's, but he would have to improvise. Crossing Beak Street, he entered Soho, the nub of the capital, a place overrun with bars, shops and internet cafes. Entering a narrow alleyway, Nicholas walked into a cafe and paid for online access.

Sitting down in front of the computer, he typed in a website name and watched, relieved, as the site came up. He had prepared it weeks earlier, entering copies of the Bosch papers and a photograph of the chain in which the papers had been found, together with explanations of the text and relevant translations. The information had been updated, ready to go live. He accused the Church of deception in concealing the death of Hieronymus Bosch and named The Brotherhood of Mary. He explained that many of Bosch's works had been faked by his family in the interests of making money, with the collusion of the Catholic Church. The whole sordid and bitter tale of Bosch's incarceration was laid out in the words of a contemporary, someone who had witnessed it.

Next he checked his blog, also ready to go live. Finally, he checked the emails he was about to send to newspapers, websites, radio and television stations around the globe – and to various eminent members of the Church. It was all complete, ready. When he pressed Enter, the world of art and of religion would find itself under blistering scrutiny, called to account for a deception perpetrated centuries earlier.

The cafe was dense with noise and the humming of computers. Relieved that he was not being watched, Nicholas glanced around him as a waitress approached. She was very young, with heavy eye make-up and a sleeve of tattoos, but she was friendly.

'You want something to drink?'

'No,' he said. 'Nothing. I'm fine.'

She was persistent. 'But we've got everything,' she went on.

Distracted for a moment Nicholas looked up at her. 'Honestly, I'm fine—'

He never saw him, just felt the punch land on the side of his ribs, as Sidney Elliott grabbed him and the waitress watched, horrified, as Nicholas was knocked to the floor. Desperate, he tried to reach up to the computer, but Elliott took hold of his arm and twisted it.

'Press Enter!' Nicholas shouted to the waitress.

She stared, transfixed.

'Press the button!' he shouted. 'Jesus, *please* . . .'

She was moving in suspended time. Her gaze went from Nicholas to the computer and back to him again. The heavily made-up eyes blinked, her mind processing what was going on and the instruction she had been given. Then, like a leaf unfurling, the tattooed arm reached out, one finger extended.

And pressed Enter.

Seventy-Nine

Someone had called the police and now an officer was heading towards the struggling men. As Elliott saw the policeman he panicked, pushing over tables in his hurry to get out, computers crashing to the floor as people watched him run into the street. He was moving so fast he couldn't stop in time, and a delivery van slammed into him and threw him several yards along the road. Panicked, the driver jumped out of his cab and ran over to the dying man.

'I didn't see him! He came out of nowhere!' the driver babbled to the onlookers. 'I didn't see him!'

It was only seconds before the police officer reached the scene, but it was obvious that Sidney Elliott was dead. His eyes were open but blank. His limbs were contorted, his neck bent at an angle. Blood pumped from his smashed chest and oiled the street, speckles of vermilion flecking the white face.

'Why did he run like that?' the waitress asked Nicholas, bemused.

He shook his head. 'I don't know. I honestly don't know.'

She glanced at the policeman who was bending over the body, then looked back to Nicholas. 'You in trouble?'

He didn't lie. 'Yes.'

Nodding, she beckoned for him to follow her, taking the alleyway and then a sharp turn to the left. He didn't question why he was following her, he was just glad of the help as the girl pushed open a back door and ushered him in. The place smelt of curry and joss-sticks, stirring an old memory of incense.

'Come on,' she said, showing him into a shabby sitting room. 'It's not much, but you're welcome to doss here a bit. Wait 'til things quieten down.'

'Why are you helping me?'

'Why not? I was on my uppers once and someone helped me. Always said I'd return the favour one day,' she replied, putting out her hand. 'I'm Tyra, and the man snoring next door is my brother. If he wakes up, say you're a friend of mine and he'll be fine with it.' She tilted her head to one side. 'Who was the man who attacked you?'

'Somebody who never got over becoming a nobody,' Nicholas replied wryly.

Tyra pulled a face. 'Well, anyway, the telly's over there and there's some food in the kitchen. I'll be back later.'

'Don't tell anyone—'

'You're here?' she grinned. 'Don't worry. No one tells anyone anything round here.'

Eighty

From the safety of Tyra's flat, Nicholas dialled 141, to withhold the number he was ringing from, and then called Hiram Kaminski.

'Sidney Elliott is dead,' he said without preamble. 'I think he was the man who tried to break into your gallery. He tried hard to stop me going public, but he didn't manage it. The Bosch deception is out there now.'

'What happened to him?'

'He was spooked by the police. It's funny: when he saw them he completely overreacted, ran off and got hit by a van before anyone could talk to him.'

'He didn't want to get caught—'

'That's what puzzles me,' Nicholas replied. 'To outsiders, it was just two men fighting. He could have explained it away, bluffed his way out of it. No, there was more to it than that. When he saw that copper, he lost it. Bolted.'

'But why would he do that?'

Nicholas thought for a moment. 'Maybe he couldn't risk being caught. Maybe he had more to hide than just attacking me.' He paused, thinking back over everything that had happened, piecing it together. 'Sidney Elliott was a desperate man. He was banking on finding out about Bosch. He was acting as though everything depended on it and got more and more unreasonable. Every time I spoke to him he raised the stakes: he went after my sister, he threatened me. He was a mess. Frenzied, dangerous. Oh God . . .'

Hiram pressed him. 'What is it?'

'I think it was Sidney Elliott who murdered Thomas Littlejohn, Sabine and Claude. Then he went after Father Luke to frame me.'

'Why would he do that?' Hiram was taken aback. 'He was an academic—'

'—who was one of the first to know about the conspiracy. I went to him, remember? I only gave him one piece of the Bosch papers, but it was enough to whet his appetite. Elliott was a bitter man, his life a failure. I think he saw the conspiracy as his last chance. *He* wanted to expose it. *He* wanted the glory of the discovery – so he had to silence everyone else who knew about it.'

'But he didn't kill you.'

'He *needed* me,' Nicholas explained. 'Elliott never knew the whole deception – I was the only person who could tell him that. He couldn't kill me, he could only threaten me.' He thought back, slotting the pieces into place. 'Didn't you tell me that Thomas Littlejohn dealt in paintings and antique books?'

Hiram nodded. 'Yes, he did.'

'So Elliott might have worked with him before on a manuscript.'

'It's possible. Sidney Elliott was an expert. We all used him,' Hiram admitted. 'But it doesn't make sense. Why would a man like him suddenly become a killer?'

'It wasn't sudden,' Nicholas explained, his voice rising. 'Bit by bit, Elliott's life had soured. I remember him almost begging me for "an adventure". My rejection was another blow to his ego.' He paused, thinking back. 'He wanted one more shot at glory, and he failed. I think that was the turning point.'

'And Thomas Littlejohn knew someone was after him,' Hiram said hurriedly. 'That's why he wrote me the letter—'

'Which Elliott didn't know about. That's why he didn't kill you – he wasn't sure how much you knew. So he scared you into silence instead.' Nicholas thought of the dead man. 'He wasn't going for honour any longer. He'd killed, crossed the line. He was going for the money instead. Sidney Elliott was working for the person who would pay him the most for the secret—'

'Conrad Voygel.'

Nicholas took in a breath. Then he asked, 'Who bought the chain at the auction?'

'The buyer was anonymous, but we all know it's Voygel. The place was buzzing. And everyone's looking for you. Your sister came to the auction trying to find you—'

'Has the chain left the auction house?'

383

'No. When I spoke to Philip Preston he said that it was being collected later tonight. There was some rumour about it being taken out of the country, but that could just be hearsay. One thing's for sure: Preston's got guards all round the place, security up to the hilt. He's scared. Maybe he thinks someone will try to steal it before it gets to its new owner.'

Nicholas thought for a moment, then nodded. 'Maybe he's right.'

Eighty-One

The news of the Bosch deception hit the art world just after the auction had finished and Philip Preston was collared in his office by a couple of journalists demanding the whole story. Had he known about it? Had he any idea of the up-heaval it would cause among the dealers and the galleries who would now start questioning their Bosch acquisitions. Composed, he met their questions with equanimity, steering the conversation over to his exclusive discovery that the famous *Tree Man* was, in fact, a portrait of Hieronymus Bosch.

'But *was* he abused?' one journalist asked. 'And what if it's true that Bosch's family and the Church just kept churning out the paintings?'

'The writings were hidden in the chain you've just sold,' another man said. 'I saw it online. A Nicholas Laverne posted it and wrote to the press. Who is Nicholas Laverne anyway?'

Philip's expression was strained. He was surprised that Nicholas had managed the exposé and was now determined to curtail the damage. 'Mr Laverne is a . . . man with a vivid imagination.'

'You saying he's lying?'

'I'm saying that he could be mistaken. Look into his background and you'll see what I mean. Mr Laverne relishes the role of whistle-blower. He also has a great animosity towards the Catholic Church. He was excommunicated ten years ago.' Philip could see them all listening, scribbling or holding their recorders up to his mouth to catch every word. 'Mr Laverne was also questioned by the police—'

'*What?*'

'– about the death of Father Luke. Late of St Barnabas's church, Fulham. Apparently he was one of the priests Laverne accused of abuse.'

'And the police think he had something to do with the murder?'

'How would I know? Ask them,' Philip said loftily. 'But I think being cut off from the Church unhinged Mr Laverne.'

The seed was sown and took quick root.

Philip Preston wasn't the only person to damn Nicholas. Within an hour of the news being posted online, Gerrit der Keyser gave an interview in which he intimated that no one believed anything Laverne said, and that he could easily have constructed the deception himself. Nicholas Laverne's exposure was an irritant, he went on, but would not turn out to be the disaster people feared. His credibility was dubious and already one high-ranking member of the Church had labelled him 'a poor, misguided fantasist'.

Only one person came to Nicholas's aid. Hiram Kaminski gave an interview to be published in *The Times* the following day, going public to say that the Bosch deception was real. How did he know? Thomas Littlejohn had told him.

'If it wasn't true,' Hiram said on BBC radio, 'why would four people involved with it have been murdered?'

His words caught the attention of everyone listening, including the authorities. Within minutes of Hiram's interview at Langham Place, he was being questioned by the London Metropolitan police. At the same time, Nicholas was leaving a thank-you note on Tyra's table in Soho, together with some money – enough to pay for the black hoodie he had taken from her brother.

Patiently, he had waited until it was dark. Tyra's brother was a heavy sleeper and his snores kept Nicholas company until 6 p.m. With the hood pulled up over his head, Nicholas left and made his way across town towards Chelsea. Sidney Elliott was dead, but that didn't mean someone else wasn't following him. Conrad Voygel had enough money to hire an army of watchers. Repeatedly changing buses, Nicholas headed for the auction house of Philip Preston.

It was almost 7.15 p.m. when he arrived, climbing over a wall and securing a vantage point from the roof of a garage. Almost concealed behind a series of steps, Nicholas watched the auction house. Hiram had been right: the doors and the fire escape were being patrolled by almost a dozen security men, the back exit monitored by a dog handler. He waited. An hour passed, then finally, around 8.20 p.m., a security van drew up. A moment later the white-haired figure of Philip Preston emerged carrying a small wooden box which he handed to a guard. After signing a document, Philip watched the van pull away, then turned and moved back into the auction house.

Leaving his hiding place, Nicholas jumped down into the alleyway and made his way out into the street, hailing a taxi and clambering in. 'You see that dark van?'

The driver nodded. 'Yeah. Want me to follow it?'

'That's exactly what I want you to do,' Nicholas replied.

When the van finally arrived at Palace Gardens, Nicholas tapped on the glass which separated him from the cabbie. 'Can you pull over?'

He did so, looking at Nicholas through his rear-view mirror. 'Don't tell me you live here? I mean, no offence, but this address is a bit rich for your blood.'

Nicholas smiled, watching the van continue along the road, then paid the driver. Keeping to the shadows, he moved down the Gardens, walking next to the high hedges and walls, aware that most of the embassies or private properties had intruder lights which would give away any trespasser. He could see the van draw up to the gates of a large house, then pause. The driver spoke to someone over the intercom and a moment later the vast gates opened to allow the van to enter. As it did so, the powerful outside lights came on, illuminating the drive and the front of the house. Drawing back, Nicholas waited. Ten minutes passed, then finally the van left, the gates closed, and the lights went off again.

Nicholas didn't need to be told that this was Conrad Voygel's house. Voygel, the man who now owned the Bosch chain; the man who had hired Sidney Elliott; the man who had approved murder to keep a secret. And all for what? Nicholas thought. He had published the exposé and now the world knew about the Bosch deception. Four people had died for nothing, and he had nearly been one of them.

'Mr Laverne,' a voice said suddenly, 'will you come with me?'

Eighty-Two

Conrad Voygel's house, Kensington, London

The room that Nicholas was shown into was surprisingly intimate, with soft lighting. A coal-effect fire burned in the grate and a Piranesi architectural drawing, ornately framed, hung over the fireplace. Next to a walnut desk was a statue of a blackamoor and beside it, incongruously, a child's drawing book. Only moments after Nicholas had been shown into the room, the door opened and a man walked in.

Conrad Voygel was tall, dressed casually, his smile hesitant. The surgeon had done well. Despite the severity of his cancer there were no obvious scars, just a faint, hollowed area on the left side of his face and the overall appearance of tightened flesh. But when he spoke his voice was hoarse, the disease having affected his vocal cords.

'Did you want to see me?' he asked, sitting at the desk, the lamplight blurring his features.

Nicholas wasn't fazed. 'You bought the Bosch chain. It cost you a lot, not just in money.'

'It cost me well above the reserve, yes.'

'I don't mean that,' Nicholas replied. 'Four people are dead because of you.'

'No,' Conrad replied. 'But I should congratulate you – after all, you managed to expose the deception. Although no one's taking you seriously – people think you're a bit of a nutter.'

'At least I don't kill people.'

'But you think I do?' Conrad smiled awkwardly, the flesh pulled tight around his mouth. 'No, not me. But I believe the police want to talk to you, and to Mr Kaminski—'

Nicholas bristled. 'Why him? He's done nothing wrong. He's just backing me, that's all.'

'Backing you doesn't seem a wise move, Mr Laverne. Backing a loser never is. You see, one thing I've learnt in life is that people don't change. If you're a whistle-blower, you stay a whistle-blower. If you're reckless, you stay reckless.' Conrad paused. 'Why did you have to attack the Church?'

'What they were doing was wrong!'

'But it's a haven, religion. You could have stayed safe, a beloved priest, living a quiet life. If you had, no one would ever have heard about Nicholas Laverne. But instead you had to create chaos. And where did it get you? Excommunicated.' Conrad shrugged. 'What amazes me is that you didn't learn your lesson—'

'What's that supposed to mean?'

'For a while you seemed to. You were quiet for ten years and then – boom! – back you came with the Bosch deception. I tried to stop you, but you just kept going.'

Nicholas stared at the figure in the chair. Conrad Voygel knew a lot about him, but that would be easy to find out. There was something else, something about him which disturbed Nicholas and stirred an old memory. He was back in his teens and early twenties, the disgrace of the family, the kid that no one could control. Mixing with crooks and petty thieves.

'Do I know you?'

'I think you would remember my face if you did.' Conrad replied as a telephone began to ring beside him. Smiling, he picked it up. 'Hello, darling . . . No, I won't be much longer. Just a little while . . .' He was listening intently. '. . . what am I doing? Nothing much – I'm just talking to my brother, that's all.'

Eighty-Three

The carpet seemed to be shifting under Nicholas's feet, the walls sloping away from him as he watched Conrad Voygel lean forward into the lamplight. But it still took him several moments to recognise the old face under the reconstructive surgery. There *was* a flicker of some vague recall, then he stared into the eyes and the years fell away. Nicholas was suddenly back in the past. He and his siblings were living with the irascible David Laverne, and Henry was just leaving university, flushed with his success at acquiring a position at a prestigious architectural firm in Paris, secured on the glowing recommendation of Raoul Devereux.

It had been a much vaulted and much envied position. Any flicker of scandal or ineptitude would have meant disgrace or even dismissal. Henry Laverne would have to be, and behave like, a gentleman . . . Nicholas looked at his brother, an old memory returning.

'*You killed our parents—*'

'*I didn't—*'

'You missed the last train! If they hadn't had to pick you up they would never have had the crash. It was your fault. It was all your fault and I'll never let you forget it.'

'Their deaths weren't down to me! I was fourteen years old,' Nicholas said, facing his brother and remembering his accusations. 'I was fourteen and you made me feel like a criminal!' His rage almost choked him. 'You held that over my head for years. You played me, relied on my guilt. And you could, because you were perfect. But you weren't, were you?' Nicholas leaned towards his brother over the desk. 'You fooled everyone but me.'

'I got away with it though, didn't I?'

'Only because you had a ready-made scapegoat,' Nicholas said bitterly. 'How many times did I cover for you? Took the blame for that assault on the woman in Milan. I remember that group you fell in with – the ones who were faking and dealing in stolen art. *You* stole that landscape painting from Raoul Devereux – and you made me the culprit. And why did I let you? Because you were the father figure. I admired you, I wanted to be like you, I couldn't say no to anything you asked. I remember you, you bastard!' he snapped. 'Crying like a kid and begging me: *"Tell them it was you. They'll throw me out of the company if you don't. Please, Nicholas, please . . ."*

'And so I said it was me. Always me. Every rotten thing you did, I took the blame. And everyone believed it. How could you be responsible for theft? How could you take drugs, be violent? No, not Henry. But Nicholas – well, I was the wild card, wasn't I?'

'You were a difficult boy—'

'Because you screwed me up! You made me believe that everything was my fault! In the end I believed it myself. I was nothing, the boy no one liked or cared about. I had nothing, so why not sacrifice myself to the burning light that was Henry Laverne? And you relied on that, didn't you?' He paused and looked around him, incredulous. 'We thought you died in that fire. We buried you—'

'You buried a gardener.'

Nicholas sat down and stared at his brother's altered face. 'I see you now. I see every rotten part of you. Why did you let us think you'd died?'

'I didn't want to be Henry Laverne any more. It was limiting. I wanted more, and suddenly there was a way I could get it.' He grimaced. 'You think *you* had it hard. Try being perfect – it gets wearing after a while. I wanted a new life—'

'As Conrad Voygel?'

'Oh, he came a little later. For a while I just drifted, got into a bit of trouble, but that didn't matter any more because I wasn't anyone. Not Henry Laverne, no one. Slowly I began to build up a property business abroad, then I went into computers. I heard about you exposing the Catholic Church because of what happened to that boy.'

'Patrick Gerin.'

'Did he remind you of yourself, Nicholas?' he asked. 'You wanted to save another lost boy. Then the scandal was over. Suddenly you were banished and disappeared – and my star was on the rise. I chose a new name, and when I got cancer

I saw it as a plus. My face changed, my voice too. Henry Laverne might not have been buried, but he was well and truly dead. And my reputation grew. No one knew where I came from, or anything about my past. I'm a respectable, revered, philanthropic tycoon. I am on a par with politicians, royalty, celebrities. People admire me.'

'You're a crook—'

'No, Henry Laverne was the crook.' He paused, smiling that tight smile. 'But you had to ruin it, didn't you? You had to come back, because you had another cause to fight for – that bloody chain. Who cared what happened to Hieronymus Bosch? Well, you did, because here was another lost boy. Of course you couldn't give up on it – it would have been like giving up on yourself.' He laced his fingers together. 'I had to stop you.'

'You were going to kill me?'

He seemed genuinely taken aback. 'Kill you? No.'

'You hired Sidney Elliott—'

'Only at the beginning, to find the chain. Elliott approached me after he'd worked for you. He told me about the Bosch conspiracy and the chain. But he was unstable, crazy, – anyone could see that. So I fired him. What he did has nothing to do with me.' Conrad paused. 'I killed no one and I had no one killed. I'm a respectable businessman with a fortune; my reputation is everything.'

'Which you'd do anything to protect,' Nicholas said coldly. 'And I was the only person who could ruin you. The

396

only one who could expose you for who – and what – you really are.'

'Exactly,' Conrad agreed. 'With this latest passion of yours you were all set to be a celebrity again. People would want to know you, know all about you – and, by extension, your family. I couldn't risk it. I know how it works, Nicholas: secrets always get sucked out. Like Bosch. I had to stop you, and the only way I could effectively do that was to discredit you. Make the world think of you as a barmy ex-priest with another conspiracy theory. People knew you were confused. You had bad dreams, you saw things—'

'*You hired Father Michael?*'

He nodded. 'And Carel Honthorst. Who does have a mighty faith. Honthorst would have ripped you limb from limb just for betraying his Church. But I wouldn't let him go that far. I didn't want to kill you—'

'Just drive me mad.'

'It was the lesser of two evils. People don't listen to lunatics or fantasists. You would have been a laughing stock, almost as good as dead.'

'You had me poisoned, drugged. I kept wondering about the dreams, why they were changing. I thought I'd done something unforgivable. Something I couldn't, or wouldn't, remember.' Nicholas looked at his brother. 'But that was just guilt, wasn't it? That guilt you instilled in me when I was a kid took over. I felt responsible, like I always had done.'

'It was a good plan—'

'Which should have worked.'

It was Conrad's turn to look surprised. 'It *did* work.'

'No, the story of the Bosch deception is out. It's gone global.'

Sighing, Conrad rose to his feet. 'No one believes you, Nicholas. And when they dig deeper into your past they'll discover your crimes and misdemeanours. You mixed with crooks and fakers; how suspect does that make your theory? And then they'll wonder about the death of Father Luke and how you're involved with three other people who died. It doesn't look good for you, Nicholas. Not good at all.'

'I'll expose you!' Nicholas snapped.

'Another exposure? Do you really think anyone will listen to you claiming to be the brother of Conrad Voygel?' He straightened up. 'By morning you'll be fully discredited. Probably in jail.'

'I never killed anyone!'

'Ah, but you have to prove that, don't you?' Conrad responded. 'You hated Father Luke. You were close to Claude Devereux, you had access to Sabine Monette—'

'She was killed in Paris while I was in London!'

'You could have had an accomplice. Someone like Sidney Elliott . . .'

Nicholas was too shocked to speak.

'. . . By the time you've been arrested, people will be baying for your blood. The art world wants to discredit what you're saying about Bosch. And the Church – well, the Church isn't going to come to your aid, is it? As for Hiram Kaminski, he's already being pressurised. I dare say he'll withdraw his support before tomorrow's out.'

'But I have the papers!' Nicholas blustered. 'The evidence of what happened to Bosch. *I have proof!*'

'Which Gerrit der Keyser will authenticate. After all, you're not a specialist or an art dealer and Mr der Keyser is. He will publicly state that an associate of yours stole the chain from his gallery. That it was all part of your plan.' He shrugged. 'Bring out your bits of paper, Nicholas. Wave them in the face of the world. Der Keyser will swear you took them from him. Once a thief, always a thief. Admit it, you've lost.'

'Why are you doing this to me?'

'I wouldn't have hurt you, Nicholas, if you'd stayed in the Church. Out of the world, out of the public eye. Unknown, without any embarrassing connection to me. I *had* to do it.'

'So what now? You're going to let me walk out of here?'

'Why not?' Conrad replied. 'You're not going far.'

Eighty-Four

Honor was staring at her computer screen, reading the website Nicholas had put up, together with his blog. The responses had been quick and often vitriolic, some calling Nicholas a fantasist, others accusing him of sensationalism. It didn't take much imagination to guess that most of the comments had been made by members of the art world. And BBC TV was trailing portions of Hiram Kaminski's interview, followed by a mention that the police 'would like to talk to Mr Nicholas Laverne with regard to accusations made against him'. In trying to support Nicholas, Hiram had inadvertently thrown suspicion on him. And now he was on the run.

If he had hoped for recognition, he had got it. Nicholas's face was in the news and the papers, his image all over the internet. Not so much a whistle-blower, more a common fraudster. And worse, a suspect in the murders of four people.

Eighty-Five

It was Judith Kaminski who picked up the phone, without recognising the number. Nicholas was using the new mobile he had bought. With an outward appearance of calm, she glanced at the police officer sitting next to Hiram and smiled.

'What's the matter, darling?' she asked the caller.

Nicholas picked up on his cue immediately. 'I need to talk to Hiram.'

'He's busy – just a minute.' She looked at her husband. 'It's Helen, my dear. She's a bit upset.' Covering the phone mouthpiece, she gave the policeman a whispered explanation. 'She's our daughter. Lovely girl, but having trouble with a man. She wants to talk to her daddy.'

She passed the phone over to a puzzled Hiram. 'Hello, darling?'

'It's me,' Nicholas said, hurrying on. 'I know there's someone there, but just answer yes or no, will you?'

401

'Yes,' Hiram replied, smiling at his wife.

'You said that many dealers used Sidney Elliott?'

'Yes.'

'Did he ever work for Philip Preston?'

Hiram could feel the eyes of his wife and the police officer boring into him but kept his tone steady. 'Yes, he did. You don't want to trust him, sweetheart – he treated you badly four years ago, with that business in Holland.'

Nicholas understood immediately what he meant. 'Holland?'

'You ask his wife – he has a mistress,' Hiram said, feeding Nicholas information while pretending to talk to his daughter. 'He's no good, no good at all.' Shaking his head, Hiram put down the phone, shrugging. 'Women. What can you do?'

Moments later Nicholas received a text from Hiram. It was a phone number and Nicholas rang it immediately. A woman picked up, her voice agitated.

'Philip! Is that you?'

'No, I was wanting to talk to your husband.'

Gayle Preston was almost hysterical. 'He's gone! He's left me for some bitch.' She was crying, hopelessly desperate. 'The bastard, the bastard . . .'

'Do you know where he is?'

'He thinks I don't have any idea,' Gayle said, her tone sly, unbalanced. 'He thinks I don't know about his little hiding place. He thinks I'm a fool. Running off with that woman—'

'Where has he gone?'

Gayle didn't stop to ask who she was speaking to or why he wanted to know about her husband. Distracted, she blundered on. 'Our lawyer let it slip. Milan, he said. *PHILIP PROMISED WE'D GO THERE!* she screamed. Nicholas could hear a voice in the background. A woman's voice, with the soothing intonation of a nurse. 'You tell that bastard I hate him!' Gayle hissed. 'Tell him not to come back here. *I DON'T WANT HIM!*' And with that, she slammed down the phone.

Nicholas knew he had to move fast. The police were looking for him and his face was in the papers and on the internet as a murder suspect. A man who merited the warning *'Dangerous to the public. Do not approach.'*

Leaving the safety of Kensington Gardens, he moved out on to Kensington High Street. It was still raining as he hailed a taxi and asked to be taken to Heathrow airport. He had been outsmarted and outmanoeuvred. Der Keyser wasn't the villain, neither was Conrad Voygel. Sidney Elliott had been the killer, but his paymaster was Philip Preston. Nicholas had been tricked by the auctioneer, trussed up like a Christmas goose. If he didn't stop him, Philip Preston was going to escape punishment and leave the country.

While he was going to jail.

Eighty-Six

Heathrow Airport, Terminal 5

Running across the concourse, Nicholas checked the flights to Milan. The plane was due for boarding in thirty minutes, the passengers milling around the departure hall or in the the large VIP lounge. He glanced inside, spotted Philip Preston's white head of hair in the distance and approached the door. He was stopped immediately.

'Your boarding pass, sir.'

'I'm not flying, I'm meeting a friend here,' Nicholas said, knowing that he wasn't going to get into the lounge and unwilling to attract any more attention. Instead he backed off and headed for the Customer Service desk.

'I have a message for one of your passengers, a Mr Philip Preston. He's flying to Milan on the ten p.m. departure.' Nicholas was talking quickly, nervously. Knowing he was giving himself away, he took in a breath and slowed himself down. 'I have to talk to him. His wife – my sister – has gone

404

into labour early. I can't get into the VIP lounge because I don't have a valid ticket.'

Behind the desk, the woman listened, her eyes widening. 'Don't worry,' she said, smiling. 'You wait here and I'll get a message to him. Mr Philip Preston, you said?'

'Yes, that's right. Don't tell him what's happened – he might panic. He's a lot older than his wife. If you could just get him out of the lounge, I can explain.'

Nicholas waited by the desk. He could see the member of ground staff talk to someone and then heard a tannoy announcement for a Mr Philip Preston. A minute passed, then a couple more. Jesus, he thought. Had Preston panicked? Thought the police were on to him? Or had he simply left the airport? But only seconds later a harried Preston walked out of the lounge. He was talking so earnestly to the member of airport staff that he didn't look up until Nicholas touched him on the arm.

'It's about your wife,' Nicholas said, gripping him tightly and smiling at the staff member. 'Thank you.'

'What the hell—' Philip began, Nicholas clinging on to his arm as he steered him away. 'What the hell are you up to, Laverne?' he snapped. 'I've got no business with you.'

'The police are after me. They think I killed four people. But we both know I didn't. You arranged their deaths.' Nicholas tightened his grip. 'You aren't denying it.'

'You're crazy. Everyone knows that.'

'So why aren't you calling for help? An innocent man in the grip of a lunatic would be screaming blue murder.'

Nicholas guided Preston towards a corridor that led to the men's toilets, set back from the departure hall. 'You want to get on that plane, don't you?'

'I *am* getting on that plane.'

'You hired Sidney Elliott. I thought it was Conrad Voygel, but I was wrong. It was you that planned all of it. When did you think it up, eh? When I came to you that day with the chain?'

Preston shook off Nicholas's grip and smoothed his hair, apparently unconcerned. 'I'd heard a rumour about the Bosch conspiracy and then you came along and dropped it in my lap. When you got spooked by Carel Honthorst, I thought you weren't coming back, so I took matters into my own hands.'

'You killed Sabine.'

'No, I didn't kill her. Sidney Elliott did.' He looked around him, checking that no one was listening. 'He was working for Voygel at the time and that was useful: it meant I could feed him gossip about the chain. I knew Voygel would want it, and I wanted the big sale. I needed that sale badly.'

'And you were prepared to do anything to get it?'

'I don't suffer from feelings of guilt, Nicholas. That's your speciality,' Preston replied. 'Sidney Elliott was a strange man, twitchy, always on a knife edge. In the past people put it down to his brilliance, but as his career faded he became unstable. When I heard about the death of Thomas Littlejohn I knew he'd done it – the rest was easy.'

'Easy?'

'I blackmailed him. Guessed that he had killed Sabine Monette to get the chain and the papers and told him I'd expose him. Have him put away. He did everything I wanted after that. Mind you, he was a treacherous bastard – tried to do a deal with Voygel even after he'd fired him. He was demented, had some idea that Voygel's money could buy back his life, but he was too far gone. Sidney Elliott killed once and then he couldn't stop.'

'You were never working with the Catholic Church?'

'To stop you going public?' Philip shook his head. 'No. Killing Father Luke was all my idea. I didn't want any suspicion to fall on Sidney Elliott and, by extension, me – so I shifted the focus on to you. You were the most likely suspect. You'd exposed Father Luke ten years ago, so why not come back and finish the job? After all, what would a Catholic priest have to do with the art world?' He paused, listening to a tannoy announcement before continuing, 'You were the perfect scapegoat.'

'You weren't working with Conrad Voygel?'

'Never,' Preston said, smiling. 'I relieved him of a large amount of money, nothing more. He paid a fortune for the Bosch chain.'

Nicholas struggled to understand. 'And by blackmailing Elliott you got him to kill four people?'

'He didn't want to go to jail.' He shrugged. 'Besides, he liked killing. He liked all of it. Following you, threatening people – it gave him power. Something he'd lost a long time ago.'

'You know he's dead?'

'I wondered why I hadn't heard from him,' Preston said coldly. 'I'm glad. He was a very chilling man.'

'The police suspect me—'

'Not for long. Elliott's DNA will be everywhere. In London, Paris – everywhere he went he will have left traces. That'll clear you.'

'*That's it?*' Nicholas asked, his voice hoarse. 'You tell me all this and expect to just leave? Fly off?'

'You can't stop me. You can't prove anything. By all means, Mr Laverne, call security now. But then again, they'd only arrest you. *You* are the suspect, after all.'

An announcement came over the tannoy again and Philip listened. 'Time for me to board my flight—'

'What about the other chain?'

'There was no other chain,' he said, laughing. 'I set up the two-chains scenario to throw suspicion off myself. Someone as wily as Gerrit der Keyser had to think I was a fool, running scared. I had the original copied in every detail. To someone like der Keyser, who has little knowledge of gold work, it looked convincing. And of course he brought it to *me* to validate. He even thought both of them might be fakes. He'd be so disappointed to know he'd been tricked.' Preston smiled with genuine amusement and turned to go.

Nicholas grabbed hold of his arm again. 'You're responsible for four deaths and you're just going to walk away? Leave me to take the blame—'

'It will only be temporary. Like I say, investigations will prove you innocent.'

'While you escape punishment?'

'There you go, talking like a priest again. There *is* no punishment, no Heaven, no Hell. There is no moral code. The strong chew up the weak, they prey on the consciences of others. You fly your banners and follow your principles. Fight for the likes of Patrick Gerin and some old painter – and where's it got you? You're washed up, Nicholas – a deluded ex-priest with nowhere left to go.'

'You'll get what you deserve.'

'Is that a threat or a prophecy? You have two choices, Nicholas.' He stared at him coldly. 'Either you defend yourself or you go on the run. I know which one I'd choose.'

Eighty-Seven

Milan

It was colder than expected when Philip Preston arrived in Milan. Carrying his suitcase, he took the lift to the third floor and entered his apartment, calling for Kim.

There was no reply.

They had made arrangements to meet in the city and spend one night together, then travel into the countryside to the farmhouse Philip had purchased, using the services of a London solicitor his wife had never met. Tired, he yawned and kicked off his shoes, then padded into the bedroom. The shower was running. Philip smiled to himself. So Kim had already arrived and was getting ready for him. Taking off his clothes, he moved into the steamy bathroom, fumbling to turn on the fan, but before he climbed into the tub he felt a sudden and violent punch to his back. Surprised, he gasped, flailing around, blood pumping from him as the knife came down again.

She stabbed Philip Preston seventeen times. Fourteen times in the back and three times in his chest. When Eloise Devereux finished, she cut initials into his skin – C D for Claude Devereux and S M for her mother, Sabine Monette. Then she showered the blood off her naked body and dressed herself. Before she left, she wiped the knife and every other surface in the flat, including the door handle.

Gerrit der Keyser had been right – his daughter *was* terrifying.

Eighty-Eight

Six months later

His head thrown back, Nicholas felt the winter sun on his face and smiled for the first time in weeks. Choosing the second option, he hadn't run but had left Heathrow and gone straight to the nearest police station. There he told them everything. The fallout was spectacular, and when Philip Preston's body was discovered Nicholas was finally believed. He explained everything and gave the police names and details, and for a while he had police protection. Terrified of what Nicholas might know, Gerrit der Keyser threw his support behind him and Hiram Kaminski also gave evidence to the police. But there was no trial, no sentencing. Sidney Elliott was dead, as was Philip Preston, and the case was complete. For the police anyway.

But not for Nicholas. Stirring himself, he rose from the bench and looked around. Then he walked back up Palace Gardens and rang the intercom of Conrad Voygel's house. This time he was admitted immediately.

Conrad was sitting in his study, wary, staring at his brother. 'What d'you want?'

'Does Honor know who you are?'

'No.'

'Good. Keep it that way.'

Unnerved, Conrad repeated the question. 'What d'you want?'

'Nothing.'

He frowned. '*Nothing*?'

'Nothing. Now.' Nicholas paused, watching the altered face of the brother he had once known, the brother who had terrorised him as a child. The man for whom he had lost his good name and his peace of mind. 'I just want you to know that at any time I could change my mind. I could expose you, ruin your life. I want you to live with that. You might find sleeping difficult, Henry. I certainly did. You might find yourself sweating at times, unnerved for no reason. I did that too. And if you think of some way to stop me, don't. I've written down everything – your real name, what you did, everything. And if anything ever happens to me, the police will hear about it. And they'll come for you.' He paused, watching his brother. 'It's illegal to fake your own death. You'd never recover from the scandal if that came out. You'd lose your wife, your daughter, your money.'

'You wouldn't dare!' Henry blustered. 'I know you. You're not that kind of person.'

'I *wasn't* that kind of person,' Nicholas corrected him. 'But I've changed. Remember, Henry, we're brothers, and treachery runs in the family.'

Back out in the sunshine, Henry walked across Kensington Gardens and paused by the urchin statue of Peter Pan before moving on to the Serpentine, where he stopped and stared into the running water. Nicholas Laverne was no longer an outcast. Indeed, he was now a wealthy man. When Sabine Monette's will was read it was a private affair, and to his surprise the French country house was left to Nicholas. Also a confidential letter – in which Sabine explained that she was the mother of Eloise Devereux. It was the last piece of the mosaic and it told Nicholas who had murdered Philip Preston. A piece of information he had no inclination to share.

As for Eloise, Nicholas had seen her a few months later. 'I'm glad my mother left you the country house—'

'I don't need it.'

Her eyes had been calm. 'Yes, you do. In fact, you need it more than anyone. I've inherited Sabine's apartment in Paris and more money than I could possibly ever need. What will I do with my time?' She had taken Nicholas's hands and weighed them in her own. 'Make a life for yourself now. Secrets are only for unhappy people.'

She had been wrong about that.

Winter was starting to shift, the cold letting in a little warmth. Before too long it would be spring. Reaching into his pocket, Nicholas pulled out an envelope and opened it. Inside were two tiny scraps of paper, written in an antique language, in an antique hand.

'The Pedlar'

After Hieronymus Bosch

The two last papers written and secreted in the Bosch chain. The ones Nicholas had kept back and shown to no one. The papers he had had laboriously translated, word for word, by four different people in four different countries. The papers that revealed the conclusion to the Bosch deception.

The incredible secret papers.

Paper Twenty-Nine

The boy lies in his winding sheet
But feels no earth upon him.
The sacking holds no man.

And then the last:

Paper Thirty

Let no man living know of this. Let chimeras and
his devils keep him company, let angels keep him safe.
I who watched his torment
set him to be a free man.
Soli Deo Gloria.

Hieronymus Bosch had not perished in 1473. This time, his father and the Church had been duped. While believing him dead, he had, in fact, been freed. Nicholas liked to believe it was Goossen, his brother, who had helped him,

416

but he would never know the truth. Just as he would never know where Hieronymus went, what he did, or how he lived. His life was a secret, like so many others'; but unlike others, he had cheated the grave.

Nicholas folded the papers, replaced them in the envelope, and pushed them deep into his pocket. As instructed in writings centuries old, he would keep the secret, as he had kept so many others.

Soli Deo Gloria, he thought, walking on. Yes, Glory be to God alone.

Bibliography

Belting, Hans, *Hieronymus Bosch: Garden of Earthly Delights* (New York, Prestel, 2002)

Bosing, Walter, *Bosch: c. 1450–1516*, Basic Art series (Los Angeles, Taschen, 2000)

Devitini Dufour, Alessia, *Bosch: Master of the Grotesque – His Life in Paintings* (London, DK Publishing, 1999)

Fomin, G., *Hieronymus Bosch* (Moscow, 1974)

Franger, J., *Hieronymus Bosch* (Dresden, 1975)

Gibson, Walter S., *Hieronymus Bosch* (London, Thames & Hudson, 1985)

Harris, Lynda, *The Secret Heresy of Hieronymus Bosch* (Edinburgh, Floris Books, 2002)

Koldeweij, Jos and Vandenbroeck, Paul, *Hieronymus Bosch: The Complete Paintings and Drawings* (New York, Harry N. Abrams, 2001)

Linfert, Carl, *Masters of Art: Bosch* (New York, Harry N. Abrams, 1989)

Zeri, Federico, *Bosch: The Garden of Earthly Delights*, One Hundred Paintings series (NDE Publishing, 2001)

Painting of Europe, *XIII–XX Centuries, Encyclopedic Dictionary* (Moscow, Iskusstvo, 1999)

The Columbia Electronic Encyclopedia, 6th edn. Copyright ©2012, Columbia University Press. All rights reserved.

National Gallery information, London